The Reunion Party

Also by Penny Batchelor

My Perfect Sister
Her New Best Friend

The Reunion Party

Penny Batchelor

embla books

First published in Great Britain in 2024 by

embla books

Bonnier Books UK Limited
4th Floor, Victoria House, Bloomsbury Square, London, WC1B 4DA
Owned by Bonnier Books
Sveavägen 56, Stockholm, Sweden

A CIP catalogue record for this book is available from the British Library.

ISBN: 9781471416354

This book is typeset using Atomik ePublisher.

Embla Books is an imprint of Bonnier Books UK.
www.bonnierbooks.co.uk

For my wonderful and sorely missed dad,
David Kenneth Batchelor, 1944–2023

Facebook Messenger

Remembering Tania Reunion group

Jeannie – Hi guys, I'm really excited to see you all again a week on Friday at Bluebell Lodge. It's been too long! You all OK with directions? I think you'll love the hotel. I've been managing it for over a year now and it's in such a lovely part of North Yorkshire. A world away from St Mark's Uni! Check in is from 3 p.m., please let me know what time you're planning on arriving. I've a delicious dinner sorted for the evening, made with organic ingredients sourced locally. It's our speciality. Oh, and don't forget Bluebell Lodge is a digital-detox hotel. No mobiles or internet allowed! But why would we want to be scrolling or texting when we've got so much to catch up on?? J

    Keren – thanks Jeannie. Adam and I are planning to set off on Friday morning after dropping the kids off at school. My parents said they'll look after them for us over the weekend. Depending on traffic, and how long we spend stopping for lunch to break up the drive, we should be with you about 4-ish?

    Johnny – planning on being there at 5 p.m.

    Saira – I've looked the route up on Google Maps and it looks quite complicated once you turn off the M1. I'll aim to arrive about the same time as Keren and Adam but it might be midnight if I get lost and you have to send out a search party!

WhatsApp message from Saira to Keren: Digital detox?? WTF!!! 😵

    WhatsApp message from Keren to Saira: I know, total marketing con to bump up the price of the rooms . . . thank goodness we're not paying for them!

    WhatsApp message from Saira to Keren: I wouldn't be going if I had to pay! This weekend better be good because the petrol's going to cost me a fortune.

Part One

The Reunion

Chapter 1

Saira

On its website Bluebell Lodge is described as a boutique, country-style hotel. Got to say I was a bit cynical on what to expect, but after driving along twisty roads and across ancient, vacant moors with grass scalded by the recent sun, I get my first glimpse. The building's yellowy sandstone is basking in the afternoon light, looking proper posh. The gravel road takes me around the side of the house to a car park at the back, no doubt so my old banger doesn't spoil the vista for other visitors.

I hope it's not a case of all fur coat and no knickers. I should have googled reviews to see if it's any good, but I didn't get round to it. I'm a last-minute sort of person, I only just manged to pack my suitcase in time and write the hotel's postcode on my hand to insert into my phone satnav before setting off. Unlike me, Jeannie was always a stickler for punctuality and getting things right, so I can't imagine she'd appreciate my tardiness, or be the manager of a place where everything isn't kept in tip-top condition.

I never wanted to come to this mini reunion party in honour of Tania, but Keren kept going on about the Messenger group invite Jeannie sent and strong-armed me into tagging along too. She's been such a support to me with everything that's happened in the last two years that I felt too guilty to say no.

Just because you used to be friends with people twenty-five years ago doesn't mean you'll have anything in common with them, or even like them, now. For a moment I seriously consider a sudden impulse to do a three-point turn and head back down to London but then shake my head fervently to send these negative thoughts scattering across the wind. I promised Keren.

It's a free weekend in a hotel. I might as well make the most of it.

Looking out of the car window, the view is incongruent. I don't know if there ever was a bluebell meadow nearby but there certainly isn't one now. The fields behind Bluebell Lodge aren't festooned with wild flowers and gambolling lambs, instead I hear cows bellowing and wrinkle up my nose when the stink of cowpats hits me through my wound-down window.

I think of the £5.99 bottle of screw-topped wine packed in my case, OK then, two, and the bath bomb I received last Christmas which I was saving for a special occasion.

Bit sad, isn't it, that there hasn't been one single cause for celebration in the last six months.

Parking up between a motorbike and a huge, gaudy Range Rover that puts my ten-year-old slovenly Fiesta to shame, I wait a couple of minutes to compose myself before I open the car door and venture in. It's almost twenty-five years to the day since I left St Mark's Uni, the Russell Group university purpose built in the 1960s on the outskirts of Bristol, and I'm not one for reunions. I binned all the uni post about group gatherings and requests for money, then told them to take my name off their database. Right now I want to look forward, not back.

The only uni friends I'm still in touch with are Keren and Adam, but I usually see Keren on her own when we both have some spare time for a catch-up. Sparky, down-to-earth Keren. Funnily enough, although we shared a house and hung out together in the same group at St Mark's, we weren't really close friends, but that changed when we both ended up living in London some years later and it was just the two of us – a gang of six reduced to two until Adam moved in with her. I never see him on my own, he was always quite quiet, keeps to himself. It's usually just Keren and me. What with us both having kids, when we meet up we like to go 'out out', letting our hair down and snatching a couple of hours for some fun.

If I'd wanted to keep up properly with the others I could have, but as time went on I suppose didn't. After I got stuck into adulthood and settled down with Hannah, I was caught up creating a new life for myself, meeting new people through work and my social circle expanding to include Hannah's family and friends too. That's the way life goes, isn't it? You grow up, move on and end up gradually drifting apart from your adolescent friends, making new ones in each stage of your life.

At least on the plus side, this weekend will fill another whole forty-eight hours that I would have otherwise spent at home with nothing to do. There's been far too much dead time these past twenty months since Hannah and I split up. This weekend it's her turn to have our daughter, Emily. My cruddy-barely-pays-the-bills admin job fills my days but the evenings, which I used to enjoy as precious family time, are now just me and the telly. Hannah's much better at feigning enthusiasm for getting up early for hockey practice and matches, for chauffeuring Emily round to friends' houses and goodness knows where else on her social calendar. Plus, being the higher earner and having enough cash to buy me out, she kept the family home whereas I'm now in a two-bed rented flat further away from Emily's friends. Free lifts and the familiarity of home makes her Golden Mum to a teenager, while I can't help but think that behind her smile Emily sometimes sees me as Gold-Plated Mum where bits have rubbed off and the base metal is showing through.

I don't let on how much I miss Emily when she's not with me or tell her that nothing I try and do to keep busy stops the bleeding in my smashed heart. She was just as devastated as me when we split. Hannah and I agreed to put Emily first and make sure we handle co-parenting amicably, but it's hard, so hard to keep up the pretence and fight the urge to lock the door when she's due back with Hannah and instead keep her all to myself.

I've got no idea what there is to do at this phone-free hotel, and what else Jeannie has planned aside from dinner tonight, so I've packed a couple of books just in case. I'm only here as a favour to Keren and have every intention of sneaking off with her and Adam after making the bare minimum of pleasantries with the others. Or if small talk becomes excruciating, I can always sunbathe on my own somewhere if the weather holds as the forecast says it should.

Right, time to go in. Let's hope my room has a bath and not a shower. To be honest, as awful as it sounds when it's a reunion in memory of a dead person, I wouldn't have come if it wasn't free. What with me now struggling to pay the rent all on my own there's no way I could justify spending money on two nights in a hotel, especially when Emily isn't here to enjoy it.

I open the car door to get some fresh air and instinctively pinch my nose to keep the smell out. You don't get manure in south London. Still, at least I can tell Emily I've been away, done something different, got myself out. I'm looking forward to having a long soak without fretting about the gas bill or leaving enough hot water for my daughter. It's about time I pampered myself. God knows I deserve it.

I unbuckle my seat belt and step out of the car, stretching my muscles that argue back like a tantrum toddler straightaway. My jeans feel slightly clammy around my legs and I pat them down to get rid of the crinkles. I wonder if I'm the first to arrive. Perhaps not – I imagine the gleaming Range Rover is the sort of car that a grown-up Johnny would drive, just like his dad did when he came to pick him up in the holidays. No change there then.

My handbag is where I slung it on the back seat next to my small, cabin-sized wheelie suitcase. I slide the driver's seat forward and lean in to pull them out then shut the door with a bang and lock it. I jump as a bird – a black one, I've no idea what species – caws loudly to make its presence known and flies off into the distance. The noise, coupled with the chorus of cows, unsettles me. I'm far more at home with a soundtrack of police sirens, neighbours' car alarms and next door's TV. Is seeing a black bird bad luck? A quick shiver shudders down my spine involuntarily, despite the sun still having lots of warmth left in its rays.

I suppose I should make my way to the front door. Right now, I wish I'd arranged with Keren to meet up with her beforehand so that we could go in together. I don't know why I feel nervous, it's just the old gang. They'll all be familiar, only twenty-five years older. We used to get on so well together, or so it seemed at the time.

With hindsight, maybe not so much during those final, fatal weeks at St Mark's.

Being here has got me thinking about Tania again after all these years. Tania, who died so young. Tania, whom I looked up to, as if she were high up on a plinth in Trafalgar Square. Tania the self-declared leader of our gang. Tania who back then I didn't question. Tania about whom some things I tried to forget long ago. That night that I've packed away tightly in a box in the backwater of my memory, firmly shut with a heavy-duty padlock.

Positive thinking, Saira. I shut my eyes and envisage a long, scorching hot pampering bath, beside which will be a glass of the wine I'm smuggling in. I doubt booze is included in the weekend – that's where hotels make their profits, charging outrageous prices to trapped guests.

Well, if I'm going in, I want to look my best. I take out my lipstick from the silver canvas handbag, one of Emily's cast-offs she gave me when the strap broke on my old chain store one. My full lips have always been my best feature. The fuchsia lipstick shade contrasts well with my light brown skin and dark hair, which I decided to cut short when Emily was a baby because she constantly used to reach up and pull it. I liked the style so much that I've kept it cropped ever since.

I take a few steps forward, pulling my case behind me. A slight breeze caresses my skin and I wonder whether I should have packed a warm jumper. June weather can be unpredictable, seemingly interminable sunshine can turn to rain clouds as quickly as the moods of my thirteen-year-old daughter. It's colder up north. Goosebumps appear on my arms despite the orange T-shirt I'm wearing. Maybe I'll get my cardigan out of my suitcase once I've checked in.

Pulling my shoulders back, I plaster a big grin on my face. Fake it till you make it, as they say. My stomach does a loud rumble, the chocolate bar I ate on the journey obviously hasn't satisfied it. Or am I nervous? I shouldn't be, it's not like I care about what the others think of me. They may see things differently but, apart from Hannah leaving me, a decision I had no control over, I'm happy with the life choices I've made.

The noise of tyres screeching over loose gravel jolts me out of my thoughts. It's an oldish family estate car that, like my old banger, is in need of some soap and water. I'm about to roll my eyes at its need to be speeding on a driveway when I spot who happens to be getting out of the driver's side of the car. It's Keren. She waves excitedly like a semaphore signer on speed. I drop my bags and walk to greet her, which takes a little longer than normal as I've left my stick in the car, thinking I wouldn't need it inside the hotel.

A grin involuntarily lights up my face as I take in her joy at seeing me. I hadn't realised quite how lonely I've been since Hannah and I split up and how solitary my life has become. It's been too long since Keren and I last met up, our communication usually happening over text or WhatsApp these days. I've gotten so used to my own company that I hardly know what to say now in social situations.

Fake it till you make it, I remind myself.

'Saira!' Keren shouts loudly. She jogs the few steps over to me and seizes the initiative, pulling me into a tight hug, rocking me side to side as if we were a pendulum, her head reaching up to my shoulder. She may be older now, sporting a sleek shiny dark blonde bob and skinny jeans with a stylish jumper rather than a band T-shirt, ripped baggy jeans and DMs, but inside, the leopard hasn't changed her spots. Same old lovely Keren. Many moons ago her constant energy and enthusiasm occasionally grated on my nerves but today her greeting reassures me. It has been a while since someone has been pleased to see me. Emily with her teenage mood swings can't be relied upon for that.

'I'm so glad you're here!' I say back, laughing at her shenanigans. While others at uni had long-term boyfriends or girlfriends back home or were coupled up with other students, Keren and I didn't have a great deal of luck, not for the want of Keren trying, and we spent the majority of our time hanging out with the whole gang. Tania, however, seemed to attract romantic attention like flies to a carcass. It became our game to pick out which man-boy would chat her up next. Indie swots, footballers, rugby players and a couple of lecturers, they all tried it on, even when she settled with Johnny.

Rich Johnny.

'Where's Adam?' I say pulling away, taking in the scent of her perfume. I don't know what she uses but it always smells like her. Vanilla with a hint of soap and rose. Fresh and clean.

There's a wham of a car door shutting and Adam appears out of the passenger seat, unfolding his long legs into the fresh air then rubbing his knees gently, as if he were shining a pair of best shoes.

'Saira!' He waves and lollops over to us, still slim but not quite as gangly as the old days. He hugs me awkwardly and Keren joins in, almost as if we're about to start a rugby scrum.

'Steady on, I don't want to fall,' I say as I grip on to Keren's shoulder so I don't lose my balance.

'Sorry, forgot. You OK? Not got your stick?'

'It's in the car.' I go to the boot to get it out. Better safe than sorry. I'm not having a rheumatoid arthritis flare-up at the moment but my joints still hurt. Adam starts to talk about the journey and how they had to rush here because they were late dropping off the kids at his parents and Keren laughs along. He kindly grabs my wheely suitcase without me asking and we start to walk towards the hotel's entrance.

'I thought we'd never get rid of them,' says Keren. 'A weekend, a whole weekend kid free! Hopefully they'll come back better behaved and appreciate us more. Mum and Dad don't take any nonsense. I think that's why they played up about going.'

'You're exaggerating. They're not that bad,' Adam butts in. 'Jim and Moira won't put them in the naughty dungeon for longer than an hour.' For a split second I'm shocked before their laughter prompts me to realise they're joking.

'Anyway, Saira, you been in yet?' He points his head towards the hotel. 'Seen the ghosts of uni past?' With that his smile falters as we remember the reason why we're all here. Adam clears his throat and quickly backtracks. 'I mean have you met the others yet?'

'No, I've only just arrived.' It hits me that out of the three of us, this get-together must be the hardest for him. What's past is past, but it doesn't mean it hasn't left an imprint, like an acne scar from a spot you couldn't help but pick.

'Great,' Keren jumps in. 'If I don't recognise anyone you can help me out. Johnny's pic in the Facebook Messenger group looked nothing like the late-nineties version of him I knew.' She looks pointedly at Adam who shuffles between his feet nervously, then briefly pats his hand. I wonder what sexual favours Keren had to promise to persuade him to come face to face with his former best friend again?

Throughout most of our time at St Mark's, Johnny had blond hair that skimmed his shoulders, which he often wore tied back with an elastic band. The girls, much to my amusement, all thought he was gorgeous. In our final term, just before he went for a job interview, he appeared one day with a short back and sides. His photo on his Facebook profile shows a middle-aged man with a shaved head.

Some men grow into their looks with age. Others, well, they don't.

Keren hooks her right arm around my left and gives it a squeeze that makes me jump. These days I'm not so used to physical affection. It occurs to me that for all her confidence maybe she's nervous about going in too. Are we walking into a fun reminiscence of times past, or a lion's den?

'Ready?'

'If you are!'

The front door is locked. I press the doorbell, which chimes as if it were Big Ben's little brother.

There's no going back now.

Chapter 2

Jeannie

I want everything to go perfectly this weekend. Tania deserves that. Usually, it'd be Grant or Bethan answering the door (it's my policy that we welcome all our guests personally as we would if they were entering our own home) but today I want it to be me. My hotel, my event. I'm running the show.

Bet they didn't think that I'd end up a successful hotel manager, although it's not as if they ever got in touch to ask. It was only a few months ago, when I tracked the others down through Facebook and started the Messenger group, that we've been in contact again. Social media might be something we frown upon at Bluebell Lodge, but it does have its uses. Without it we all may never have seen each other again and I'd have remained plain old Jeannie in the background to them, not an award-winning business woman.

I run my palm over my head to smooth down a flyway hair I know doesn't exist because I checked in the mirror two minutes ago. For five seconds I close my eyes, slow my breathing and count backwards. I can do this. It's important for me to honour Tania this weekend.

I always felt like the outsider in the group, the hanger-on. Not with Tania, no, she was my best friend, but the others seemed to tolerate me rather than include me. It was rare that I'd be invited to something if Tania wasn't going. They weren't all as bad as each other, a few of them had their moments, but today I'm going to show them who I am now and who I was then – Tania's closest friend. I've never had a friendship like that since. Perhaps I'm lucky to have experienced it once in a lifetime.

I oversaw the refurbishment of the inside of the hotel two years ago, and it was my idea to rebrand as a boutique, digital-detox hotel. The owners poached me from a rival chain, promising me a large budget and the full run of the show.

My eyes do a quick scan of the entrance hall. Like the rest of the interior, it is immaculate. Run your fingertip over the coving or skirting board and you won't find a speck of dust. I had the hall carpet deep-cleaned last week – it gets dirty quite quickly when people don't wipe their shoes on the doormat that's so obviously placed in the doorway – and there are fresh lilies in two vases on the reception desk perfuming the hall. Close your eyes and we could be in a cottage garden. Scent is very important when it comes to well-being and relaxation, and I pride myself that our guests leave us refreshed and renewed.

Lilies for the dead, my grandma used to say. They grow, they bloom, they exhale their delightful scent from between their petals but then they fade. I bought them especially for this occasion of remembrance. Lily pollen leaves its mark on whoever touches them, like Tania did to us. Anyone who met her couldn't fail to forget how special she was, the dust of her personality clings indelibly on to our skin.

The doorbell chimes and, walking towards the large wooden front door, I wonder which one of them it will be. I turn the lock and pull the door open wide, clenching my facial muscles so the corners of my mouth upturn. My pre-prepared greeting comes out a little too loudly: 'Saira, Keren, Adam, welcome! How lovely to see you all again.'

I step aside to allow them in, sweeping my arm back theatrically to beckon them inside. Adam moves forward first and holds out his hand for me to shake. 'Jeannie! Long time no see. Thanks for inviting us.'

His grip is rather firm and I hope my palm isn't sweaty with nerves. I think quickly to the stock phrases I've memorised and smile. 'It's my pleasure. Thanks for coming. Tania would be very pleased.'

Before he can reply, Keren thrusts her hand forward for me to shake, followed by Saira, who is clutching on to her walking stick, wrapped in a rainbow ribbon, with her other hand.

Handshakes all round. Very formal, no? Both women are middle-aged versions of who they used to be, making me wonder how they'll perceive me. Facebook shows that Keren and Saira are still in touch. No doubt they'll be analysing my life to gossip about later when they're alone together.

There's a short, toe-curling silence, which I proceed to fill brightly with more phrases I thought of earlier. 'How was the journey? Did you find the hotel all right? We are quite remote, which is a popular selling point for guests. Deep in the Yorkshire countryside.'

Adam answers in his deep voice. 'Satnav worked fine, thanks. Have you worked here long?'

A question I anticipated and had already prepared for. 'Nearly two years now. I was brought in to relaunch the hotel as a detox destination. Like I said, we ask that you hand in your mobiles if you don't mind, not that they'll work here but it stops you from trying! This is a weekend for you to truly refresh and reboot.' I know the script off by heart, I've said it brightly enough to guests time and time again.

Out of the corner of my eye I see Keren raise her eyebrows at Saira. She thinks I'm looking at Adam, not her. I smile even wider showing my veneered front teeth. I'm not the woman I used to be.

'Keren, if you don't mind?'

Keren makes a big fuss of emptying her huge handbag full of tissues, receipts, a makeup bag and more junk onto the side table. She'll give herself a bad back carrying all that around. Posture is key according to my Pilates teacher. I stand up even straighter and roll my shoulders back. Presence is important.

'Here it is,' she says, eventually passing me a battered old smartphone with her name sellotaped onto the back. When she sees me look at it, she says, 'I didn't want mine to get confused with my eldest's.'

I doubt that any self-respecting child would want to admit to owning that phone but keep smiling anyway.

'Thanks.'

Adam pulls a black iPhone out of his jeans pocket and Saira's mobile is in a pink glitter case that says 'Emily' on the back. I take them and put them in a drawer in the reception desk, turn the key in the lock and place it the side pocket of my knee-length tailored grey dress, the uniform I chose for female front of house staff, who are also issued with a fitted grey trouser suit. Stylish yet corporate. We represent the brand.

'I'll put them in the safe in a minute but first let me give you your room keys. They let you in the front door as well.' They are behind the main desk and are credit card-style, pre-programmed for each room. I hand two to Adam for him and Keren, and one to Saira. 'It's a single, snug but very comfortable.'

Saira examines hers then slides it into her back jeans pocket. 'They're like the ones they have at a Travelodge,' she laughs.

'I think you'll find we're not like a Travelodge at all,' I start to bristle, 'Bluebell Lodge is a unique, boutique hotel.'

'It looks lovely, thank you,' jumps in Adam, ever the conciliator.

Keren is looking round at our impressive entrance hall. 'Very swish,' she comments.

'What if we lose the card or leave it in the room?' Adam asks, looking at his wife. I get the impression Keren has done this before.

'Don't worry, we've got a master key behind the desk that opens all the rooms. We don't usually tell our guests that though as we don't want to encourage them to be lax with their keys. It costs us to replace and reprogramme them. Why don't you all come through to the lounge and Grant, out barman and waiter, will fix you a drink? The lounge is the place to come when you want to go to the bar, meet others, relax generally. There's a huge bookcase full of books to borrow and the cupboard below has a selection of board games. Old school, but perfect for passing a relaxing afternoon.'

I'm babbling I know, so I decide to close my mouth to smile in that professional yet friendly fashion I've developed over the years.

Adam's forehead wrinkles. 'Has anyone else arrived?' he asks.

By anyone else I assume he means Johnny.

'Johnny's in the bar. I'll take you all through,' I reply brightly.

I lead them through the oak door from the hall to the bar, Adam bringing up the rear. The afternoon sun is streaming in through the huge bay windows, in front of which is Johnny, clad in what looks like quiet luxe designer chinos and a short-sleeved, open-necked tailored shirt. He's lounging on a leather sofa with a whisky in one hand, and a copy of *Yorkshire Life* magazine that he's taken from the bookcase in the other.

'Keren, I think I'll take our bags up to the room first, freshen up after the long drive. See you up there.'

Adam shoots off before Johnny has a chance to look up and greet the new arrivals he hasn't seen for twenty-five years.

For a moment I let my gaze linger on his dark eyelashes, butterflies fluttering in my stomach, a sign of old feelings resurfacing that bring a warm flush to my cheeks. When he looks up, I dart my eyes towards the door and make my excuses, saying I must go to the kitchens to oversee dinner preparations. It's imperative that I behave as the consummate, irreproachable professional. I really don't want more minutes of agonising chit-chat with Keren, Adam and Saira, as I'm running out of things to say. At least by dinner, I'll have had time to think of some more topics to discuss – and obviously we'll speak about Tania, the whole reason why we're all gathered here.

What did we used to talk about all those years ago at university? I can barely remember. I suppose I said very little. Looking back, there were seemingly endless hours to hang about in the kitchen, someone's bedroom or the library café, fingers wrapped round a steaming hot chocolate. I was rarely alone with Johnny. He shared a house with Adam and another boy – Imran I think? – but he spent most of his time over at the house I shared with Tania, Saira and Keren. When Johnny was there, he and Tania were usually closeted away in her room, a pair of tights strewn casually over the door to prevent it shutting and jamming in the warped frame, letting the sounds of their laughter and the scent of dope sneak through like footsteps of naughty children.

In the kitchen there's the delicious scent of food bubbling away in a large pan. Just as I asked for. Eerik, our chef, is preparing for this evening's meal, a flavoursome soup made with home-grown vegetable stock. I smile politely. Thankfully, as I don't speak any Estonian, his English is perfect.

'Have your special guests arrived, Jeannie?' he asks, his lips curling around the words as if he's tasting them for their succulent flavour. He wipes his forehead with the back of his hand and, before I reply, turns to the knife rack and slides out a large, sharp one, the edge of which gleams under the kitchen's strip light, and proceeds to dice an onion on the chopping board.

I shudder without thinking, the sight of the knife causing my skin to crawl. I've never liked knives, blades or even sharp scissors for that matter. If it cuts, I shall bleed. You would have thought that by now I would have got over my aversion, particularly having overseen kitchen staff for many years. They say that people who are scared of spiders can be cured by some sort of befriending therapy, learning to be near a spider for just a little longer each day. I don't believe a word of it. It only makes it worse.

'Yes, I'll be joining them for dinner at seven thirty in the private dining room as we discussed. Smells good, Eerik. Grant is around to make the after-dinner drinks, so after you've prepared the desserts your time is your own.'

He carefully puts down the knife, resting it on the chopping board next to the shards of onion and twists his waist in my direction to look at me. A laugh escapes from his thin lips, lighting up his face from his eyes, a moment that reminds me how young he is. Now in his early- to mid-twenties, he started cookery training at sixteen, worked his way up a few rungs of the ladder then moved to England for more job opportunities back in the days when we opened our arms to Europeans for the cheap labour. He's currently applying for citizenship and plans to marry his boyfriend. Right now the boyfriend, I forget his name, lives in York and Eerik lives here, York being too far to travel to and from every day. I know all this because he tells me, chatting away amiably whether I show that I'm listening or not. He's not a man who likes quiet. Usually, unless he's really concentrating on a dish or supervising one of the casual staff I bring in at busy times, he plays the radio in the background, singing tunelessly under his breath.

'What?' I ask, wondering what could possibly be funny.

'You said dessert. Ian told me on the phone last night that people in Yorkshire don't say dessert, they say pudding. With an "uh" sound. He taught me how to say it. Puuuding.' He chuckles again at the sound his pronunciation makes.

'Well I'm not from Yorkshire, I'm from Surrey.'

'Where's that?'

'Further south.'

The knife is still lying on the chopping board. How strange that such a deadly weapon lies in a drawer in every kitchen in the country. We have permits and licences for guns yet the humble knife roams free, never mind the damage it could inflict on skin, muscle and tendon.

Tania used to laugh at me hiding behind a cushion when we watched a violent fight scene. A gunshot, now that didn't bother me; there's something impersonal about watching a character raise his or her arm and pull a trigger, with a bullet hitting or missing its quarry. But a knife; to cut someone you have to get up close to your victim, hear their breath and cries when you force it through flesh with a little extra force as Eerik does to overcome the meat's natural resistance when jointing a chicken.

'Jeannie, you've got to toughen up!' Tania would say, trying to pull the cushion away from my eyes. 'It's not real. If you're this scared, imagine what you'll be like with a horror movie!'

When I shut my eyes I can picture it so well, as if it only happened yesterday. Tania hasn't faded in my memory. She shines as brightly as she always did.

Eerik's voice pulls me back into the present. 'Jeannie, did you hear me? I said is Surrey a desert?'

I haven't got a clue what he's on about. My mind is lingering in the shared student kitchen-cum-lounge where there was a battered old red-wine-stained sofa that we'd laze on to watch the portable TV in the corner. It was Saira's, I think. Her parents bought it for her, she said, to encourage her to stay in rather than go out drinking alcohol and meeting boys.

'Pardon?' I reply.

Eerik laughs again. 'Desert, dessert, see? A dessert,' he says, putting the stress on the double 's', 'is a puuudding and a desert has lots of sand. Is there sand in Surrey?'

'No. It's land locked. There's no beach.' I wonder what it must be like to see life through Eerik's eyes, finding good and humour in everything. He doesn't have a bad word to say about anyone. Try as I might, I do. I'm just built that way. Not that I'd say it out loud. My thoughts stay safely imprisoned in my head. That's the way to try and fit in.

'Aah, no beach? You should come to Estonia! We have lots of them. Beautiful ones. And I don't mind working late tonight if you need help. Just tell me. It's not like I have anywhere to go!' He chuckles again and I can't help but smile, this time naturally.

'Thanks, but I'll try to avoid it. You deserve some time to yourself.' The latest human resources training course I went on emphasised the importance of manager/staff relations in retaining good workers. I don't want to lose Eerik, he's an excellent chef.

The menu is prepared, two choices for starter, main and dessert, or puuuding. I smile inwardly at Eerik's joke. I've put a lot of work into making this weekend special, especially for Tania's sake. People forget so easily but every day I remember she's not here. We should honour her. The five of us were the closest people to her, though of course the four others didn't have the friendship that Tania and I shared. They didn't see her on that first day at St Mark's when she knocked on my bedroom door, the room next to hers, to introduce herself. There she stood, wearing a long flowery dress, her messy brown hair tied back in a ponytail, a prototype of what she would soon become. For the first term we spent nearly all our time outside lectures together. She was quiet, shy like me, and wanted someone to explore campus with, go to the refectory with and talk to about this strange new world we inhabited. The friend she chose was me. I wasn't used to being chosen, at school I drifted in and out of friendship groups but never belonged. The others on our corridor weren't around much. One had a boyfriend in another hall and spent all her time at his. There were a couple of third years who were pleasant enough but had their own friendship groups. And the others? I can't remember. Just that Tania didn't rate them much and therefore I didn't either.

And then she went out without me for end-of-term Christmas drinks, and got in with Adam and Keren, with Johnny and Saira soon following. Sometimes I used to wish she hadn't, and that things could have stayed the same as that first term, so long ago, when there weren't the others wanting her attention.

Adam used to be joined at the hip with his best friend Johnny, well until our third year anyway. My mind flashes back to the first time I saw Johnny, when he came with Adam to meet Tania in her room, smiling slightly too widely, and I was already there, drinking a cup of tea and reading a set text in companiable silence . . .

I feel my cheeks becoming hotter. There's no time to dwell on all that now. What have I got to do next? Oh yes, lay the dining tables for this evening. Grant's behind the bar. Our housekeeper has gone home. She asked for the weekend off to attend a wedding and I thought that, seeing as we don't have any new guests booked in until Monday, if there are any housekeeping requests in the meantime, I can easily step in and save the cost of paying for temporary agency staff. Bethan, our receptionist, is off sick and I've routed internal guest calls through to my contraband mobile, with external booking enquiries going to the hotel chain's reservation number. I can only call in, not out, on the phone and I don't answer it in front of guests (it's on silent and vibrate mode) because I don't want them to know I've got a phone that works. They'd be pestering me to use it and our USP is that this is a digital-detox hotel. No mobiles, computers, laptops, tablets or anything that can connect to Wi-Fi allowed. We have had a few guests trying to sneak in those watches that connect to the internet but they don't work here anyway. Technical wizardry that the owners set up – which I don't quite understand myself, I just use it – enables me to have a working phone with internet access, though we do have a secret router that's protected for staff only, with our phones strictly not to be used in guest areas.

I'm about to turn on my heel and leave Eerik to his soup in the kitchen when my eyes home in on the knife, still unleashed on the chopping board.

'Eerik, if you've finished with the knife would you mind putting it away, please? Health and safety.'

'Yes, boss,' he says and picks up the knife by its handle, walks to the sink to clean it, taking care to avoid the sharp end, then sheaths it in the block. My muscles relax, and as my shoulders drop, I let out a deep breath.

Health and safety, you can never be too careful. Who knows when something terrible might happen? Tania didn't.

Chapter 3

Johnny

This Scotch tastes good, nectar for the gods, burning my tongue and slipping down my throat with speedy delight. Bugger the blood sugar, today I need it. In her email Jeannie said that the weekend is complimentary. I hope that includes booze. I certainly intend to partake of a barrel load. I need it to settle my nerves at seeing the others. Adam shot out of the room as quickly as a ferret with a firework up its backside rather than say hello. I've been looking forward to seeing him, catching up with my uni best mate, but no, looks like time hasn't defrosted that water under the bridge. Is he going to avoid me all weekend?

At least I don't have to hand back the keys to the Range Rover until next week or I'd never have got here. I haven't sunk as low as the Megabus. Not that I'm going to tell the others about my motor's repossession. The funny thing was that I hardly used the 4 x 4 in London, what with the Tube and cabs on account I didn't need to. It was parked outside my house ready for weekends, holidays, taking my girls out of the city at half-term to keep them occupied.

Now the stucco-fronted Georgian terrace belongs to my ex-wife and the Range Rover is usually parked wherever I can find a space near the block that houses the bedsit I temporarily live in. It's worse than late-nineties private student accommodation and hopefully I'll be waving it cheerio not too long after the Range Rover. I'm praying it won't be long before another bank recognises my potential and offers me a position with the customary health, share and pension benefits. The alternative is something I can't bear thinking about, but I do.

I partake of the last mouthful of Scotch left in the tumbler, willing it to block out the worry that keeps coming back to punch me in the face. What with the whopping maintenance I have to pay to Olivia every month, and no job, my savings are seeping away and the well is almost dry. I couldn't face not being able to provide for my daughters. It's what dads are supposed to do, and not being able to pay up would give my ex another reason to try and stop me from seeing them, while she swanks about with her new boyfriend in the house I paid for.

Bugger blood sugar. Bugger Brexit. Bugger recessions. Bugger management restructuring. Bugger off the lot of you.

A bourbon next I think. I smile when the barman I've been chatting to tops me up with an extra measure. 'Last of the bottle,' he says. I hope there's another one in the cellar or whatever this woke, touchy-feely gaff uses to store the booze. The Connaught or Brown's, it definitely isn't.

No mobiles? I should have thought about smuggling in a cheap pay-as-you-go phone, not that I've got the spare cash to buy one, but I didn't read the messages about the digital-detox tosh properly before I arrived and Jeannie, like a schoolmistress confiscating contraband, asked me to hand over the iPhone I 'forgot' to hand back to my former employer. I haven't seen Jeannie since graduation. She greeted me warmly and was keen to settle me in the bar while we waited for the others to arrive, although there's still something nervy about her, like in the old days, as if she panics when you talk to her in case you might bite.

I suppose I should count my blessings. I made it here and have enough petrol left in the tank to get back. I've got a damp-free room for the weekend, well at least it looked that way when I dropped my bag off and saw where I'll be sleeping for the next two nights. No dance music thumping through the walls or bed banging as the couple next door try to recreate a porno film. Even if Adam and Keren are in the next room I doubt that after the length of time they've been together there'll be much of that going on. There certainly wasn't with my ex. Thanks to the quiet location and the brandy I should actually get some kip for a change, certainly an attraction of accepting Jeannie's invitation. When I look in the mirror, I notice I look like hell, all receding shaved hairline and black eyebags. Hopefully a couple of good nights' sleep will do me good.

My upper arm itches and I scratch it through the fabric of the Bond Street shirt my wife gave me for Christmas a few years ago. If it fitted her no doubt she'd have requisitioned it when she threw me out and changed the locks before I could come back to fill my suitcases. When there was a glitch in bankrolling the lifestyle to which she'd become accustomed she decided I was persona non grata and surplus to her requirements. Later, when she finally let me back inside the house I mainly paid for, anything she'd decided belonged to her had mysteriously disappeared, apart from the painting my parents bought us for our wedding present, which she's always hated. It's an old school, classical English landscape, not modern or arty. It's hanging in my bedsit now, covering a damp stain on the wallpaper. If I get really desperate I can always pawn it. I doubt Mum and Dad would have given us anything cheap and cheerful; they wouldn't have wanted to look tight. They know about the divorce but not about my lack of employment. Father would never be able to live it down at his club. His son on the dole. I couldn't bear to see the disappointment and disgust on his face.

I'm not just here for the free bed and booze though. Jeannie organised it for us all to remember Tania. How could I forget her, my former soul mate, for she pops up now and again in my dreams where I'm young again, kissing her soft, nubile body while she gasps with pleasure. It doesn't seem possible that she's been dead for so many years – more years than she'd been alive. 'Tarn-ee-ya' she used to say if people mispronounced her name and called her 'Tan-ee-a', fixing their gaze with her chiding ice-blue eyes. My Tania. My first love, not counting the girls at school or ones in my first term at uni who I met in clubs and were never more than a one-time thing. My inquisitiveness and desire to think about her again after all these years was too strong to turn Jeannie's invitation down. This weekend, well, call me sentimental, but it feels like the memorial for her we never had.

The drink is making me uncharacteristically philosophical, playing 'what if' scenarios in my mind. What would have happened if Tania hadn't died? Would we have stayed together starting out our adult lives in London, or would we have had more rows and drifted apart? Was I destined to marry Olivia anyway? Who knows? I was certainly under Tania's spell. We all were. We're all here twenty-five years later, aren't we? She had the knack of making whoever she was talking to feel like the most important person in the world, but it was only me who really understood her, who she was truly herself with. Or at least so I thought until those last few weeks . . .

So long ago and yet if I close my eyes, it's clearer than yesterday.

'Can you watch my glass for a moment, mate?' I ask the barman who nods. He probably thinks I'm going for a slash. Instead, unseen, I slip around the corner and through the door marked 'staff only', which I guess leads to the kitchen. The hinges squeak as I push it open and a young, tall bloke turns round to look at me, opening his mouth to speak. He isn't wearing a white hat but, due to the fact he's standing near a steaming pot of something on the stove, I guess he's the cook. I talk before he can, turning on the charm I still have a little left of.

'Hi, mate, I'm a guest here. Is it OK if I store this in your fridge? Medical supplies.' I flash my 'all boys together' grin but I don't think I needed to because no look of questioning or disbelief crosses his face.

'Sure, put it in the bottom left-hand drawer. Tell me when you need it. Guests aren't supposed to come in here but you're one of Jeannie's old friends staying here, aren't you? A VIP!'

You wouldn't get that in London. Country people are so naive, though from his accent I think English is his second language. I place the package double wrapped in Sainsbury's orange carrier bags at the back of the drawer, shut the industrial fridge's huge door firmly then raise my right hand in thanks.

'Cheers, mate, will do.'

The man turns back to the stove and I return to my drink. I'm still alone in the bar, my other three 'old friends' are upstairs unpacking in their rooms, and Jeannie's off doing whatever hotel managers do. She's done well for herself, good for her. Out of all of the gang back at uni she was the one I spent the least time with and I never asked her what she wanted to do with her life. Perhaps that says more about me than about her.

I brace myself for forty-eight hours in the company of these people I used to see every day but now barely know, or even recognise, at all. Keren, Jeannie and Saira look a lot different from our student days, though I suppose I do too. Less hair, bigger stomach. When they came into the bar, Saira was the friendliest, tactfully not pressing me when she asked me about my family and I changed the subject. She's walking with a stick but I returned the favour and didn't ask her why. I felt it's too much of a personal question to ask. Perhaps she broke her ankle or something.

Keren chattered on to fill the silence, updating me on her kids' lives, before announcing that she was keen to see her and Adam's room – probably to check on him after his rapid disappearance. I take another gulp of my drink to quash my discomfort at his reaction to seeing me (or not) again. Funny he and Keren ended up together, I wouldn't have bet a ton on that. They got on well as friends but I never saw a romantic spark between them at the time.

I swirl the last few drops of liquid around the bottom of my glass and watch it slide back down as easily as it did down my throat. If this is how we are set to spend the weekend, surrounded by awkward silences and small talk, then the reunion is set to be a barrel of laughs. Maybe Jeannie will surprise us all by livening things up with the suggestion of holding hands and connecting with Tania through a Ouija board. I chuckle at the thought but then if Tania wanted to come back and haunt us, she'd have done so already. If anyone could make something happen by force of will it was her. But no, Tania's ashes are in the grave she was buried in after the private, family-only service her dad had insisted on when I asked about going, although she didn't have any siblings and her mother died when she was a young child. Mr Armstrong-Jones was always very protective of his daughter, some might say controlling. Perhaps he wanted to avoid any gossip. Questions would have been asked, unspoken rumours shrouding her coffin. I don't think he ever approved of me very much. Tania never invited me back to Devon.

Maybe it was best after all that I wasn't there.

I jump when for a split second I feel a sharp pang as an image of Tania, lying still as if asleep, slips into my mind. I shake my head, like a shaggy dog ridding its fur of rainwater, to dislodge the image. Yes, we were all captivated by her even though with Tania, you never quite knew where you were. That was part of the fun of it, the game. We had a spiritual connection. Life with Tania was never boring. Unlike my ex-wife Olivia, Tania had an urge to push boundaries and bend the rules whenever the mood struck her. She never seemed to care about what other people thought.

Jeannie comes back into the bar with some instructions for the barman and I see her tweak the beer mats as she's talking, turning the three of them so the writing is parallel to the edge of the polished wood bar top, exactly in line. Then she runs her forefinger very quickly along a couple of centimetres of wood to the left-hand side, as if she's checking for dust, while asking him to bring up two crates of beer from the cellar when it's quiet. Perhaps she is, her mind working on two things at once.

At St Mark's, Jeannie was quiet, reserved, a thinker not a doer; Tania's exuberance seemed to make Jeannie fade further into the wallpaper. She was the sort of girl I probably would've walked straight past in a bar. The only reason we really spoke was because she was Tania's friend. Looking back, I did used to be a bit of an arrogant wanker. Today, Jeannie is dressed smartly, corporately, all proper yet flattering her slim waist and figure. I think grimly that she's certainly aged better than me – now I'm the one women wouldn't look twice at. I take a quick glance at her left hand out of curiosity. No wedding ring, though of course that doesn't mean she's single. I still wear mine, I got used to it I suppose. Sentimental attachment. Absent-mindedly twirling it around my finger, I think I probably ought to make the break and take it off for good. What's past is past. If I get truly desperate it might raise me a few hundred down the pawnbroker's.

'Everything OK?' Jeannie asks me, with a steady smile on her face that I assume is the standard look she reserves for the hotel's guests rather than delight at our reacquaintance. It's been a long time since anyone's looked genuinely happy to see me.

I raise my glass to her. She nods and says she'll see us all at dinner, then strides purposefully out of the room.

I realise that, apart from graduation, and when I arrived today, that's probably the first time I've been in Jeannie's company when Tania wasn't there too.

Or at least the first time I've noticed it.

Chapter 4

Saira

My room is a single with a tiny bathroom carved out of the end of what probably used to be a double room. I think in the brochure they call it 'bijou'. That's what you get for being a single woman. I bet Johnny has got a bigger one, even though he's come solo too. I'm looking forward to gossiping with Keren about what Johnny and Jeannie have turned out like.

As soon as I get in, I lock the door, heave my case onto the bed then flop down and test the mattress. Firm yet comfy, no bedsprings sticking out or saggy dip in the middle.

I'm sweaty and ruffled after the drive and decide to take my toiletry bag, and the wine, into the bathroom, filling the sink with cold water to chill the bottle. The bath is smaller than a usual size, presumably so it fits into the space under the skylight where bathers can look up and see the sky.

The hot tap runs more quickly than I expected, and I top it up with a bit of cold. In goes the whole mini bottle of complimentary bubble bath. Fancy stuff, doesn't look cheap. The scent of aromatherapy oils reaches my nostrils and I take in a deep breath, my knee shaking as I stand leaning over the bath to reach the taps. My hands grip the side of the bath more tightly to steady myself. Aah! A jabbing pain shoots up my leg causing me to cry out. My eyes flick instantly towards the wine bottle in the white, art-deco style sink, nestling under the tap.

I shouldn't really, it's not six o'clock yet.

Oh sod it. This whole situation is awkward and we haven't even had dinner yet. The thought of the five of us together talking about Tania, the knot that's tightening in my stomach, makes me crave a glass. One bottle for today and one for tomorrow.

I pivot on my better leg and sit down on the loo until the bath is three-quarters full then stand up again to turn off the taps, swishing my hand in the water to test the temperature. Perfect, hot but not scorching.

Baths are great for pain, and so is wine.

My leg is throbbing. I wince as I feel the hot, achy pain pulsate to the timing of a silent beat. I need a quick fix. Dinner won't be for a while, I expect. I unscrew the bottle cap and savour the satisfying glug as I pour the light-yellow liquid into a small glass tumbler on the shelf, the type hotels expect you to put your toothbrush in, then gulp it down in two mouthfuls. It won't be long before the warmth kicks in and it dials down my discomfort. The GP doesn't prescribe me enough painkillers. Says I need to alter my lifestyle to cope with the RA, which came on suddenly just less than a couple of years ago. Bet he wouldn't be saying that if he had to put up with it. As if meditation and mindfulness is going to make the pain go away.

I pour another light amber glass, screw the cap back on carefully – wouldn't want to waste any – and I'm about to place the bottle back in the sink when I realise that I'll have to get out of the bath again to top up my glass; it's more practical for it to stand on the floor beside the bath instead. Once I've undressed, I put the tumbler on the shelf above the bath where the toiletries are, then sit on the side and swing my feet into the water before lowering myself in.

As I lie back in the bubbles I exhale deeply, enjoying the warmth of the water against my skin and its spa-like scent. Not that I can afford to go to spas. The label on the bubble bath bottle said it's a lavender blend, ideal for relaxing. That's exactly what I need. One by one, with each mouthful of wine and top up of hot water in the bath, my muscles and joints start to loosen up, uncurling like fat fingers used to clinging on to a safety rail, letting go a little of my pent-up frustration, difficulties and discomfort. My thoughts meander from the now to the then, back to when stresses were writing assignments on time, my housemates using up the last bit of milk I'd bought, without replacing it, which meant I had to take my morning coffee black, and pain was something I only really experienced when it was my time of the month.

I didn't know I had it so good.

It's not long before the tumbler is empty and I reach over and pour another.

I never drink when Emily is with me, of course not. Trouble is, now I share access with Hannah, my daughter and I spend a lot of time apart. The mediator we saw said 50/50 custody is the fairest way to proceed with parenting, with Emily knowing she's loved and wanted by both her mums. My head knows it's the right thing to do but my heart wants to grab on to her when it's handover day, keep her all to myself and savour every minute of being her mum, teenage angst and mood swings included. Give it a few years and she'll be flying the coop, finding her own path in the world, like I did when I went to St Mark's.

A shadow crosses the room as a cloud moves in front of the sun distracting me from my thoughts. The temperature has cooled and I start to feel a slight chill in my shoulders where they peek out above the water. I raise my knee above the surface and shuffle up to the taps to top up the heat. There's a gurgle as lukewarm water flows out. I leave it a minute but the temperature stays the same. Oh for goodness' sake. It can't be a heat-on-demand boiler. You'd have thought a hotel would have enough hot water for all the guests. Or is it because I'm in the smallest, least important room?

Never mind, I suppose I ought to face up to start getting ready for the evening meal, the big reunion for Tania. In my mind's eye I imagine her throwing her head back and laughing at Jeannie rushing around, trying to make everything perfect, just so. She did like to poke fun at Jeannie's quirks when she wasn't looking. A memory resurfaces in my consciousness of how Tania would never do her washing-up because she knew Jeannie would crack when she saw unclean dishes by the draining board and wash them herself. 'Why wash up when we already have a cleaning genie?' Tania would joke when our housemate was out of earshot. The rare weekends that Jeannie went home to visit her parents I'd do Tania's washing-up for her, which usually included Johnny's mess as well. She didn't ask me to, I just did it, as if I accepted that someone as special and disorganised as Tania couldn't be expected to keep on top of menial tasks. I suppose it seems odd now.

I wonder where that memory popped up from? I deliberately haven't thought about those three university years for a long time. A tide of guilt sweeps over me – I've been busy getting on with my life, despite the fact that Tania lost hers.

My tumbler is empty. Dangling my arm over the side of the bath, my wet fingers clasp the glass bottle and I lift it up to see how much wine there is left. Enough for a quick refill and to leave a couple of centimetres in the bottle. That way I haven't drunk a whole bottle by myself and there's a bit left for a nightcap. I unscrew the cap and take a quick swig for good luck before topping up my tumbler, which I balance on the side of the bath while I use both hands to screw the cap back on.

Despite the tepid temperature I feel warm inside, as if I could float on top of the now rather forlorn-looking bubbles. Hot water situation excluded, this freebie weekend is turning out to be better than expected. I wish I could stay in this room tonight with the fluffy robe and my book, instead of having to make conversation with Jeannie and Johnny, but I promised Keren I'd support her. If I don't hurry up and get dressed I'll be late. I ponder on the two outfits I brought with me – which of them shall I wear tonight? I say outfits but they are both more than a few years old and were the only clean and presentable items in my wardrobe. I don't get to go out very often or have the spare cash to buy anything new.

A knock on the bedroom door snatches me from my sartorial thoughts and I jump in surprise, my arm shooting out to pull myself up in the bath.

Smash. A split second after hearing the sound I look over and see with horror that I've knocked the tumbler on to the floor and it has shattered into a multitude of sharp-edged, glittering pieces. I step out of the bath gingerly and throw a hand towel over the detritus but, when I feel a sharp stab in my big toe, I realise I haven't been careful enough. With a larger towel wrapped round me I sit on the loo and inspect the damage, my leg not complaining as loudly as it usually does about the effort it takes me to bend my knee to bring my foot closer to my eyes.

There's a tiny piece of glass sticking out of my big toe's padded flesh. A thought flashes in my mind: Is this karma? Payback time, my just deserts brought on by being here?

I'm being stupid, it was just a silly accident. I pull the shard out with my thumb and forefinger quickly and throw it in the bathroom bin. Small globules of oozing blood appear, causing me to press loo roll onto my toe to stem the flow. That's better. No harm done.

The noise coming from the bedroom door starts again: rap, rap, rap, louder this time, more forceful. Who on earth is it? I don't really want to show myself wrapped in a towel.

'Coming!' I shout as the knocking continues. I walk out of the bathroom and towards the brown panelled door. Whoever it is, is pretty impatient.

All of a sudden, the violent knocking kicks another dusty memory into my mind. The bangs on the door. A jolt into consciousness, then a few sweet seconds before everything changed and I found out Tania was dead.

Chapter 5

Adam

'You didn't want to talk to Johnny then? You know you're going to have to at some point, hun. I thought you said it was all in the past?' Keren asks me as she zips open the large holdall we've brought with us. I'd be quite happy leaving it all in the bag and picking out what I need as and when, but Keren busies herself with unfolding the clothes we've packed, hanging her dresses and the jeans she keeps for best up in the wardrobe along with my couple of shirts and pairs of trousers. She puts our T-shirts in the chest of drawers and lays out her pyjamas on the right side of the bed, the side she claimed since we first got together and I hoped she'd never get out of.

Her tone is light but I can tell she's in concerned, protective wife mode.

'No, I needed the loo, that's why I carried the bags up to our room. I'll talk to him at dinner. Everything's fine.'

'Did you see how much he's changed since uni? He might have money and privilege but age has not been kind to him,' she replies straightaway, kissing me on the top of my head where I have hair and Johnny, by the brief glance I had of him, now has a bald spot.

I change the subject. 'Great room, isn't it? I'm certainly planning on getting lucky,' I say warmly at her loyalty.

Keren lets out a high-pitched giggle and bends over where I'm sitting on the bed, wraps her arms around me, her fingers still clasping a pair of knickers destined for the drawer. 'Chance will be a fine thing. Two whole nights without the kids.'

'And the mornings.' I wink.

The bed is one of those fake four poster ones with wooden poles at each corner supporting a high up canopy but with no curtains or material attached. There's something odd about the rest of the room, despite its floral wallpaper and deep carpet, and I can't work out what it is until I realise there's no TV.

'Have you been worrying about seeing him again?'

'Not really,' I mutter.

'I just want you to enjoy this weekend, darling. Honestly, he's not worth stressing about.'

'Like you said, it was all a long time ago.' I detach myself from her arms and turn to reach the paperback I threw in the holdall earlier, signalling that the conversation is over. I flip through the pages of the sport biography, trying to remember where I'd read up to. There are lots of corners turned over and I try to find the most recent.

My wife looks in my direction and I avoid her eyes, something I've been doing rather a lot of lately. She knows me. If she looks into my eyes, she'll see my soul and right now I want to keep it hidden.

I'm pretending to read while Keren carries on putting everything in the place she wants it to be in. For someone small she has always made a lot of noise. That's one of the many things I love about her, you can literally hear her presence.

She sucks in a breath, is about to speak but then falters. Then she tries again.

'Is everything OK?' she asks. 'You've been, well, not yourself recently. Quiet.'

There's silence, a strange nothingness that you never get in our house in London, where there are always voices, music, sirens, car alarms or the TV creating a background score to our everyday life.

'Adam?' she prompts.

'I'm sorry, love, I'm just really tired. Work's been non-stop, what with Helena on board.'

My eyes remain firmly focused on the black type.

'They were mad not to give you the job. She sounds like such a bitch. You'd better keep me away from her at the Christmas do!' Keren consoles me.

I lift my book up so she can't see the guilt cross my face. A wave of exhaustion at my pretence crashes over me.

Keren pats my knee tenderly. 'I know you weren't bothered about coming here this weekend, I hope I haven't forced you into it. It's just that, as I said, Saira wanted to come and I didn't want her to be here on her own.' There's a slight tremor in her voice, an uncertainty she rarely shows.

I lower my book, place my best sales director smile on my face and try to sound enthusiastic.

'She wouldn't have been on her own, there'd still be Johnny and Jeannie here. Anyway, a free weekend away with my gorgeous wife? What's not to love.'

Now I look up. Keren is smiling, eyes crinkling with pleasure at the compliment. Her voice reverts back to near its usual confidence. 'When you put it that way . . . I reckon we can do without the pyjamas,' she says, throwing them back in the bag and laughing. 'Why bother putting them on tonight when I'll only be taking them straight off?'

I make an appreciative sound and reach out and hold her left hand, running my fingertip over the cold smoothness of her wedding ring.

'I'm a bit knackered after the drive to be honest. It's been a busy week,' I say, trying to use the excuse of the drive not to worry her more.

'It did seem never-ending. Why is the north so far north?' she laughs.

'I might just lie down for a bit, rest up before whatever Jeannie has planned for us at dinner tonight.'

'Good idea. I think I'll go and explore the place, have a nose around. Find out what there is in the local area for us to visit tomorrow. A walk to a country pub or something. Surely we won't have to spend all our time in the hotel, will we? Mind you, I don't know if Saira will be able to manage a walk. We might have to go in the car instead. I expect there'll be leaflets downstairs somewhere on places to visit nearby.'

I smile internally. Keren's earlier concerns have all but disappeared now and she's springing across the room, excited about exploring the Yorkshire countryside. She's always enjoyed visiting new places and we don't get to do it very often, mainly because I prefer my home comforts. But I'd do anything to make sure she's happy, even it means trekking up a hill or two.

'It's a bit weird seeing Johnny in the flesh again after twenty-five years, isn't it? He looks so much older. Do you think he's thinking the same about me?' She laughs, screwing up her face into tight wrinkles.

'You are as gorgeous as ever,' I reassure her. 'We all look different from our student days. Remember the blond streak I had?'

Keren snorts with derision. Tania had wanted to experiment with my hair, and I'd have let her do anything, even though the results were abominable. Thank God there are no photos kicking around as proof. I've never liked having my photo taken. The kids take selfies all the time, but I'm glad I grew up in an age when camera phones hadn't yet been invented.

'And Jeannie's changed her hair colour too,' I add.

'Oh yes, Jeannie. I always forget about her,' adds Keren nonchalantly. 'Even though we're here because of her.'

'We're not though, are we? We're here because of Tania,' I reply, thinking of the Facebook Messenger invite we'd all received. I'm only on it for work. It was Keren, whose phone pings constantly with notifications, who saw Jeannie's post first. A gathering to remember Tania. Twenty-five years after her death.

'Tania. Everything always was about Tania, may she rest in peace,' Keren replies.

'Was it? I suppose it was,' I say. We hardly ever talked about her. I always thought it best not to, considering Keren knows how I felt about Tania when we were at St Mark's, and despite the fact that she occasionally haunts my dreams. It would be disrespectful somehow to my wife. Let the past remain in the past, an old box of memories and emotions best left closed. Especially what she doesn't know.

Unlike me, Keren accepted Jeannie's Facebook Messenger group invite straightaway. I hardly ever log on to my account and I only did so when Keren told me the invite was there and we could have a free weekend away. My wife is on more social media platforms than she knows what to do with, but she says she has to be on them to be in the know as to what's going on with the kids' school and to organise things with other parents.

'Looking back, whatever she did, we were all quick to follow,' continues Keren. 'She liked organising things and being the centre of attention. Unlike me. I suppose it was great to have Tania leading the way.'

She pauses for a second, as if she's deep in thought, before carrying on. 'Right, I'm off downstairs then. I've got my key card. Rest up and I'll be back to put a dress on before dinner.'

The bedroom door closes with a satisfying click. I'm all alone, physically, but not in my head. Tania is there, more vivid in my memory than she ever could be in a photograph. Keren's right, I did follow her like a cat crossing a busy road, too blinkered to worry whether I'd be hit by a truck.

It was all such a long time ago, and I've done my best to move on from it. Do I really want to dig it up and let it burn?

In front of me the printed words make no sense on the page. I can't concentrate on reading and toss the book to the end of the bed. I briefly look for a TV remote but then remember that this is a digital-detox hotel and television is a banned activity.

The idea of no phone or internet was a bonus for this weekend. Work can't contact me, I've got a blissful forty-eight hours of peace. The new MD of the company – where I've been for twenty years and worked my way up to becoming sales director – wasn't impressed when I told her that I was off limits this weekend. Her fingers grasped her knees more rigidly than usual while she droned on about potential emergencies and important clients. When I played my trump card, that the weekend is to commemorate a dead friend and it was important for my well-being (on the hoof I remembered the two-hour self-care seminar she'd forced us directors to take time out of our day for, so she could tick a caring employer check box, and then expected us to work late to make the time up), she realised she had to smile and agree. *Just this once and sorry for your loss.*

What did she want, me to shove an iPhone up my backside and smuggle it in?

I reach for the pillows behind me and plump them, folding one in half so I can lie back half supine. The cotton feels cool and soothing against my neck. I've got about sixty hours before Helena will expect to micromanage me again, smartphone on, ready to jump at her whim.

I wince as the guilt I'm suppressing comes back to haunt me. Keren thinks I applied for the MD job and was beaten to it by Helena. The truth is that when the previous MD announced he was retiring, he suggested I take on the role. I knew the company inside out, he said, and was popular and well respected by my colleagues. It felt like a family then, a well-oiled machine where everyone had their place.

That evening when I told Keren that Ray was retiring, her face instantly lit up. My wife has always championed me and insisted I'm undervalued at work. Before I could even mention the job offer to her, she'd told me about the latest estimate a building firm had quoted her on getting a small extension downstairs. Our plans of making the kitchen open plan and adding a downstairs loo were slowly becoming unachievable. With the kids getting older, we're pushed for space and can't afford to move up the housing ladder. I hadn't seen Keren this excited in so long, already working on her mood board, and we'd hoped to find a builder to start work in the autumn.

But then came the letter from our mortgage company reminding us that our fixed term deal was soon up for renewal. The best rate we could find was a few hundred pounds more a month than what we were paying. Keren tried to hide the disappointment on her crumpling face when we realised there was no way we could afford both the mortgage and the extension. The kitchen dream had remained that for a while, just a dream.

'Look, the estimate is three grand cheaper than the others,' Keren said brightly, chattering away about how the firm had done a good job at one of her friend's houses and they'd got credentials.

'If you get the MD job you'll get a big pay rise, won't you, and a larger annual bonus? Didn't Ray buy a new Jag last year? And he and his wife went on a Caribbean cruise. We'll be able to afford both the mortgage and the extension. Now you'll finally get the promotion you deserve and we'll have more space in this house, it's a win-win situation!'

I couldn't bear to ruin her happiness by saying how unsure I was about taking the job, so I hugged her, keeping my reservations to myself. Then, as time went on, Keren threw herself into renovation planning and it became harder tell her the truth. Perhaps I could have said yes, taken on the extra work and responsibility, and provide for my family like my father never did for my mum. Yet every time I imagined myself sitting behind Ray's desk my stomach churned and dread overcame me. I'm the wrong side of forty. I want to do less work before I meet the Grim Reaper, not more. I've got an eight-year-old and a ten-year-old whom I want to spend time with while they still want to be seen with their dad, and my mum, who lives fifty miles away, is needing more help from me as she gets older.

So I bottled it. I let Keren believe that I'd applied for the MD role but Helena beat me. At the time it felt easier than explaining my inadequacy, crushing her dreams and admitting I'd lied, then having to watch her loyally hide her disappointment and tell me it's OK.

I've only ever lied to her once before.

A beam of sunlight shines through the hotel bedroom window onto my face, causing me to squint. Maybe I should have taken the job. How I wish I'd been able to look into the future and foreseen the arrival of Helena, who marked me down at my staff evaluation as requiring improvement just because I don't subscribe to her American corporate management bullshit. I'm stuck in a job I hate with little hope of finding a similar role at the same salary.

I shut my eyes tightly and try and block out thoughts of my two lies, or omissions of the truth, that are threating to seep guiltily out of my pores. Should I have come this weekend? Keren wanted to, and I couldn't bear to let her down once more, and Tania, how could I resist the chance to overtly remember her again? But what if the long-buried truth comes out?

I must have dozed off, alternating between that half-asleep and half-awake phase where you're not sure where you are, because my eyes snap open when I hear a knock on the door.

'Keren?' I shout out, pulling myself off the bed and padding to the door to open it.

There's no one there. The corridor is empty apart from a table with a Chinese-style vase on filled with summer flowers.

'Hello?' I call. Nobody answers. I turn back into the room and try to pull the door closed but there's something preventing it moving smoothly. Looking down, I see a white A5 size envelope whose corner must have furled up when I tried to shut the door.

I pick it up and sit down on the end of bed, wondering if it's a dinner menu or some schedule for the weekend from Jeannie.

Sliding out what the envelope contains I gasp involuntarily. In my hand is a slightly faded photo of a woman with a short shock of bleached blonde hair, with one arm around a tall, skinny youth with a blonde streak in his dark brown hair and the other holding an alcopop bottle. Tania and me. I don't remember this photo ever being taken but, looking at the background of the bar in my first-year student halls, with its sticky grey carpet tiles and green wallpaper, the time and place of this photo comes back to me. It was during the few weeks Tania and I were dating on and off, before I knew that my feelings towards her were much stronger than hers, the night she'd wanted to go to a gig at a nearby pub and we'd started drinking in the bar beforehand, me too enamoured to tell her I disliked rock music and crowds.

Like I said, I'd have followed her anywhere.

Was I a fool?

I look into Tania's eyes, obscured by an orange ring from the flash. So young. So full of fire and anticipation.

Who put the envelope under my door? Was it Jeannie? Or Johnny? Saira would surely have said if she'd had an old photo of me. Why would they send me this photo specifically?

A pang grabs my heart, a recollection of heady, insecure, intense love I haven't experienced for decades. Not the deep, steady, joint-parent and putting the bins out on the right day love I have now.

Tania. My first girlfriend. My first love.

If only if I'd known it wouldn't last and could have prepared for the heartbreak.

If only things had been different, I had been different.
If only I hadn't done what I did.
If only, if only . . .
I push the photo back in the envelope and hide it in my bag.

Chapter 6

Keren

Credit where credit is due, Jeannie's done a good job with the hotel. She always was pernickety about little things and I suppose that eye for detail, or what we used to think was her being anal, has paid off. Enjoying the rare peace and quiet, I forgive myself my little white lie to Adam, telling him that we're here because Saira wanted to come. It prised him away from home and a weekend away will do us both good.

This accommodation is really nice, probably the best I've stayed in apart from the ten glorious days of our honeymoon in Greece. Mind you, that had the smell of drains, now and then, that reminded you you were on the continent. What is it with this not flushing paper down the loo business? None of that in this Yorkshire hotel of course.

Tania's family home was the poshest private house I'd ever visited by a mile. In my mind's eye a memory of the huge rooms, quiet luxe decor before it became all the rage, appears; the kitchen-diner that was larger than the whole ground floor of our house, the private beach sloping down to the sea, and the nonchalant way Tania took it for granted, like she did with her studies. I suppose you would if it's all you've ever known. I had to work hard both to pass my exams and earn money to pay for my food, books and social life. Tania didn't, it all came to her for free.

I leave our room to explore. Instead of taking the lift that Jeannie had installed as part of the refurb I walk down the curved stairs, feeling the smooth, varnished oak of the banister under my palm.

My kids would have loved to have slid down here when they were younger. They probably still would now.

The walls are lined with a tasteful white wallpaper interspersed with printed trailing ivy and tiny pale pink flowers. There's no cheap art nailed to the walls like you get in those identikit hotels on the outskirts of seemingly every town. Instead, in brass frames that look elegant not gaudy, there are a couple of pictures that even to my art-heathen eye look like they've actually been painted and aren't prints.

I stand still on one step, halfway down, to peer closer at what looks like a countryside scene in summer, with sheep in a field, shading under tree canopies. With my eye a couple of centimetres from the canvas I can see the individual brushstrokes. Beautiful. It's modern but not one of those experimental Picasso-like pictures I saw on a school trip to an art gallery. Can't have been cheap. Unlike the framed IKEA posters on our lounge wall at home.

Home. We've only been gone a few hours but it seems so far away now. I've been looking forward to this trip and signed up straightaway as soon as Adam agreed to it, even though I knew it would be more difficult for him. But I couldn't think of another way to get him away, without the kids, so we could really talk. He batted away my suggestions of a weekend break. Maybe, we'll see, depends on what comes up, work's busy, he said. All the same excuses I give the children when I want to avoid the temper tantrum I'd get if I said no outright.

Something's wrong, I know it is. He thinks he's fooling me but he's not. I'm much better at it than he is.

The stairs lead down to the entrance hall. I jump, as out of the corner of my eye I think I see a moving shadow. Turning my head, I blink and look to see what it was. There's no one there. The hall is empty. Jeannie said there aren't any other guests staying. It must have been a trick of the light. I've got to admit it, this whole reunion has made me feel rather uneasy and on edge.

The hairs on the back of my neck stand to attention. I shiver involuntarily and nearly lose my footing. I grasp the banister with my now sweaty hand. Adam's in our room. Saira can't move that quickly. If I did see someone it must be Johnny or Jeannie. But why would they be creeping around?

I cautiously walk down the last few stairs and then pop my head round the bar area. It's empty apart from a white-shirt-wearing barman, who welcomes me as I come in.

My shoulders lower a couple of centimetres as I breathe in the pleasant scent of polish. Of course, a place like this must have quite a large staff. It'll be one of the hotel employees who I saw.

This place is calm, ordered and relaxing. I can see why they made it a digital-detox hotel, even though I already feel a bit itchy that I can't check my social media. It's the sort of place I can imagine that producers would use to film period dramas. Imagine the days when all this space was one family's house, and they had a cleaner, cook and maids to do all the donkey work rather than just two frazzled working parents.

Johnny with his flash Range Rover still seems to be as well-to-do as ever, born into the same privileged world as Tania. It's probably why they were well suited. At St Mark's he acted like any other uni student. You wouldn't have thought he came from money, though we all knew that in the holidays he went home to his parents' mews house in central London. I expect he owns a similar one too now – I heard on the grapevine that, like me, he's married with a couple of children. But he's not like Adam and me – we haven't had everything handed to us on a plate. Johnny didn't have to get a job when he was at St Mark's to help support his student loan. Easier to get good grades when you can spend your spare time studying rather than pulling pints behind the student bar, isn't it?

Money breeds money. We live in the same city yet no doubt he owns a multi-million pound house in a sought-after area, while our mortgage hardly seems to go down every year despite what we're paying for a semi smaller than the one I grew up in and we can't even afford a kitchen extension anymore. If only bloody Helena hadn't beaten Adam to the MD job.

While I appreciate having the freebie trip, staying in a bedroom twice as large as ours at home with the holy grail of an en suite, there's still a petty part inside of me that resents Johnny's privileged lifestyle, reminding me of what I haven't got. I suppose psychologists would have a theory for it. This is how marketing experts sell you things you never thought you wanted or needed – seeing them plants a worm in your mind that starts to eat you up inside.

'Can I get you anything, madam?' the barman asks. If I were ten years younger I might think he was cute in a muscles-under-his-shirt-and-friendly-smile kind of way.

Jeannie said that breakfast and dinner are included but she didn't mention if alcohol was. I bet it costs a fortune here. Mind you, it's too early anyway. If I have a G & T now I'll start to fall asleep at the dinner table.

'Tap water please,' I reply.

'Take a seat and I'll bring it over for you.'

Yes, I'd definitely think he was cute if I were on the market. I'm thankful I'm not though, particularly after seeing what Saira's been through since her wife ended their relationship. I love Adam to bits and our noisy, busy life with the kids. It's not fashionable to say you're happily married, but it's true and I don't want anything to spoil it. My thoughts run to the time alone Adam and I will have this weekend. Child-free sex. I hope the barman can't see the blush that's creeping onto my face at the scenario which is popping into my head.

I thank the cute barman and walk to a leather armchair by a rack of tourist information leaflets. I choose a few then sit down. Breathing in, I notice the subtle scent of vanilla in the air, much nicer than the air freshener in our loo at home. I look to see if there's a plug-in one in the wall, then laugh at myself for being daft. This isn't a cheap B & B. They'll be pumping out the fragrance somewhere unobtrusively like they do in swanky spas – or so I read in a magazine.

The barman brings over my water, dressed with ice and lemon, and a bowl of pretzels. I try not to show my excitement at free snacks and spend the next half an hour unwinding, enjoying the time to just daydream, even though it feels weird not being able to check my phone and scroll aimlessly, which is what I usually do if I get a break from the kids. I don't know if Jeannie has anything else planned for the group, apart from dinner tonight and tomorrow, but I certainly want to explore the countryside and make the most of being out of the city. One leaflet shows a waterfall a car ride from here that looks gorgeous. Maybe we could take a picnic. I packed some crisps, chocolate, our refillable water bottles and fruit in my case to make sure we don't have to buy any supplies. The petrol to come here cost a fortune.

A thought flutters into my head like a welcome butterfly. I'm being ridiculous thinking about money. What am I worrying about? Nature is free. I'm away for the weekend with my husband whom I still love and fancy, and trust not to suddenly leave me – like Hannah did to Saira. Our children are happy and healthy. We have enough cash coming in each month to ensure we can live comfortably. So what if I can't buy loads of crap that I'd like but don't need? I'm manufacturing a fake problem for myself. I'm here, I'm alive. The reason we're at this hotel is to commemorate Tania, who never got the chance to experience life as a fully-fledged adult.

My mum used to say that she grew concerned when everything was going right for once in our house. My brother and I were happy and doing well at school, Dad's teaching job was secure, my grandparents were all well, she felt she was making a difference with her teaching assistant job at a primary school and volunteering at the local Brownie pack.

'Things never stay the same. Something's bound to go wrong,' she'd say to my dad, who would tell her not to bother stressing about things that hadn't happened yet. She was right though. One year a Brownie fell and broke her ankle at camp. In another, Grandma was diagnosed with breast cancer. My brother came down with gastroenteritis. I spent two weeks crying solidly after being dumped by my first, and only, school boyfriend.

There's an old adage that women turn into their mothers. I touch the wood of the side table next to me in superstition, hoping that nothing will go wrong. The kids are fine with their grandparents. We're all happy and healthy. Except . . . Adam. I can't shake the feeling that there's something he's not telling me. What if it's something that will prove my mum's theory right?

Besides, we're here in this hotel for Tania, the friend I'd adored, a visceral reminder that no one knows what lies in their future. She was just about to start her adult life, with so many opportunities ahead of her, when she died; went from having it all to having nothing.

I shudder involuntarily at the morbid thought.

My glass is empty and only a few crumbs remain in the pretzel bowl. There's a rumble in my stomach. I look at my watch. It's not too long before Jeannie has asked us to meet downstairs for dinner. I should check on Saira to see if she's OK and have a quick gossip before quickly getting changed myself and picking up Adam.

The sound of a creaking floorboard breaks my thoughts as I walk back up the stairs, causing me to look round. Like before, there's no one there. The hairs on the back of my neck start to prick up again, the feeling you get when you go into survival mode as if a caveman has detected a sabre-tooth tiger in the vicinity. No tigers here thankfully. I'm being silly, paranoid even.

And yet that's the second time it has happened this afternoon. Jeannie couldn't be watching me on CCTV. I saw a little security camera in the entrance hall. Are there more around, hidden so guests don't notice them? Surely not, it's a far too creepy thought. Why would Jeannie want to watch her guests? I shake my head to try and get rid of my ridiculous thoughts. Adam would think I'd lost the plot if I told him, and anyway, I can't put a damper on being here because it was me who wanted to come this weekend.

At the top of the stairs I hear a faint sound, like a smash. The noise came from not that far away and the nearest room to the stairwell is Saira's. Shit, has she fallen? Concerned, I hurry and knock on her door, the rap echoing down the corridor. Silence. There's no one else around who could have caused it. Why isn't Saira answering? Can she not move? My heart speeds up and I knock on the door repeatedly. Maybe the bad thing is happening now and Saira is hurt. She had a nasty fall a couple of months back when she lost her balance and that's when she started using a stick.

'Saira, are you OK? It's Keren,' I shout. Despite my turning the doorknob, it won't open. I don't have the key. I try and force it with the weight of my shoulder but this isn't a Hollywood movie, I'm not that strong and the door stubbornly doesn't budge.

'Saira!' I must be shouting loud enough for the whole floor to hear now.

Sickness starts to rise up in my gullet. The only thing I can do is run downstairs, find Jeannie and get her to open the door. Or maybe get that master key she mentioned. I start to turn when I hear a familiar voice from the other side of the door. 'It's OK, I'm coming.'

The lock turns with a sound so sweet. Saira opens the door just wide enough to let me in, then swiftly locks it behind us. She's damp with a towel wrapped round her and is leaning heavily on her stick, not putting one foot to the ground.

'Just a little accident. Nothing to worry about. Give me a few seconds to sweep it up and I'll be fine.' Am I imagining it or is she slurring her words slightly?

'What happened? Can I help?' She's avoiding my gaze. I can smell wine on her breath. 'Have you hurt your leg?'

'I stood on a piece of glass. I treated myself to a glass of wine in the bath and accidentally knocked it over. You know how clumsy I am with this RA.'

I don't say that wine won't help clumsiness. It's not for me to judge. Saira's had a rough two years, so what if she wants a glass of wine in the bath when she's on holiday? This is probably the only hotel she'll get to stay in this year. Hannah's taking Emily to Spain for a fortnight in the summer holidays to a villa with her parents, brother and his family. Saira cried down the phone to me when she said she can only afford four nights in a B & B in Dorset for her and Emily. She's worried that Emily will want to spend more time with Hannah than her because her ex can afford foreign holidays and meals out.

I look round, my nosey streak kicking in. Saira's single room is a lot smaller than ours, and it looks even pokier with her clothes thrown over the bed and wheely suitcase unzipped, its contents spilling over on to the floor. I step over it as I walk in.

'You got a plaster in here? Or I can always go downstairs and ask at reception.'

'No, please don't do that.' Saira shakes her head violently. 'I'd have to explain why I need it and I don't know if I'm supposed to sneak wine in.' She perches her bottom on the end of the bed and lifts her leg up, resting her foot on the chintzy-but-cool bedspread.

'I think I've got a mini first aid kit in my handbag. Have had it in there since Emily was little. Can you have a look please?'

She gestures towards her canvas shoulder bag that's sitting on the right-hand bedside table. I walk round, squeezing past Saira to pick it up, then have a quick look in. There's something that feels a bit wrong about rifling through another woman's handbag. We've all got the same stuff: purse, keys, old receipts, lipstick, hairbrush (no phone, of course), but there's something quite intimate about someone else's day-to-day things. I put my hand in to see if I can find a plaster.

'Oh, chuck it all out on the bed, it'll be easier to find. Just pretend you haven't seen the used tissues,' Saira laughs loudly. I wonder whether it was just the one glass of wine she had but then tell myself again that it's none of my business.

'If you don't mind?'

Saira nods.

'Here goes then!' I tip the contents of the bag out over the pillow. It's a smallish bag, probably not the one Saira uses when she has to go into the office for work, and there isn't that much in it. I have a quick rummage, avoiding the snotty tissues, and spot a little plastic ziplock bag. Inside I find a few different-size plasters, a blister pack of paracetamol and a couple of antiseptic wipes.

'What do you reckon Jeannie's got planned for tonight?' I ask Saira as I take charge, wipe her big toe with the antiseptic wipe and then wrap a plaster round it. It doesn't look too bad at all, the little cut has started to clot already.

'Good food, I hope. And talking about Tania I guess, considering that she's the reason Jeannie organised this weekend. I can't believe she's been gone twenty-five years.'

We both stay respectfully silent for a minute, then Saira restarts the conversation.

'Very fancy hotel, isn't it? Jeannie's done a good job. She's certainly changed her image too, hasn't she?' We chat for a few minutes and then I notice the time. Not long until dinner is served, and I can't imagine Jeannie will be pleased if we turn up late. It'd be rude to anyway considering that she's paying for it. 'Meet you downstairs in fifteen minutes,' I say to Saira, then shut her room door gently behind me and walk to my own.

The first thing I notice when I enter is that Adam looks gorgeous. He's wearing a navy, checked, open-neck shirt with navy trousers that flatter his peachy bum. The second is that his face is pale, almost ill looking.

'Are you all right?' I ask, concerned, and he draws me into an embrace. The woody scent of his aftershave smells like home and I'm happy to linger there.

'Yeah, I missed you though. I'm not sure what to expect tonight. Bit nervous really. What have we all got in common anymore?'

I stay wrapped in his arms. I don't tell him the enjoyment I felt earlier on in the bar has evaporated, replaced by a sense of foreboding disquiet.

'I missed you too . . . I found a waterfall though for us to visit tomorrow.' I try and lighten the mood and don't mention what happened earlier. The eyes on me. I keep quiet about Saira's accident too. That's her business.

'We'll eat Jeannie's food, make polite chit-chat and talk about what everyone's been up to since St Mark's. We'll honour Tania's memory, like Jeannie wants us to, but we don't have to stay up late. Come ten o'clock we can excuse ourselves and come right back here. That's the part I'm looking forward to.'

Adam squeezes me, like he does with the kids to signal that the hug is over, and lets me go. My skin feels cold where he's stopped touching it.

'You're right.' He smiles and I'm about to relax, thinking that I've reassured him, until I notice that the smile doesn't reach his tired eyes. I take his hand and hold it.

'Everything will be fine. Before we know it'll be Sunday and we'll be driving back home. You never know, we might have such a good time that we want to come back!'

We chat about what the children might be up to with their grandparents while I quickly change into a knee-length green shift dress and Adam zips me up at the back. It's a few years old but still fits. I'm bigger built than my still-svelte husband but the dress's shape flatters my boobs and bum and a thin black belt accentuates my waist. I brush my hair, put on some blusher, mascara and lipstick, then we're ready to go.

When we're in the corridor Adam tries our room door to check it's locked. I look at him quizzically. It's not something he does at home. Usually I'm the one who wants to double-check I've shut all the windows and put the full lock on.

'Not quite sure how these key cards work. Much simpler with just an ordinary key,' he says and sets off towards the stairs.

The entrance to the private dining room on the ground floor is along a corridor we've not been down before. Jeannie explained earlier where to go. It's quite dark along the corridor, what with there being hardly any windows or natural light to illuminate it, and the only small window being at the far end. The wall lamps, despite it still being a sunny evening outside, are on but their dull yellow glow doesn't illuminate a great deal. They're probably those eco-friendly bulbs that take ages to heat up and still leave you squinting, wondering if your eyesight is getting worse and you're going to start needing varifocals.

Outside of the dining room door stands Johnny, wearing exactly what he was earlier. He nods at me but focuses on Adam. 'It's great to see you again, mate,' he says, proffering his right hand for my husband to shake. I hold my breath. For a split second it looks like Adam is going to ignore him and leave Johnny standing with his arm outstretched, but then I exhale as he shakes it politely.

'We've got a lot to catch up on, haven't we?' Johnny continues.

In my mind's eye I can see the two of them back in the day, best friends, as thick as thieves until, all thanks to Johnny, suddenly they weren't.

Johnny's words draw me back to the present day.

'I'm sorry for being a dickhead back then at St Mark's. It really is good to see you.' There's an unusual flicker of nerves in Johnny's voice, a slight neediness, and I wonder if Adam's picked up on it.

'Ah, well, we all were dickheads at some point,' my husband replies unconvincingly, and turns away.

Some more than others, I think.

Part of me, if I dwell on it, is still angry at Johnny on Adam's behalf for what he did, but then I think it was all in the past and should stay there. We were all barely out of childhood ourselves back then. What's the point in holding a grudge? Hasn't Adam got a successful life, a well-paid job, me and our kids, anyway? Then again, I sometimes used to think that Adam was too nice, too slow to realise when others were taking advantage of him, before he got together with me and I had his back.

'No Jeannie?' slurs a voice from behind our little group. It's Saira. She's wearing black leather trousers and a bright, multi-coloured blouse. It suits her. When I stand next to her I smell a waft of mint on her breath.

I shake my head and delicately hold on to her arm in case she's wobbly on her feet. Did she drink more wine after I left her room? It's not for me to tell her what to do but I don't want her to fall again.

We all stand awkwardly as if we're schoolchildren lining up outside a classroom waiting for the teacher. The dining room door opens from the other side and Jeannie walks through, shutting the door behind her.

'As if by magic, Jeannie appears,' I say nervously, causing a little laughter.

'Thanks for being on time. Dinner's ready to be served. Please come through, we've got the private dining room to ourselves,' Jeannie says, with an awkward smile on her face, a mixture of anxiety and excitement.

She opens the heavy wooden door and stands by it to let us through, one by one. No one moves a step, us all looking at each other in that polite, British, 'no you go first' irritating way. Jeannie looks at us all expectantly. No one else is budging, so I break the impasse and lead the way, purposefully ignoring the jitters in my stomach. It's only dinner after all and those jitters are probably because I haven't eaten much since breakfast. A woman needs more than a few pretzels to sustain herself.

What I see at the end of the room, at the head of the table, stops me in my tracks. I open my mouth, rooted to the spot, but no words come out. I'm rendered mute in shock.

'What the hell?' shouts Johnny, following right behind me.

There, directly facing us, is Tania.

Chapter 7

Johnny

When I get my breath back, I realise what I'm looking at, what's staring at me with those open turquoise eyes I adored drowning in so many years ago.

The atmosphere in the room is electric. Behind me deep heavy breaths resonate with shock. No one moves, it's as if we're all rendered immobile.

'Jesus Christ, that's sick,' I say, then remember that my children use the word sick as a compliment, and clarify hurriedly, 'Poor taste. Really poor taste, Jeannie.'

'Bloody hell,' says Keren's voice as she walks next to me. 'It's so realistic. For a moment I really thought it was her.'

Someone behind me stifles a sob. Saira, maybe?

In front of us, at the head of the dining table, is a life-size cardboard cut-out of Tania. For a split second it had me fooled, made me think I'd seen a ghost, until I noticed her unblinking eyes and the fact that she is aged about twenty-one, fresh-faced, unlined, with her signature cropped bleached hair. This image of Tania is unravaged by time, from when she was less than half the age we are now. A captured moment from our shared past.

Who knows what she would have looked like if she were alive now? The thought that she never got to age pricks my eyes with a threat of a few guilty tears that I stop myself shedding. Man up, Johnny, I tell myself. It's the whisky talking, and the shock.

This really feels like a cruel trick. I can't believe it's something

Jeannie would do on purpose. She must have thought we'd be pleased to see it.

Adam walks around the table to look at the cardboard figure up close. He picks it up and shows us the plastic stand it's slotted into to make it stand up.

'What are you playing at, Jeannie? Why did you do this?' he asks our host, seeming as put out as the rest of us. 'Were you trying to give us a heart attack?'

Jeannie rushes over to him, pale-faced and slightly lost for words. It's obvious our reaction wasn't what she was expecting.

'I, er . . .' She brushes down the front of her jacket to rid it of imaginary creases. Her eyes dart between us all. We're the Greek chorus judging her.

Jeannie takes the cardboard Tania from Adam and moves it to the side of the fireplace that's the dining room's central focus point. She takes a deep breath, pulls her shoulders back and starts again.

'We're all here this weekend to remember Tania, so I thought it's only right that she be with us in some form. Remember when, back in our student house, we'd show each other the developed photos we'd taken on nights out? Even the ones that had someone's finger in or where we had our eyes shut? I looked through old photos and found this lovely one I took of Tania the night we'd all completed our finals. Remember we all met in the students' union? Tania and Keren were the last to finish among all of us. We'd made a pact that none of us would celebrate until we were all free.'

I'd forgotten about that, but Jeannie's prompt brings the memories rushing back. My last exam was two days before Tania's and at that point we were firmly back together again. Instead of sleeping over at Tania's place, I stayed with Adam and Imran in our student house where we drank beer and caught up on our sleep before the real celebrations began. Two nights without Tania. I'd thought it didn't matter because we'd have the rest of our lives together. After what happened I wished I'd spent every moment I could with her.

'I know you meant well, but it's a bit macabre. You really did give me a shock,' Adam says.

We all stand around not sure what to do. The tension in the air is palpable.

Keren walks up to her husband and puts her arm around him. Is it to comfort Adam or herself? 'Gosh, she looks so young,' she says wistfully, staring at the static cardboard. Tania's eyes are like those in classic paintings where they seem to follow you around the room, always looking, always probing into what you're thinking.

'I'm sorry if my idea upset you. How about we all sit down, I'll pour the wine and then Grant will come and serve the starter. I think our chef Eerik would like to pop in and say hello too. I've told him he's cooking for extra special guests! There are name cards by the place settings. Red or white?'

Jeannie's switched firmly to professional hostess mode, probably hoping we'll move on from her mistake, and goes to fetch one of the open reds from a brass drinks trolley on wheels near to the table. Next to it is a huge wine bucket filled with ice and two bottles of white.

I hope there are more bottles where they came from as I'll be needing a few stiff drinks after that surprise. And I hope there are no more shocks in store.

The table is set for six. The head of the table, where the cardboard cut-out had been, doesn't have a place name by it but is fully set with plates, cutlery and a wine glass. Very weird leaving a seat for a dead person. Jeannie's place is at the other end of the table. I'm on her right, Keren on my right, and opposite us are Adam and Saira. We all take our seats bar Jeannie, who bustles around filling up wine and water glasses. The only thing we say is 'red' or 'white, please.' Other conversation is cut dead.

Saira's eyes look a bit red. I can think why, as she stinks of booze, but don't say anything. I'm here for some fun this weekend, not dealing with a drunk woman and having a cardboard cut-out induced heart attack.

The barman I chatted to earlier comes in carrying the starters we ordered this afternoon, followed by a tall blond-haired bloke, and Jeannie fills the silence talking about sourcing local produce and all the food being organic.

'I bet you charge a tenner here, Jeannie, for a few rocket leaves and a couple of tomatoes from Tesco!' I joke loudly, hoping to cut through the excruciating vibe in the room.

Keren starts to giggle, then, after seeing the thunderous look on the chef's face and Jeannie's jaw start to wobble, she covers it up with a coughing fit.

'All the food I cook is fresh from farms within the county. I wouldn't go anywhere near the rubbish English supermarkets sell. Jeannie sets very high standards here,' the chef firmly says to me, hovering next to his boss as if to shield her from the detritus of my lead balloon inappropriate remark.

'Thank you, Eerik. The food looks delightful. We provide top quality service for our guests, Johnny,' Jeannie retorts.

Grant delivers the starters carefully to each guest but plonks my plate down in front of me with a slam. Serves me right, I suppose. I keep my head down, concentrating on my sticky chicken wings, while they leave. Adam has ordered them as well, while Keren, Jeannie and Saira went for soup, far more ladylike to eat than gnawing on chicken wings. It reminds me of our regular stop-offs at the chicken takeaway on the way home after a night out at the students' union, when Adam and I would drunkenly compete against each other on how many wings we could get through. Good times.

I take another mouthful from my wine glass. This Chianti's decent, medium-bodied, not cheap I'd bet. At least Jeannie hasn't stinted on her guests and tried to palm us off with some sort of 'house red' decanted from an Aldi value wine box.

'I hope you enjoy your meal,' Jeannie says, signalling that we can start, though Saira and Keren have already started tucking into their starter. To be fair, I should have thought of doing the same – that way, it's easier to avoid making polite conversation and drawing any more attention to the elephant, or rather the cardboard cut-out, in the room, like when we discussed the circumstances around Tania's death all those years ago. I wonder, with a cold shiver, if the others are thinking that too.

I notice with a pang that my starter is a dish that Tania loved, although it's a fancier version. The chicken wings accompanied by a green salad and spicy sauce on the side are delicious. I hadn't realised how hungry I was, too caught up by the tense atmosphere of the dinner. It seems I'm not the only one. Keren jumps at the sound of my knife and fork clinking on the plate. I wipe my hands on my napkin and look round at my fellow guests. They're all eyes down on their food, still avoiding conversation. As I've finished first I no longer have that luxury.

Oh well, needs must.

'Great starter, thank you,' I say to break the silence and try and get into Jeannie's good books. She smiles with pleasure. She's quite pretty when she does this, I notice. Gets little dimples in her cheeks.

I take another swig from my glass, there's only a few blood-red dregs left now, and carry on talking to liven the mood a bit. A fun memory hits me of Tania at her best. 'Do you remember when Tania was studying Ancient Rome and she decided to throw a Roman party? We all came in togas and there were bunches of grapes to feed each other with along with a huge jug of wine?'

'Yes!' says Keren, putting down her spoon hastily. 'That was hilarious!'

'And I ruined my only bedsheet by using it as a toga and spilling red wine down it,' adds Saira, rolling her eyes. 'Oh and Tania wrote us each a typed note giving us a Roman name for the night and telling us why we were so special to her? If my memory serves me right, I was Sabia, meaning "sweet".'

'I was Juvenus, meaning "youthful". I wouldn't get called that today!' I quip.

We all start to laugh and the tension breaks, like a rainstorm following a heatwave. I mentally pat myself on the back for my good call.

'I spent ages looking up the names and writing the cards,' says Jeannie. 'I thought it was a fun touch. I tried to match the name with the person.'

'It was you? I thought Tania did it?' asks Adam swiftly.

Tania had told me she'd written the cards too.

The mood in the room hurtles back down.

Jeannie looks round at us all, slightly startled, backtracking. 'I helped her out, she had a lot to organise for the party. Tania wanted them – if she'd had enough time she'd have done them herself.'

'Tania always did take you for granted,' Keren says tartly. There's a hush. Jeannie's face falls as if someone's told her that her fluffy kitten has been run over. I glance at Keren's glass. I think she must have downed a few in quick succession during the starter to be this blunt.

Most of us look at her. 'Sorry,' she says quietly, and drains what's left of her glass of white wine.

'There's nothing wrong with Jeannie helping Tania out is there? You and Tania used to help each other out with essays and revision too, seeing as you were on the same course.' Adam jumps in. 'The Roman night was great fun. I was Antonius. Apparently, it means "invaluable".'

Keren huffs as if her husband has annoyed her. 'It was more me helping Tania than her helping me. I never did her washing-up and laundry though, like Jeannie did. Tania always seemed to remember at the last minute that she didn't have any clean clothes for the night, and was always mysteriously too busy to do it herself.'

'Keren,' Adam says softly, shooting her a look that I assume is meant to beseech her to be quiet.

Jeannie's cheeks have turned pink, the wine's effect perhaps, or is she upset? Probably so after Keren's comment. So much for me trying to lighten the atmosphere.

'I had my own washing to do anyway,' Jeannie retorts with a put-on bright smile that doesn't reach her eyes. 'It's cheaper, isn't it, to do one big load rather than two.'

Adam's warning seems to have worked. Keren looks down at the table, her mouth shut, while Saira nods in agreement.

Jeannie pulls back her chair and stands up, the same smile still locked in. 'Let me refill your glasses and I'll ask Grant to bring in the main course, after which I have another surprise. A party game, like the infamous one Tania made up for us with photos.'

Keren looks at Saira and shares a smirk.

None of us had a video camera at uni so at least it's not going to be a home video. Or a drunken smartphone selfie like kids these days, because they weren't invented then.

God that makes me feel old.

When Jeannie bends beside me to refill my glass, I thank her. 'Why don't you leave the bottles on the table so we can all help ourselves? Save you getting up and waiting on us?' I suggest.

That way we can drink as much as we like without having to ask. I've a feeling that the way this evening is turning out we're all going to need more booze to get through it.

'Yes, good idea, thank you for thinking of me,' Jeannie replies. She's so close to me now that I can smell a hint of her flowery perfume rising up from the arch of her neck. I can tell this weekend means a great deal to her. She always was kind-hearted. Perhaps I took her for granted like Tania often did.

Grant the barman comes through with the main courses, again Tania's favourites: two lots of vegetable ravioli and three fish fillets with crushed potatoes and veg that was probably dug up this morning by a local peasant.

'Johnny, what are you up to these days? Still a hotshot city banker?' Keren asks me.

To avoid the question I fill my mouth with food and give a brief shrug, miming that I'm not able to answer right now. They don't need to know I've just about hit rock bottom and I'm wearing years' old clothes. My bruised and battered ego can't bear to tell them. Let them think I'm a hotshot like I used to be. No harm done. It'll probably be another twenty-five years at Tania's fiftieth anniversary before I see them again. A lot can happen in that time.

Jeannie steps in. 'Saira, what are you doing work-wise now?'

'This and that. Temp jobs in admin mostly. Hannah, my wife, well, she's my ex now, although the divorce hasn't gone through yet, is a dentist and she's always worked full time. I stayed at home and looked after our daughter Emily until she'd settled into school and then got part-time jobs here and there.'

'How old is Emily?'

'She's thirteen.'

'And you've been in temp jobs all that time in London? Couldn't you get anything more permanent?' I ask, a wave of horror coming over me at the thought of my being stuck in a low-paid temp job for the rest of my life. If I can't get another banking job soon I'm going to have to do something else to pay the bills. My bank balance is as dry as a bar during Prohibition. When my car is repossessed, I won't even be able to be a gig economy delivery driver. Not that I'd want to have to resort to that.

Another swig of wine. Saira looks at me, put out. 'I did have a permanent part-time job but had to leave because I had too much time off sick.'

'What was wrong?' I ask, the Chianti loosening my tongue and reversing my previous decision not to pry. Keren elbows me in the ribs.

'Sorry, I apologise, you don't need to tell me,' I say, contrite.

This time it's Saira's turn to take a gulp from her wine glass. She's on the Sauvignon Blanc. I'd think she'd had enough if it weren't the pot calling the kettle black. Beside me, Keren looks at Saira with concern but she doesn't seem to notice.

'I was diagnosed with rheumatoid arthritis nearly two years ago. I get flare-ups. I find temping easier because I can try and get jobs where I can work from home.'

'Tough. Sorry to hear that,' I say. That explains the walking stick. So there are two of us in the wars in our own way then.

'It's more than tough. Saira's had an awful time. Can you believe her wife left her because of her illness? She forgot the "in sickness and in health" part of their vows,' Keren pipes up, her voice a bit too loud. I turn towards her and see her cheeks are flushed. A minute ago she seemed concerned at the amount Saira's drinking but it isn't stopping her keeping up. The wine must have gone straight to her head – well, we've all drunk a lot during the meal. Apart from Adam, he's only on his second, I think. He never was that much of a drinker.

'Keren,' he says to his wife, like earlier, offering her a friendly warning look.

'Well it's true,' she replies, 'Saira's our friend and she's been treated badly.'

'That is awful. Could she not cope with your illness?' I ask Saira, feeling the subject has become rather personal for both of us.

'She, well . . .' Saira stumbles on her words.

'She is a two-faced cow. Sorry, I've held my tongue before, but she is,' Keren proclaims.

I chuckle inwardly. I don't remember Keren ever being this forthright before. Must be the wine. Or the peri-menopause that Olivia was always talking about.

Adam looks down at the table.

'She isn't, she had her reasons,' Saira says.

'What were they, ditching you when you were in pain and needed her help?'

'I never said she left because of my RA.'

'RA?' I ask.

'Rheumatoid arthritis,' Adam fills me in.

'You did, I'm sure you did. That was the impression we got, wasn't it, Adam? You said she wanted you to move out and it was all around the same time you were diagnosed.'

Saira's eyes blaze like a trapped deer's bargaining with her hunter. 'I'm sorry, I suppose it was easier to let you think that. It was a difficult time for me.'

'So why did Hannah leave you then, if it wasn't because of your RA?' Keren presses.

Ouch, now I'm not the only one to have asked a rude question.

'More wine anyone?' interjects Jeannie. The others shake their heads and I top up my glass myself from the ever-diminishing bottle. I shouldn't, I know, but I do.

Saira speaks quietly. 'I had a one-night stand with a friend of ours. It was a huge mistake. Hannah couldn't forgive me.'

'What? You cheated on her?' Karen asks, astonished. I imagine she wouldn't spare her words if Adam went astray, not that he ever would. He's not that sort of person and he hated his dad for walking out on him and his mum.

Saira nods. 'I've regretted it ever since. I'm sorry I let you believe it was Hannah's fault. I was ashamed to tell you the truth.'

Keren sits in stony silence. Adam pats Saira on the arm. 'Not for us to judge. Can't have been easy for you.'

I'm still sober enough to keep my mouth shut and not pour oil on the fire. At least I never played away from Olivia. Chance would have been a fine thing.

'Let's not forget why we are here today,' Jeannie jumps in. 'I can't believe it has been twenty-five years since she died. I remember when I met her in halls on the first day of term. It was just us two until she met you four. Can you believe it's all that long ago? What do you think she'd be doing now? I always imagined you and Tania would be married, Johnny, both in high-flying jobs, taking the world by storm.'

I don't say that it's something I've thought a lot about myself. Instead I reply, 'Who knows?'

It might be only me that sees the pained look in Adam's eyes following Jeannie's rather blunt retelling of events. Back then, when we were best mates, I knew he and Tania had spent a few nights together, but he told me it wasn't anything serious, and then it fizzled out. When I asked him if he minded if I asked Tania on a date, and that I wouldn't if it bothered him, to my relief he insisted he was cool with it. Even so, I felt a bit guilty when Tania and I became serious. I couldn't shake the feeling that Adam wasn't as cool with it as he'd said he was.

There's a loud scrape as Adam pushes back his chair, uncurls his legs from under the table, and stands up, placing his white napkin by the side of his plate.

'Excuse me.' With that, he walks out of the room.

'Nature calls probably,' Keren says in attempt to smooth over her husband cutting off Jeannie's conversation dead. None of us remaining choose to join in with Jeannie's reminiscence. We all carry on finishing our main course. God, this is awkward, not like when we used to get together in the old days at St Mark's. There was always Tania there to keep everything jolly.

A few minutes later, Adam saunters back in, a pang of sadness and regret hitting me when he doesn't meet my eyes as I watch him take his seat. We used to be as close as brothers.

'Adam, so how did you and Keren get together then?' I ask him in friendly banter style, attempting to kill two birds with one stone: breaking the ice with him and making safe small talk to fill the silence. At least I hope it's safe small talk and that they both weren't married to someone else at the time or met at a swingers' party. I chuckle at the thought of salt-of-the-earth Adam at one of those. He'd probably be eaten alive.

At last Adam looks at me and speaks. 'After Keren left St Mark's we kept in touch a bit. I moved to London a couple of years later for a promotion and Keren soon followed when she got a new job in the history department at a London school. She didn't know many people at the time and looked me up. It was the best decision she ever made.' Adam winked at Keren, and they shared a private smile at the memory of it.

'I didn't have any hint at St Mark's that you fancied each other,' says Jeannie.

'It caught me by surprise, that's for sure. We were just mates at uni but in London we started spending a lot of time together and then she jumped on me.' Adam grins.

'Hardly! You were so slow at making the first move that I had to do it,' adds Keren. 'He felt like home. Marriage, house and two kids came later.'

They look at each other across the table in a way that I don't remember my ex-wife ever looking at me before. Tania did, or is that a figment of my imagination? It was so long ago that it's hard to remember clearly her smiling at me, whether it's an actual memory or something I've constructed in my mind over the years. She certainly didn't look at me with adoration during those last few difficult weeks. There she appears in my mind with red-rimmed eyes and tears angrily streaming down her soft cheeks. No, I won't go there. I clasp my eyes shut and change the picture to that of her sleeping softly next to me in her bed, looking like a slumbering short-haired angel.

'You mentioned you have children?' Jeannie asks Keren politely. Her voice brings me back to the present.

'Yes, two and they keep us on our toes. My parents are looking after them this weekend. Nice to have a bit of peace.' She smiles, though as a parent myself I know that as much as it's good to have a break once in a while she'll be looking forward to seeing them again. I miss my daughters, far more than I think they miss me.

Adam jumps in. 'They're great kids. Boy and a girl. Noah and Maisie.'

'And you're management now, mate? A company director, aren't you?' I ask him.

'I'm a sales director.'

'Good job. Done well for yourself.'

'He's done brilliantly, should have been the company's MD but they brought an awful woman in from outside instead. Not an electrical engineer though, is he?' Keren says tartly.

Guilt washes over me. I deserved that one. I made the wrong decision there, but I can't turn back the clock now, even though with hindsight I've long wished I could.

Jeannie delicately pulls back her chair and gets up. It's still light outside, although twilight is beginning to draw in. She walks to the wall, presses a switch and the chandelier overhanging the dining table switches on, each crystal dancing in the light of the seemingly hundreds of individual bulbs. Must be an optical illusion. Or I'm drunker than I think I am.

'Everyone ready for dessert? I'll ask Grant to bring in the trolley and then it's time for our party game!' With that, she goes out of the room.

'At least we know it's not pin the tail on the donkey. There's no photos with that!' Saira jokes, and we all laugh nervously. Considering Jeannie's surprise earlier on, which is still standing in the corner of the room looking at us, I have no idea what to expect.

There's an unopened bottle of red on the table. Thankfully it's a screw top. I do the honours. Bottoms up! I'm in need of Dutch courage. This evening is bringing back memories of Tania that perhaps were best left forgotten, not the ones Jeannie, or Tania herself, would have preferred us to reminisce over.

I walk to the cardboard cut-out, stare Tania in the face, then turn her round to face the wall. It gives me the creeps looking at it, as if it were an effigy on top of an Egyptian mummy that has rotted inside.

The barman pushes the dessert trolley into the room and he's swiftly followed by Jeannie.

'Right then, shall we begin?' she says brightly.

My stomach lurches guiltily. The game is about to start. Bring it on.

Chapter 8

Adam

So I've done it, I've talked to my former best friend. Strangely enough those few snippets of conversation, once I'd started, felt easy, comfortable even, just as it used to be before he screwed me over – again.

The last time I saw him before this weekend was at the pub after St Mark's graduation ceremony. We were both a bit drunk, not steaming – I can't remember getting home pissed – but we'd both had enough to make the time pass, for him to get through the day's formalities and for me to blot out that, by rights, if my family had money like the others', I would have been up there wearing the obligatory mortar board, black cape and whatever you call the coloured material that goes on top.

Before the news about Tania's death, there was no way I was going to go, not for me the self-torture of what should have been – her and I graduating together, boyfriend and girlfriend.

I didn't want to watch the students who had parents with cash, rather than a single mum with two sons surviving on casual work and benefit top-ups like mine, graduate. Working hard and getting an electrical engineering degree was supposed to be the route to a great job where I could help out financially. Instead, I had to drop out in my final year to take a job a sixteen-year-old would have had the qualifications for. Mum lost her job and couldn't support herself and my brother, never mind me. Without me working full time and sending money home, she and my little brother would have faced eviction.

'Rough man, bad luck,' a few of the others on my course said, adding, 'you can always come back and do the last year,' with a commiserative frown transforming into a pep-you-up. As if Mum and my brother were going to stop needing the money I brought home and I could stop working just like that with thousands in the bank to keep me going for a year. For all their complaints about finals I bet they were glad they actually got to sit them and then go home to the Bank of Mum and Dad for a layabout summer before looking for work and not just any old job, but a vocation, a *calling*. When you're rich, working is all about self-fulfilment, not survival.

There were rumours too that the government, despite being socialist, was going to start charging tuition fees. How on earth was anyone without parental help going to be able to afford to pay those on top of everything else? If I knew then that universities would be charging a grand a year, and much more later on, for the privilege of an education I'd have been even more pissed off at having to drop out when my course was free.

I tried hard not to blame Johnny for what he did, it's not in my nature to be unkind, but I couldn't quite manage it. Eventually it killed our friendship, that and Tania, the glue that held us all together, dying. Without our ringleader we all went our separate ways into adulthood, but that didn't stop me guiltily missing them both, despite what they'd done.

I met Johnny in the first year at the football society. At St Mark's his money and his family's status hadn't mattered, though in the real world of course it did. I ended up doing a basic job instead of becoming the electrical engineer I'd have been if I'd finished my degree, and Adam went back to his posh family home in London and a graduate traineeship at an international bank. I took the bus and a packed lunch into work, he got cabs and wined and dined clients on an expense account. Or so I imagined on the many occasions I thought about what had happened to him. The bridge between us was too far for me to ask. I couldn't afford a mobile phone.

Johnny sent a letter with his new contact details to my mum's house. I thought about replying, getting my old mate back. It wasn't as if in those first couple of years I made any new ones other than a quick drink with workmates, but what would I say when I knew deep down bitterness still brewed? And anyway, what would we have in common anymore?

I never did go back to university, though I kept my student room on for somewhere to live for the rest of the academic year while I worked. I socialised with the gang sometimes though it felt like going through the motions, trying not to resent them when they complained about the pressure of revision and exams. I'd have swapped that for the pressure of making enough money to keep myself and send some back to my mum and little brother any day.

Tonight is stirring up those memories. Johnny, he might look a lot different but he's still the same as before in many ways. He's trying to be friendly and part of me wants to fall back into it but then the memory of what he did bursts into my brain. I remember how I felt back then and think that I wouldn't be in this situation, wouldn't have had to work in sales in the first place, if it weren't for him. Then again, I know I am being unfair. I'd thought I'd grown up and was long over it, like I'd accepted it when he asked me if it was OK if he started seeing Tania – not that long after she made it clear that our fling was over, and whom he only met because I introduced them. At the time I clung on to the friendship she offered as a consolation prize, and though seeing them together stamped on my heart, I thought it wasn't worth losing the two people I was closest to in my life, and maybe Tania would get bored of Johnny and realise the grass was greener on my side . . .

It was the kind of autumn day when the summer is giving out its last gasps when I confided in Johnny about the financial dilemma I was in. We'd not long been back at St Mark's for our third year. He'd asked me a few times if I was OK and I brushed it off, too embarrassed to talk about money with him in case it looked like I was fishing for cash. Now though I only had a couple of days before I'd have to leave if I was serious about dropping out to help my family. Mum had encouraged me to return for my third year and not to worry about her, but before I left I saw the red letter bills in the kitchen drawer and how the food cupboard was nearly bare. My summer job in a factory that made rolls of Christmas wrapping paper meant I had enough money to pay the rent for my student bedroom for the first month, and also pay Mum's gas and electricity bills, but there was little left over for anything else, including the new football boots that my little brother needed. He was only ten. He shouldn't have had to miss out or, God forbid, lose his home.

Johnny was my best mate and I needed to talk to someone. Besides, I couldn't just disappear or pretend I was still attending seminars and lectures.

I'd chosen one of the quieter bars at the students' union to talk to Johnny, but in the heady throws of a new term, with freshers not having much work to do yet, it was still hard to get a seat. I bought a couple of pints for us and found a small table in a corner underneath a framed band poster from the eighties. No one had put any money in the jukebox yet, meaning that the hum of background chatter was our soundtrack.

'Are you sure you're OK, mate? I'm a bit worried about you,' Johnny said, tucking his long hair behind his ear. We'd not had chance for a proper catch-up on our own since we'd got back. The six of us had spent the majority of the time together, falling back into the same routine as the previous year. I didn't want to talk about my financial problems in front of them. It was too personal, too raw. They all had parents who could help them out with cash and they might not understand. Johnny, despite being loaded, would though, I knew.

I let out a deep sigh then bit the bullet. 'To be honest, mate, I'm not. It's money. Mum's not doing so well, she's lost her job. I've given her what I can but she's still behind on her bills. It's hard for her finding work to fit around looking after Bobby, there's not much about, and she's not well herself. She needs help. Dad's not paying maintenance.'

Johnny looked at me sympathetically, waiting for me to go on.

'She can't give me the money the council said she should to top up my grant. Without it, even with my weekend job at the supermarket, I can't afford to carry on here and support Mum as well. I don't want to leave but if I get a full-time job then I can give more money to Mum and Bobby. I'm worried that if I don't then she won't be able to keep up with her bills and the council could evict them.'

'But you've done two years of your degree, you should be able to earn good money when you graduate. It'd be a waste to give it up, mate . . . I understand what you're saying about your mum though. Is there another way? Does St Mark's give out hardship grants?'

'I asked yesterday and no, they don't. Even if I got a grant to help me stay on the course, I still wouldn't have enough spare to give Mum what she needs. A student loan isn't nearly enough.'

'That's totally unfair for your mum, and you. I'm so sorry. I don't want you to go,' Johnny said. We fell into silence and finished our pints.

'My round.' Johnny went up to the bar and I looked at the 'children', as Tania called the eighteen-year-olds who'd just started. I could pick them out in the bar. They were trying to make new friends, fresh-faced with the excitement of their course ahead of them, the way I felt when I first started. Despair crept in. I really didn't want to have to leave before my time. If only my mum had the same financial security as Johnny's family . . .

The thump of a pint being placed in front of me made me look up at the returning Johnny.

'Hear me out. I might have a solution,' Johnny said quickly with an excitement in his voice. 'It's stupid you giving up on your degree. How about I lend you some cash? I've got some I can get my hands on. Enough for you to be able to finish your course and help your mum. You can pay me back when you're back on your feet with a job after graduation.'

My jaw dropped. Would Johnny do that for me?

'Really?' I asked, a light appearing at the end of the tunnel. 'I hope you don't think I was trying to wangle money out of you.'

Johnny looked at me earnestly. 'Look, I'm glad you confided in me, mate, I know you didn't do it to tap me for cash. I really have been concerned about you and I want to help. Your mum's always been lovely to me when I've visited you at home and my family isn't exactly short of a bob or two. It's not fair that I get to carry on with my degree and you have to drop out. Besides, what am I going to do here without my best mate?'

For the first time in a few weeks I felt an inkling of hope. Relief. 'Are you sure? I will pay you back, get a legal agreement or something.'

Johnny patted me on the back. 'I know you will. Let me know how much you need. What are friends for? You'd help me out if the boot was on the other foot.'

Yes, I would have done, but on my foot was a four-year-old falling-apart trainer rather than a golden boot.

'I can't believe you'd do that for me, mate. That's just amazing. A lifesaver. You're the best.' I lurch Johnny into a man hug and slap him on the back a little too enthusiastically.

'Steady on!' he laughs.

We celebrate the news with another couple of pints, a lot for me, but I'm giddy with relief and grateful for our friendship.

Then a week later Johnny stamped all over my short-lived happiness, after I'd taken out a loan to give mum a month's rent money and pay my own for the term, to tide me over while Johnny was sorting out his money to transfer to my account.

I was cooking, if I can use that term when it comes to making beans on toast, in the kitchen in our shared student house, when I heard the front door shut. I knew Imran was in the chemistry lab all day. That, and the tell-tale sound of his rubber-soled shoes squeaking on our cracked-tiled hallway, meant it must be Johnny.

I sensed something was up when I turned my head to look at him as he walked into the kitchen. He seemed nervous, worried, his brow furrowing into deep trenches.

'All right, mate?' I asked.

He launched into it straightaway. 'Look, Adam, I'm really sorry but I don't think I can lend you the money. My parents would want to know where it went and I don't think they'd be too happy, and I've been thinking about lending to a friend and maybe it's not a good idea. I wouldn't want anything to spoil our friendship, you know?'

You don't want anything to spoil our friendship, but you're OK with pulling out of lending me money, which you offered in the first place, and me having to drop out of St Mark's and that spoiling our friendship? is what I wish I'd said. Instead, I was in shock and kept quiet while he apologised and asked if I was OK, but guiltily didn't wait to hear the answer, saying he was late for a tutorial. I'm not the shouting, dramatic type to have stopped him. Good old quiet, not causing a fuss Adam.

Johnny shut the front door loudly when he left. My beans boiled over. My fate was sealed.

The next day I told my personal tutor I was leaving and went straight to an employment agency afterwards. Two days later I started temp work. The irony was that it was admin in the uni's overseas recruitment department marketing courses to rich foreign students.

After that Johnny and I tiptoed around each other. I'm not one for arguments. Maybe it would have been better if I was and I could have got everything out in the open, but I felt hurt, let down and didn't know how to articulate it. Instead, I hunkered down and worked as many hours as I could get.

One night, months later, I came home from work, exhausted, to find only Tania there. It was one of the rare nights she stayed over with Johnny rather than the other way round, but he and Imran weren't back yet. Johnny had made a copy of his key for her, which came in useful as a back-up whenever one of us couldn't find ours.

It'd been nearly two years since I was last on my own with Tania, back when she said she just wanted to be friends and broke my heart. She made it sound like she was doing me a favour. She wasn't ready to get serious; I deserved someone who did. She didn't want a fling to spoil our friendship. I'd always have a special place in her heart. I thought that what she really meant was that she wanted to play the field. Loads of blokes tried to chat her up when I was with her.

I always wondered why, out of all those men at uni who were interested, she chose Johnny to replace me. They both swore they'd just been friends when we were together, but in the small hours of the morning, when I heard them having sex through the thin walls of our student house, I tortured myself with wondering if she had been lying. I believed Johnny, but had Tania wanted him all along when she was with me? Had she thought that when I introduced them? When we were together it seemed too good to be true. Who wouldn't prefer Johnny to me back then?

The first time I saw her, well actually it turned out it was the second time, was in a bar in the students' union. It was the last night of the first term, Christmas songs blared out of the speakers, and I'd joined my hall mates for a goodbye drink. My friend Caroline from my halls said she was bringing a girl from her course she'd asked earlier after bumping into her in the refectory. 'She's nice, a bit shy, doesn't usually socialise after lectures. I thought she might appreciate an invite,' Caroline told us. Imran, Keren and I got there first and bagged a table, putting coats over two stools to save them for the two girls. Johnny had gone back to London at lunchtime because it was his mum's birthday and they were having a family meal out.

The bar was packed, bodies pushing past each other to get to the bar or find a space to stand. I saw Caroline appear, her arm wrapped through that of a pretty, slim girl wearing a floral dress like my nan's curtains. 'Everyone this is Tania. Tania, this is Imran, Keren and Adam,' Caroline said jollily before leaving again to go to the bar.

Tania sat opposite me and looked, with all the noise and bustling bodies around her, like a rabbit caught in the headlights of a motor rally. Not being comfortable in party situations was something I empathised with. She looked up and caught my eye, triggering a brief memory.

'Hi, Tania. I'm sure I've seen you before,' I said, acutely conscious of my townie accent. Tania looked like she came from a posher background than me. My heart started to beat faster. I realised I wanted her to like me.

'Of course you've seen her before, she lives on campus. We're like rats in a lab, we all pass each other every day!' laughed Keren. 'Tania, we're on the same course, I think. I've seen you in lectures. How's it going?'

Tania opened her mouth and took a couple of seconds to quietly reply. 'Good, thanks. Yes, I recognise you. That's how you know Caroline then, is it, through history?'

'Yeah, but Caroline is doing joint history and politics and she's thinking of dropping the history next term to stick to politics.'

'I'm studying chemistry, I'm in the same hall as Caroline and Adam,' Imran said, offering his hand across the table for her to shake.

Then it came to me. 'I've got it! The day I arrived you were behind me in the queue for room keys. I've got a good memory for faces.'

'I thought you looked familiar.' She smiled, looking up through her thick, dark eyelashes. That was the moment when I fell for her hook, line and sinker, and tried to talk to her as much as I could without looking desperate.

Throughout the whole Christmas break I hoped Tania would come along to the birthday party Caroline invited her to and my jaw dropped when she met us at the bus stop to go to the pizza restaurant in town. Gone was the long hair, replaced by a stunning bleach blonde pixie cut. A few weeks later she said she changed her hair because she wanted me to notice her. How could any man not? When you got Tania's undivided attention it felt as if the sun was shining solely for you.

Back in the shared house in our final year, when I found myself alone with Johnny's girlfriend, this reminiscence came flooding back.

'I'm so pleased it's just the two of us,' she exclaimed in the lounge, saying that it'd been so long since we'd spent any time together on our own. We called out for a pizza. She asked me how my job was, how I felt about leaving uni and said she was so sorry I had to drop out because she knew how much studying to be an electrical engineer had meant to me. Tania always knew how to make me laugh and when we talked it really felt like she was listening to me. I could open up to her. Time flew by and yet it also seemed that the clock had turned its hands back to when we were together. I told her all my worries about my mum and Bobby.

'I've missed you,' she said to me on the sofa, an empty pizza box lounging by our feet. A fire ignited in my heart and elsewhere. Tania's gaze fixed on mine and it seemed she was looking into my soul. A stir of longing came over me, even though she was Johnny's girlfriend now. But hadn't Johnny let me down twice, the first when he went out with Tania, my ex, and secondly when he decided not to lend me the money to stay on at St Mark's?

'I've missed you too,' I replied hesitantly, not daring to think what the subtext may be behind her words. I'd dated a couple of girls over the past year or so but nothing ended up becoming serious. Neither lived up to her. Back then I doubted I'd ever find any girl who could.

She flung her arm across the back of the sofa, her fingers a few millimetres away from the hairs standing erect on the back of my neck.

'I sometimes wonder if I picked the right man . . .' she whispered in my ear.

My heart leaped. Was her smile an invitation to take things further? This was everything I'd dreamed of. I began to lean my face towards hers, so close that I could feel her breath on my lips, when SLAM! – the noise of the front door caused us both to jump back just in time before Imran and Johnny walked into the room.

'You ordered pizza and you didn't save any for me?' said Imran disappointedly. Johnny looked at me quizzically but kept his mouth shut. Instead, he bounded over to Tania, threw his arms around her and kissed her like a cat spraying his territory.

I didn't get to be alone again with Tania that night, but once my buried feelings had erupted again, I couldn't quell them. If the others hadn't come back, would we have kissed? Or maybe more? Did Tania really want us to get back together? Did Johnny get in the way? If he hadn't turned up that night, with the chain reaction it caused, would she still be alive?

I've had my fill of memories tonight but now Jeannie wants to bring up some more with a photo game. I can't take any more shocks, not after the photo under the door and seeing the cardboard version of Tania that fooled me for a split second, and Keren's already put her foot in it twice. Time for us to make a polite exit, I think.

I yawn theatrically and stretch my arms into the air. 'A game sounds great Jeannie but Keren and I have had a long day – we were up early with the kids. Probably time to hit the hay.'

Although I'm smiling pointedly at my wife, subconsciously trying to remind her of our ten o'clock bed and sex pact, she's drunkenly having none of it.

'Oh, don't be boring, Adam. I don't get to have a drink very often. Let's stay up a bit longer and see what this game is.' She's twitching her nose like a chipmunk, a tell-tale sign that she's had a few. I hope she'll lay off the wine now or she's going to feel very rough in the morning.

I shouldn't really leave her on her own in this state and God knows what this game is that Jeannie wants to play or what Keren might say to upset someone again. Everything about tonight is disconcerting but I don't want to disagree with Keren in front of the others.

'OK, a bit longer then, darling,' I reply. Her gaze is flicking randomly around the room. I don't want to embarrass her by suggesting she drinks some water. Hopefully we can get this game over quickly then we can go to bed, leaving all this uncomfortableness behind.

When Jeannie went out of the room to get her game, I made small talk about the meal with Saira, who had been very quiet since she told us she'd cheated on Hannah. I feel a bit sorry for her. I never would have guessed she'd slept with someone else. You don't know what goes on behind closed doors, do you? She's been a bit weird all evening, ever since she saw that cardboard cut-out of Tania. Keren's torn, I can tell. She hates infidelity but is very loyal to her friends. I hope she doesn't say anything she'll regret tonight. I don't want her to be upset or fall out with Saira. Life's too short.

Instead, I take another forkful of my dessert. A few minutes earlier, the barman Grant wheeled in an eighties-style dessert trolley. When he saw it, Johnny ambled back to his place at the table. We all chose between fresh fruit salad or chocolate mousse cake while Grant loaded our empty main course plates into the bottom of the trolley.

'Enjoy your sweet course. For this game I've got an envelope for each of you,' Jeannie gushes. Johnny's amused expression at Jeannie's enthusiasm makes me snicker, which I immediately try to cover with a cough and a napkin over my mouth. Johnny looks over at me and his eyes twinkle with our shared joke, just like the old days. I glance away quickly.

Jeannie picks up some white A4-size envelopes that she had brought in with her and put on the table. Each has a different initial written in felt tip on the front and she hands them to us one by one, holding one back for herself.

It must have been her who put the photo under my door. I've not got round to telling Keren about it yet. The emotions that picture stirred up are personal, newly raw again. I never mentioned to Keren how much I really felt for Tania or what I did before she died. Thank

God that Tania didn't tell anyone about it. If she had done, surely someone would have mentioned it when she died, wouldn't they?

'Did you happen to put a photo under our bedroom door, Jeannie?' I ask.

Her forehead lines in confusion. 'No. Why, did someone do that?' she asks.

Maybe she's lying, though I don't know why she would want to. But who else could have done it? Then it hits me. Johnny. Perhaps Tania did say something. He was her boyfriend after all. Despite him seeming friendly today, is Johnny actually taunting me? Is that what the mystery photograph was all about?

I look over at my wife again and try to catch her eye, but she doesn't appear to be listening to the conversation, she's too busy drinking more wine.

'Just wondered if it was all part of the game as well,' I say to Jeannie.

Jeannie looks confused before sitting back down. Johnny attentively tops up her glass. He's still got the gentlemanly manners, instilled in him at his public school, I see.

'Today we're here to remember our friend Tania who, as you know, tragically died twenty-five years ago,' Jeannie announces.

Saira raises her glass and we all follow suit to toast our late friend.

'After I organised this weekend, I went through the packets of old photos I've kept from our time at St Mark's. In each envelope there's a photo that holds a special memory of Tania for us. I thought it would be a nice way of reminiscing about our friendships with her and remember all the great times we had. I'll go first.'

Je for Jeannie. Jeannie carefully slides her left forefinger under her envelope flap, which is sealed, and neatly prises it open. She pulls out a photograph and places it in the middle of the table for us all to see.

In the image, Tania has her arm around Jeannie's shoulder and both of them are grinning at the camera. Jeannie is wearing a large badge with the number twenty on it.

'I remember that. It was your birthday party, Jeannie. We went to the Elvis tribute night where three different Elvises sang and competed to be voted the best. Remember the one that was tone deaf?' I say.

'It was a great night. Tania organised it all for me and bought me a signed copy of a book I'd told her I loved, which my mum had accidentally given to a jumble sale when I went to uni. It must have been really hard to get hold of,' gushes Jeannie.

Saira and Keren exchange glances. I don't know if Jeannie notices.

Johnny joins in. 'And there was the Chinese Elvis who was pretty good! He asked for an audience member to come up on the stage and Tania volunteered. Remember that wig he had on and the white jumpsuit! That night was hilarious.'

'Wasn't it "Suspicious Minds" that they sang? She rocked it!' I add, smiling at the memory.

'Yes, and you bought one of the Elvis wigs on sale in the foyer. You didn't take it off all night, you kept doing that wobbly knee Elvis impression.'

'Knee trembler, not wobbly knee, mate,' I remind him, laughing, forgetting myself.

'Nah, definitely wobbly knee! That was comedy gold.' Johnny, Jeannie and I laugh at the memory.

'Actually . . .' Keren says, and I look over at her. 'Saira?' she asks uncertainly.

Saira takes a deep breath and starts slurring. 'It doesn't matter now, it was a long time ago, but it was my idea to book that for your birthday, and Keren and I found the book. Tania mentioned that you might like it and we spent an afternoon searching in some second-hand bookshops to see if we could find a copy. The present was from the three of us. We all chipped in.'

'Oh. I thought Tania arranged it,' Jeannie says, looking crestfallen.

I don't know whether to be pleased that Saira and Keren are back in cahoots again or irked that they've brought this up. What does it matter now?

'Tania wrapped it up and gave it to you. And the book was her idea,' Saira adds.

'But not the restaurant?' Jeannie asks.

'It was a great night though, wasn't it?' interrupts Johnny, trying to ease the moment.

'Yes. I've still got the book.' Jeannie doesn't sound too convinced. 'Who wants to go next?'

'I will,' I volunteer, to get it over and done with, thinking back to the times I remember us having our photo taken together. 'I bet it's a photo of me and Tania at that dodgy pub we all went to a few times for the band night.' Before Jeannie can answer a loud crash from somewhere upstairs causes us all to jump.

'I'm sure it's nothing to worry about, I'll go and see what's happened . . .' Jeannie starts to say before she's cut off from the rest of her sentence by the shock of all the lights in the room going out with a pop, plunging us into darkness. Before I can take another breath, a loud scream pierces the oppressive blackness.

Chapter 9

Saira

I didn't mean to scream so loudly. I've been on edge ever since I saw that cardboard cut-out of Tania that fooled me for a moment, and the lights going out with a poof so unexpectedly made me jump in fright.

'Don't panic!' I hear Jeannie say and I try to calm down a little but the room has started to spin in the dark and I hold on to my chair so I don't fall off. I wish I were at home in my own bed, or almost anywhere else rather than here. There's something not quite right and really unsettling about tonight. The memories brought up in this hotel have given me goosebumps, like pox scars on my skin announcing my guilt. Perhaps our recollections of Tania would have been better left untouched in each of our minds, rather than sharing them to decay openly in the sun.

In the dark there's nowhere to hide. My shame suffocates me in the blackness. Thanks to Keren, I had to admit I cheated on Hannah, an act I deeply wish I could go back and erase. Keren seems furious with me. I need to talk to her and tell her what happened, how sorry I am and how I felt too ashamed to tell her the honest truth. I've already lost my wife, I don't want to lose my friend as well.

But that's not the only thing I have to feel guilty about, is it?

This free weekend really wasn't worth it.

It's as if a locked box is being opened and long-buried secrets are crawling out. I wish I'd never slept with Zainab, I don't know what got into me. Hannah and I had had a stupid row. Zainab, our mutual friend, invited me to go round to hers because she knew Emily was at a sleepover, Hannah had gone to a dental conference, and I'd be on my own. I never even fancied Zainab before, I hadn't thought that way about another woman since the day I first met Hannah in a bar.

Zainab and I had a takeaway, drank wine and everything that was bothering me boiled over and engulfed me. I talked about my RA diagnosis and how I thought Hannah should cut down on her hours at work. She's a great dentist but a perfectionist. The long hours she worked annoyed me sometimes as it meant that the mainstay of parenting fell to me and, although I'm not as skilled as Hannah or able to get as high paid a job, I didn't get the chance to have a proper career.

Now of course I long to be back in the family home, spending every day with Emily.

I wanted the three of us to be together more as a family, but yet again, Hannah was working another weekend instead of being at home with us, this time at a conference the practice owner wanted her to go to. I was so angry, I felt like second, or third best behind the job and her boss. Couldn't she have said no and told him to go himself?

I suppose I felt lonely. I was fed up with the pain in my joints and worried about what the future held. I should have waited until Hannah got home on Sunday and confided in her, but instead what I ended up confessing when she got back was that in a fit of pique I'd got drunk, stayed over with Zainab, responded to her attentions because in my drunken state it felt nice to be wanted, and I woke up in the morning in her bed regretting what we'd done.

My guilt smothers me in its shroud. There's another secret I'm keeping too, one which only Tania knew about.

'I'll sort the lights out, don't worry.'

Jeannie's voice sounds louder, cutting through the inky shadows. Must be because all my senses are on alert, ready for any hint of danger.

'It'll be the fuse. I'll get a torch and go and find Grant. He's working late because we're short staffed. He'll know what to do.'

'Anyone want to play I-spy?' jokes Johnny.

I hear what sounds like a cupboard door opening. I noticed an oak, antique-looking sideboard at the side of the room when we came in. It's probably that.

'Found it! I keep one in every room in case of an emergency.' A torch light switches on.

'Do you want me to come with you?' Johnny asks.

'No, I'm fine. You all stay here. I'll try not to be too long,' Jeannie answers and walks out of the room with her torch, plunging us back into pitch blackness again.

'I think maybe when the lights come back on we should call it a night,' says Adam next to me. I want to grasp onto his arm, grab on to him like a lifesaver, so I know I'm not all alone. That would be pathetic though and besides, I don't want to move my hands that are steadying me in my dizziness. Shutting my eyes makes it worse.

'Jeannie really wanted us to open the envelopes. She is our hostess, we should do that quickly when she comes back and get it over with,' Johnny adds.

Bang. I jump again.

'Oops, sorry, I think I've knocked over my wine glass,' says Keren.

Adam next to me speaks up protectively. 'Just leave it, darling, don't touch anything.'

This place is really giving me the creeps. I feel the urge to go to the loo but there's no way I'm leaving this room until the lights are back on. As my eyes start to adjust to the darkness, I see eerie shadows waving around on the ceiling. My cane is next to me and instinctively I grab it with one hand for security. Just in case. Why though do I feel under threat? Unless ...

'Perhaps Tania's spirit isn't happy with us,' I say. 'Or maybe she's trying to tell us something. We never really talked about how she died, did we? It was all very weird. There was the accident, her dad whisked her off to a private hospital in Devon without us seeing her, and then he calls to say she's drowned. Why didn't he want us to go to her funeral?'

I'm not usually a superstitious person, but there's something I can't quite put my finger on, a feeling that there's a malevolent air to the evening, and to all these opposite memories being dug up from her grave. Who was Tania, our best friend or a user, a confidante or someone we never really knew? I certainly found out she wasn't who I thought she was. Guilt, shame and regret mix with anger in my stomach – a toxic combination on top of the alcohol.

'I don't mean to be rude, Saira, but I think the wine's gone to your head.' Johnny's deep voice travels across the table.

Is he right? He certainly is about the wine. There's an acrid taste in my mouth and my thoughts tumble in my head, causing it to spin faster. In the dark everything seems more out of sorts. There's no background noise of clinking glasses, cutlery or eating food, just Johnny's voice carrying on.

'It *was* such a shock. First I knew about the car accident was when her dad called our house to say he'd taken her to Devon. When she wasn't around in the morning I'd assumed she'd stayed over at Johnny's,' Keren adds mournfully.

I hear Johnny sigh in the darkness. 'She didn't, but it didn't worry me then because I thought she was pissed off with me like I was with her. We'd had a stupid argument the night before,' he says.

Next to me, Adam pipes up. 'I can't remember why she had your car?'

Johnny replies quietly, 'I'd put her on my car insurance at the start of the third year in case I needed a lift after I'd gone out drinking. I'd done it for her loads of times. The night before she'd driven us to a get-together with my football mates. There was a big post-exam party at a club that wasn't on a bus route. I got a bit worse for wear and Tania thought I was flirting with a couple of girls there, when I was only being friendly, and then she went and danced for ages with a guy I knew had tried it on with her before to get her own back. I went over to stop her – it's all a bit hazy to be honest – we had a big row and she stormed off, taking the car with her. I had to get a cab back. I thought she'd come round and bring my car back the next day when we'd both cooled off and everything would be OK, but she didn't show up. I still thought she'd started it and decided to wait until she made the first move.'

'But why didn't she phone you at our house, or the girls' house to tell us she was in hospital? I always wondered that,' replies Adam in his distinctive baritone voice.

There's a pause before Johnny replies sadly, 'Who knows? Maybe her dad got to the hospital quickly and she couldn't phone on her way back to Devon from Bristol. None of us had a mobile back then.'

I hear a glug being drunk from a wine glass followed by a slight clunk as Johnny puts it back down on the table.

'You didn't raise the alarm though did you, Saira, when she didn't come back to your shared house? Or you, Keren?' Johnny adds pointedly.

'We knew she was out with you. We assumed she was staying at yours,' Keren snaps.

It's strange how the room can still spin so violently even though it's pitch black and I can't see it. 'We were supposed to be her friends. We all thought she was with someone else but didn't check,' I say. I knew there were lots of times when one of us didn't come home for the night and we didn't worry. We were free agents, sometimes pulling all-nighters at the library to meet an essay deadline, or crashing on a friend's floor after a night out.

My mind goes straight back to the knock on my bedroom door the morning after Tania had gone back to Devon, when I'd been having a lie-in, recovering from the exam stress and late-night ongoing celebrations. Jeannie had taken the second phone call from Tania's dad. She'd been released from hospital and gone for a swim in the sea on the private beach behind the posh house. She'd grown up by the sea and was a strong swimmer. Her dad was in his study, thinking she was resting on the sofa. She wasn't. Her towel was on the beach and her swimming costume gone. I remember the disbelief followed by the lurch in my stomach when the words sunk in. For a day or so we all held on to hope that the rescuers would find her and everything would be all right. When they didn't, we had to face the worst. Tania had drowned. Her body washed up months later. The inquest ruled that although she was an experienced swimmer and knew the currents there, undiagnosed concussion probably caused her to get into trouble.

My words tumble out of my mouth. 'It was all such a shock, her death was so horrible, we didn't question what happened, did we? And soon after our house rentals were up, we all went our separate ways, only meeting up again for graduation. Tania would have drawn us all together but she was dead and we just carried on with our lives. Should we have tried harder, done more for her? At least turned up at the funeral even though her dad said it was private?'

'We were young though and didn't want to upset Tania's dad. Maybe we should have organised something else, our own ceremony for her or something on that day. I suppose I thought that as Johnny was her boyfriend it was his decision whether to do anything or not, but I should have raised the idea,' says Keren.

A groan emanates from across the table followed by Johnny's voice. 'Shit, I should have thought of it, I should have taken responsibility, but her dad made it clear to me that he didn't want us there. He'd sent me a solicitor's letter with a cheque for my car, which wasn't worth repairing apparently after the crash. He said he didn't want to go through the upset of having to relive what happened to Tania if I claimed on my insurance. I was so knocked for six I went back to my parents and didn't get out of bed much for a couple of months until my job was about to start and my dad turfed me out. By the time it was Tania's funeral, we'd all gone our separate ways anyway.'

It occurs to me that there's something about the darkness that brings out an honesty we conceal in the light. Johnny had never told me all that before.

'It's not your fault, mate, none of us did anything, did we? Tania's dad was rather scary, very dominant and protective of her. I don't think he approved of any of us,' Adam says gently.

'Tania told me once her dad was worried she'd turn into her mother and steered her away from boys and drink,' I say, thinking of the photo she kept of her mum Delphine in a drawer.

'I suppose we can't blame him for that. Tania was only a few years old when her mum committed suicide,' Johnny quietly adds.

Delphine had been out drinking with another man then drove her car into a tree at high speed. A worm of uncertainty crawls through my consciousness, leaving a trail in its malevolent wake. 'You don't think that Tania *meant* to drown, do you??'

I recoil at the force of Johnny's response. 'For God's sake. Why would you say that, Saira? Why would Tania have wanted to kill herself? The inquest said she went swimming in the sea, got into difficulties and drowned. You saw her after our finals. She was happy, excited about the future and moving to London.'

'But what caused the car accident? Why didn't she get in touch with any of us when she was back in Devon? What happened there?' I ask.

'We know what happened back in Devon. That's why we're here twenty-five years later,' Keren argues.

'Horrible way to go, drowning,' Adam says quietly next to me. 'Mind you, we only have her dad's word for what happened in Devon, don't we?

The worm continues its stealthy revelation of malevolent thoughts. Could Tania's dad have been lying? Had they had an argument and he didn't supervise her properly? Was she upset and that caused her to swim out too far and lose control in the current? Tears well up in my eyes again. 'It all doesn't make sense,' I say. 'She was an experienced swimmer. If she didn't feel right after the accident surely she wouldn't have swum out of her depth?'

Johnny is the one who answers me. 'She loved swimming. Went every week to the university pool because she missed it so much. Maybe she didn't realise she had concussion and ignored the doctor's warnings to take it easy. She could be stubborn when she wanted to be.'

The chandelier flicks on for a fraction of a second, illuminating our shocked, drawn faces, before plunging us again into darkness.

'I hope Jeannie hurries up and fixes the power,' Keren cries.

'Give her a chance,' says Johnny.

Vomit threatens to rise up from my stomach. I feel blindly on the table for my glass of water, clench my fingers around its cool glass and drink the lot in one go.

Adam hesitantly breaks the silence. 'I did hear a rumour going round not long after you all left and I stayed in Bristol a bit longer until I got a job back home,' Adam says. 'I ignored it, thought it was just nasty gossip, not worth repeating.'

'What was that? You never said,' Keren jumps in.

'Like I said, it's probably rubbish. There was a police incident with some students the night of Tania's crash. When she went missing, a few people were saying that she might have been involved.'

'That's ridiculous. Why would Tania have been involved with the police? She would have told me,' Johnny replies.

'I'm sure you're right.'

'What incident with the police? First I've heard of it,' asks Keren inquisitively.

'It was in the local paper that a police officer was severely injured after a raid on The Dark Horse pub – you know the rough one on the corner in town near the train station where we went to a few times when it was band night. Some students were arrested during a drugs raid.'

A bit of vomit lurches into my mouth along with a distant memory. 'The Dark Horse?' I enquire.

'Yeah, a right dive but the drinks were cheap.'

I can picture the primary-coloured letters spelling out those words on our fridge. We'd use the fridge magnets to leave messages for each other: 'Keren's mum called'; 'Someone buy milk!'; 'House inspection on Tuesday'. With my eyes shut, I can see the blurry sentence: 'T meet me at Dark Horse 7.30 p.m.' on the side of the fridge above a freebie St Mark's Uni magnet on top of a band flyer. Or is the alcohol causing me to imagine it? My words, thoughts and memories are spinning around together.

The Dark Horse pub. I think I'm going to be sick.

All of a sudden the lights ping back on and I squint as my eyes readjust. Adam walks over to Keren and gives her a hug. Johnny throws his head back and downs a glass of water, then tops up his wine glass and raises it.

'Well done, Jeannie.'

The smell of the alcohol emanating from my half-drunk glass is too much.

I push myself up to my feet using my stick and take a couple of seconds to get my balance.

'You OK?' Keren asks protectively. 'Do you want a hand?'

'No, I'm fine, I just need, you know, the loo.' My ears are ringing and I focus on putting one foot firmly in front of the other on the uneven floor, hurrying to make it on time. I saw the ladies' sign in the corridor earlier when I walked along it to get to the dining room.

When I close the dining room door behind me, I walk next to the wall to steady myself, then stumble through the loo doors. In the cubicle my stomach brings its contents back up and I cough it all out, wishing I could expunge my guilty thoughts that easily. I flush, wipe my mouth with toilet roll then sit on the loo.

After a minute, the room becomes static and my mouth craves water. The memory comes flashing back in my head, one I've tried not to think about for years. Just an embarrassing incident, not worth remembering. And yet, if anyone else knew, would they blame me?

It all started around the time we were revising for our finals. While Keren was in the library, Jeannie was studying in her room and the boys were back at their house, Tania and I would sit and revise together, usually ending in her suggesting we take a break and watch TV or pour a vodka and orange as a treat. Ever since I'd met her at a charity fundraising meeting she'd always made me feel special, not just one of the crowd, and I was delighted when she suggested that I join her, Jeannie and Keren in a house share for the second year. She was with Johnny, I knew, and straight as a die, but in those last few weeks I looked forward to our revision sessions, hungering for her attention, the smiles she gave me, and the compliments on the way I looked. She'd get in bed next to me while we read. Once, her arm brushed the side of my boob and I held my breath, shocked by my body wanting more. I couldn't stop thinking, could she be bi? Was she hinting that she liked me as more than a friend? I'd had a short relationship that ended a few months before when my girlfriend ditched me for a boy on her course. Tania had held me in her arms while I cried, stroking my hair and telling me how great I was and that I would find someone else.

I gingerly stand up. My throat is as dry as sandpaper. I lean on my stick and walk to the sink where I desperately try to catch water in my cupped hand, willing it not to slip through my fingers, and gulp down as much as I can.

The water won't wash away the memory in my head. We both had our last exams on the same day. The night before, Tania and I lay on my bed with our notes to cram in some last-minute knowledge. Tania asked me to test her knowledge of a crib sheet she'd made listing key dates, names and points to memorise, only for her to burst into tears with frustration when she got some wrong.

There, with red eyes and without her usual makeup on, she looked so vulnerable and worried. I shuffled up next to her on the bed and put my arms around her.

'It's only nerves, you've got hours to remember it all in the exam and those subjects might not even come up,' I soothed. Her tears dropped onto the top of my T-shirt.

'I haven't done enough work, I'm not clever enough, I'm going to let my dad down,' she whispered.

I'd never seen Tania like this before, exposed and needy rather than assured and confident, the one others went to when they needed help.

'You'll be fine, I promise,' I said, holding her tight.

'I'm not really who you think I am,' she sighed into my neck. 'I'm not good enough.'

'Of course you are,' I retorted quickly. 'You're special, attractive, kind, and . . . I adore you.'

Tania snuffled in my neck. 'I wish Johnny was more like you.'

I pulled back and looked her in the eyes, overwhelmed by the urge to kiss her. I tentatively pressed my lips to hers. She started a little, surprised, but then kissed me back, running her fingers through my long hair. It lasted about five minutes, then she said she ought to have an early night to be fresh for her exam and pecked me on the cheek goodnight.

I hardly slept that night for thinking about her, desire mixed with guilt about what Johnny would say, but then I told myself that uni was nearly over, if Tania wanted to be with me then Johnny won't be around. Relationships break up all the time. I dared to hope that that night wasn't a one-off.

It was.

At six thirty in the morning there was a knock at my door. Bleary eyed, I called 'Come in', sitting up to see whether it was Tania or Keren. It was Tania looking dark eyed and sheepish. She came in and closed the door behind her but stood rigidly with her back to it.

'Saira, look, I just wanted a quick chat about last night. You're a good friend but what happened, well it was a one-off. I'm with Johnny, and you know, I don't feel that way about girls. I was upset and I got carried away. I know you'll understand, you're a brilliant friend I never want to lose. But if Johnny finds out he'll probably dump me for good and I couldn't bear that. We've had a bit of a rocky patch as you know. You won't tell him, will you? I'll probably fail my finals if he ends it with me.'

She smiled at me with imploring eyes. My stomach lurched into freefall and took my breath away. I didn't want to be responsible for her failing. She'd blindsided me.

'Um, yes. Sure.'

'Great. Good luck today.'

Tania swiftly disappeared and closed the door quietly. I crawled under my duvet and sobbed, covering my face with my pillow to mask the sound.

Somehow I managed to get through the exam, trying to block out my feelings of hurt that turned to anger and then confusion as to whether she'd led me on or not. In the evening I joined in the group celebrations, going through the motions, pretending that everything was fine. Seeing Tania laughing, sitting on Johnny's knee with her tongue down his throat, stabbed me in the chest.

The others didn't notice anything had happened.

Now, standing by the sink, my knuckles turning pale clutching the porcelain to steady me, the memories of my hurt and anger come flooding back.

No one can possibly know what I did next, can they?

Twenty-five years has passed. In the loos I stand up straight and look at myself in the mirror. My eyes are puffy and swollen, my skin blotchy and I have a black smear of mascara over my eyelids. I grab a paper towel and wet it to wipe it off.

What happened was so long ago. My bloodshot eyes stare back at me in the mirror and I see my pupils widen as a horrible thought hits me.

Perhaps they do, have pieced two and two together and are watching, waiting to expose me.

Chapter 10

Keren

For a posh hotel it has dodgy electrics. The lights going off really gave me the willies. Saira's right, there's a spooky feeling about tonight, but Johnny's correct too that it's the wine prompting her to talk about Tania's spirit and woo-woo nonsense like that.

Adam's hug is reassuring. Saira's gone to the loo but he still lowers his voice so Johnny can't hear and whispers into my ear, 'Let's make our excuses soon. Best if you drink the water not the wine.'

I push him away, annoyed. He obviously thinks I'm plastered. So I've had a few drinks, it's not like I usually get the chance to do so with two children and a house to look after. He's had a few glasses too. Let's face it, we've all needed alcohol to get through this awful evening.

Jeannie walks back in and Adam goes back to sit in his seat. He looks a bit annoyed with me. Well, he deserved it, he shouldn't be telling me what to do. The free wine is lovely. I have a few mouthfuls of water then make a point of refilling the wine glass I knocked over in the dark.

'All fixed!' Jeannie says brightly. I wonder what she's been up to, to make her so cheerful. I chuckle at the thought of her getting down and dirty with sexy barman Grant in the dark, but no way would she do that. There isn't even a crease in her suit.

Johnny stands up and pulls back Jeannie's chair for her as if he's a Victorian gentleman.

'Oh, thank you!' She smiles and sits down. 'The fuse box had tripped, the lights were off in all the rooms on this circuit. Eerik came down to help. It took us a little time to work it out and check we'd got the right fuse but everything's fine now. I do apologise, it's not the sort of thing that usually happens here. Have you been having fun?'

She's gabbling now. I realise she's on edge like the rest of us.

'Not really, we've just been sitting in the dark,' I reply.

'Yes, of course, sorry. Saira's not here, is she OK?'

'In the loo,' I add.

'Shall we finish the photo game? I don't know about you lot but I'm looking forward to taking advantage of my lovely bedroom,' says Johnny.

'Oh yeah, who with?' I quip.

I could swear I see Jeannie blush. She quickly changes the subject.

'Right then, who wants to go next?'

I volunteer. The photo inside my envelope is of Tania and I in eighties fancy dress. I pass it around the table. She's dressed as Madonna, wearing ripped tights, a miniskirt, a vest top, and a multitude of bangles up her arms. I'm dressed as a goth in all black, with black eyeliner, black lipstick and hair sticking up so high that it took half a can of hairspray to fix it in place. The photo reminds me of the fun Tania and I had together, how she could always make me laugh until my stomach hurt. I've never met anyone like that since.

After the Christmas night out with Caroline, Tania and I would team up in lectures, and we were in a couple of seminars together too. At first I thought she just seemed grateful not to sit on her own but then, after we went out for lunch post-lecture and ended up chatting all afternoon, we became proper friends and then the gang formed. Tania already knew Jeannie, and after Tania had had a few drunken snogs with Adam, he introduced her to Johnny. Saira, from RAG, soon became one of us too. At first I'd been closest to Adam, because we were on the same corridor. We spent most of the first term together, friends only. After he'd hooked up with Tania though, he annoyingly followed her around like a lost puppy dog for a while and didn't bother spending much time with me until

Tania and Johnny became an item. She still couldn't do any wrong in his eyes though.

'I remember that night.' Johnny smiles. 'I went as one of the Pet Shop Boys.'

Hmm, I bet he doesn't remember it for the reason I do.

'Fancy dress isn't my thing but Tania persuaded me to take part. We went round charity shops and found a blouse with shoulder pads and she curled my hair for me,' Jeannie reminisces.

'Who were you supposed to be?' Johnny asks.

'No one really, it was an eighties look. I remember my mum wearing that sort of thing.'

'I don't think I bothered dressing up, I went in my usual jeans and T-shirt,' Adam says. 'I put my sunglasses on and said I was a New York rapper.'

At that we all laugh. If anyone is most unlikely to be a New York rapper it's him.

'You and Tania won prizes for your fancy dress, didn't you, Keren?'

I think back to the voucher for a free drink in the students' union I got for coming fourth. Tania, who needed it the least, got a £50 supermarket voucher. 'Tania was voted first, I was fourth.'

'You two celebrated hard that night. You both disappeared. I remember Tania had said she'd walk back with Jeannie but you two didn't show up so Adam and I walked her home and left you two to it,' Johnny says.

We weren't partying hard at all. I wonder whether I should say anything. Ah, sod it, the wine has loosened my tongue.

'Well, actually, we lost each other in the crowds and I was trying to find Tania.'

'Find her? She'd not fallen asleep in the loos, had she?' laughs Johnny.

'No. Actually I found her with some bloke who was visiting a friend at the uni. They were in the second-floor bar, the quieter one that didn't have an event on that night.'

Johnny clears his throat.

'I'm sure it was all innocent,' Adam intervenes.

'He was coming on to her, trying to get her to go home with him.

She wasn't exactly slapping him in the face. I made her come back with me, which he wasn't happy about.'

'I'm sure she was only being friendly. She was stunning, men did come on to her a lot. She would have just been being polite,' Jeannie says indignantly.

'They came on to her more than you knew. Sorry, Johnny, but I think she liked the attention. It wasn't the first time I'd intervened to stop her going off with some random bloke.'

'Keren,' warns Adam, shooting me a death stare.

Johnny looks down at the table. 'Yes, she had other admirers. She was a beautiful girl and liked socialising, but she wouldn't have done anything, she was with me,' he says, slightly less confidently than usual.

Yeah right. He didn't catch her snogging blokes far away from his eyes, like a teenager behind the bike sheds. I, and I think once Saira, made sure she came back with us, didn't do something she'd regret. She usually thanked me in the morning. The first few times it was funny but after a while it became wearing, but friends look out for each other, don't they?

'Whatever you want to believe,' I say. This Sauvignon Blanc, it's like truth serum. I take another sip. This evening's been so bad, anything I say can't make it any worse. The others seem to want to believe Tania was a saint. I'm not wearing blinkers any more.

Saira comes back in looking decidedly the worse for wear. 'I've probably had a bit too much to drink. I'm off to bed now. Thanks for this evening, Jeannie,' she says, avoiding all our eyes, then leaves the room. I'd hoped we'd get a chance to talk before the evening ended but then again I still feel hurt she hadn't told me the truth. Perhaps it's better to leave it till tomorrow when I'll have cooled off. I don't want to say something I shouldn't in the heat of the moment, like I did to Jeannie earlier on. It's not worth losing Saira's friendship over and she did look really upset earlier.

'That's a shame. Saira didn't get to open her envelope,' Jeannie says, looking slightly crestfallen.

'I don't mind doing it,' Adam replies and reaches for the envelope with an S on the front. I can tell he wants to speed the evening up and get it over with. Then another thought pops into my head, remembering how adoring he was of Tania when they were briefly together. I've never wanted to talk to him about it. I don't want to make a fuss, it was so long ago, and a small part of me doesn't want to in case he says something I don't want to hear. How can I compete with the memory of a dead woman? Did he volunteer because he wants to see another photo of her? For a moment, a bolt of jealousy hits me but I swat it away like a tennis player returning a lightning serve over the net. Tania's long gone. She isn't a threat to me. This weekend is all about nostalgia.

Saira's photo is of her and Tania both holding RAG collection buckets. They're wearing silver tutus and have pink glitter sparkling all over their faces.

'That must have been taken at RAG week. Tania met Saira when she joined the society, I think,' Adam concludes.

Tania later told me she'd joined RAG to raise money for a charity for bereaved children. I knew her mum died when she was little but it was a long time before she opened up to me about how.

'They both raised a lot of money for charity,' jumps in Jeannie. 'Tania was really thoughtful of others. She might have been well off but always wanted to help people who were less fortunate than herself. Remember the time she roped us all into a sponsored egg and spoon mini marathon? And the fancy dress karaoke where we all dressed up as a famous singer and people bet on who we were trying to be before we sang a song?'

'Oh God, I felt like a total idiot that night. Tania sweet-talked us all into taking part and I insisted I'd only do it if I could do a duet with Adam,' Johnny says.

'Oh yes!' Adam laughs. 'We spent ages working out who to be and what song we might have a chance of trying to sing.'

'You dressed up as Danny from *Grease* and I bought a black dress and a blonde curly wig from a charity shop and tried to be Sandy,' Johnny adds.

'We totally murdered that song!'

They both laughingly launch into a rendition of 'You're the One That I Want', before I jokingly put my fingers in my ears and cry, 'Enough!'

'We raised a couple of hundred pounds for charity.' Jeannie smiles. 'That wouldn't have happened if it wasn't for Tania.'

I glance between my husband and his former best friend. Relations seem to be warming up. At least one good thing is coming out of this evening. I hate seeing Adam unhappy.

'I remember her collecting for local people as well as the children's charity. Like when that factory nearby shut down and they all lost their jobs,' I add. I respected Tania for that. St Mark's was hot on students getting involved with the community. In my final year I volunteered a couple of hours a week to listen to children read in a nearby primary school. It was good experience for my PGCE application.

Johnny snorts with laughter. 'Not quite. She was supposed to be on a three-hour morning shift in town with a collecting bucket but we were both so hungover we bunged a few notes in the bucket and stayed in bed.'

I should have guessed. My blinkers aren't so far gone as I thought they were.

Jeannie slams her hand down on the table. Blimey, I've never seen her do that before. We all look over at her in shock.

'I'm trying to have a lovely evening here with great memories to commemorate our friend. Why do you all keep spoiling them?'

'Sorry, didn't mean to upset you, we know you've put a lot of effort into this,' Johnny says, patting her arm.

Jeannie quietens down. 'We were her friends. This should be a happy evening. Respectful of her memory.'

My mouth opens before my brain kicks in.

'Not being funny, Jeannie, but you do seem to be remembering a different person than me. Tania wasn't perfect. She seemed like it at the time, but looking back, she wasn't at all. She didn't exactly treat you very well, did she? You'd always do anything she wanted and she knew that and played on it. She used you really for when she had nothing else to do.'

Adam holds his head in his hands.

'It wasn't like that!' Jeannie shouts.

'Keren, come on, leave it please,' my husband says to me.

'No, I'm not going to leave it. She did. It didn't mean we didn't like her but there's no point pretending she was a saint. And you *were* a bit of a lapdog, Jeannie. You let her walk all over you. You act like you're the keeper of Tania's flame, her chosen friend, but she didn't really treat you well, did she?'

Adam sticks his oar in. 'We don't know what Jeannie and Tania's friendship was truly like. They were friends before we joined the group.'

'Yes, I was Tania's best friend. I knew her better than all of you,' Jeannie cries. Tears start to roll down her cheeks. Johnny awkwardly pats her on the hand in an attempt to comfort her. No doubt he feels sorry for her after my outburst. I spot her smiling at him with thanks and start to feel guilty about what I said, even though it's true.

I look over at Adam, willing him to back me up here like I've always done for him.

He gets the message. 'It's all in the past but Tania, well, she could be a bit fickle. Lead people on.'

Jeannie looks stricken. 'Why, what did she say? Did she talk about me behind my back?'

I can see Adam mentally backtracking. 'We were all young, we all said or did things out of turn and played up to entertain others.'

'I didn't,' I interject.

Johnny throws his head back and laughed. 'Oh come on, you are one big pretence! Your name isn't really Keren, it's Agatha. That's what's on your birth certificate. Tania told me you were christened after your granny. You changed your name to Keren when you were eighteen before you came to St Mark's because you were a big fan in childhood of Bananarama!'

I swore Tania to secrecy when I told her that one night when we had a heart-to-heart. She said she'd take it to her grave.

'Tania told you that?' I say angrily.

'Yes she did.' Johnny smirks.

'Steady on, mate, my wife's name is her own business, nothing to do with you,' Adam steps in.

'I suppose. Sorry, Keren.'

'Well, you lived in cloud cuckoo land thinking that Tania was faithful to you,' I snap.

A nerve on Johnny's forehead starts to twitch.

'I wasn't a fool. What I knew and what I assumed happened is my business, just like you and your name,' he spits back.

'I always wondered if something went on with her and Saira as well before our last exams. Saira suddenly started avoiding Tania and she wouldn't tell me why.'

'Keren!' wails Jeannie. 'Please stop. This is not what tonight is supposed to be about!'

Everyone goes quiet. Oh God. What have I done? Shame begins to trickle through my veins. Tania was my friend. I shouldn't be speaking ill of the dead. I wasn't perfect either. My mind casts back to that final week, my last interaction with Tania . . .

I speak up. 'Sorry, Jeannie. Sorry, everyone. I think the combination of the alcohol and my heightened emotions this evening have gotten the better of me. I didn't mean to be so harsh about Tania. I cared about her. We all did.'

Adam sends me a conciliatory smile.

'Thanks for the meal and all the effort you put in, Jeannie. I'm sorry if I've spoilt it. We've got a new day tomorrow. Let's all do something nice then to remember Tania, shall we?'

Jeannie snaps back into professional mode.

'Yes. Thanks, Keren. Breakfast starts at 7.30 a.m. and I've got some great ideas of activities for tomorrow afternoon.'

'Lovely,' I reply, although I don't think it. I'm not giving up going to the waterfall. 'I'm off to bed now. See you all tomorrow. Adam, are you coming?'

'Yes,' he says, but then Johnny interrupts.

'Why don't you stay up a bit longer, mate? We've got loads to catch up on.'

'Just a little while, Adam? You haven't opened your photo yet,' Jeannie cajoles.

Adam looks at her, then back at me, undecided. I nod. There's no way I'm staying up to watch him open his bloody photo of him and Tania. It's in everyone's best interests if I make my escape now.

'I'll follow you in a minute. I'll open my photo first,' my husband says.

I walk over to him, trying not to do so in a wobbly line, and kiss him on the forehead, hoping my breath doesn't stink. Too late for that after all the wine I've drunk.

The corridor is deathly quiet. I quickly go to the ladies' to check that Saira hasn't fallen in there or something after her accident earlier, but thankfully it's empty.

A couple of stairs creak underfoot as I walk up them, holding on to the banister because the ground doesn't look exactly horizontal. The subdued lighting casts shadows across the ceiling. I stand still as a statue when I hear a quiet click, like someone gently closing a door. My eyes dart around. There's no one there.

This place gives me the creeps. I take back what I thought earlier about being envious of anyone with the cash to buy it and live here. I'll keep my packed semi-detached house any day of the week.

I continue walking up the stairs as fast as I safely can without tumbling back down them. The first floor is deserted. Only the sound of a faint buzz coming from the night lights breaking the eerie silence.

For goodness' sake I tell myself, it's late, of course there's no one around. There are only a few of us in this hotel. Saira's in bed. The noise I heard was probably one of the staff going to bed. I think Jeannie said that the chef lives here.

I fumble in my handbag for my key card for ten seconds and exhale with relief when my fingers clasp the cool plastic. The door opens first try. I turn the light on and lock the door behind me. Only Adam with his key card will be able to get in.

I start to walk over to the bed when my foot skids on the floor and I grab on to the edge of the desk to stop myself from tumbling over. Adrenaline shoots round my body, causing an acrid taste in my mouth. That might have been nasty, I could have turned my ankle in these heels.

Looking down at the carpet where I skidded there's a white envelope.

The initial K is on the front in thick, black ink.

Chapter 11

Adam

Let's get this photo thing over and done with. I really wanted to go back to our room with Keren. I hope she'll find her way back all right in the state that she's in, but I was torn between being with her and trying to make up for earlier rudeness towards Jeannie.

This had better be a non-contentious picture. I rip open the envelope and slide out the photograph, trying to hide the guilt and shock from my face. The picture is a little bit blurry and in shade, but it's crystal clear to me when it was taken. The night when Tania and I were alone chatting on the sofa, the night that, if Johnny hadn't walked in when he did, who knows what would have happened? The night it all started again.

At least I thought we were alone then. My eyes dart across the table to Johnny, to see if he reacts, but he's the other side of the table and probably can't make out the photo from there.

'What is it, mate?' he asks, slurring his words a bit but not as badly as Saira and Keren were. I lift it up to show him.

'It's a good one that. It was in a pack that Johnny took, along with ones of our exam celebration night. I'd asked him to get me a duplicate set. When Tania went missing, you know, I wanted as many photos of her as I could get.' Jeannie smiles sadly.

So Johnny took the photo. I'd forgotten he'd decided to try out his new camera that night, like a kid with a new toy. I'd stayed a while longer. I thought it would look suspicious if I'd upped and left straightaway, and I held a hope that maybe Johnny and Imran might go upstairs and I'd be alone with Tania again. It might be over twenty-five years since that night, but right now it feels like yesterday. My heart begins to beat more quickly. I'm glad Keren's gone up to bed, I might not have been able to hide my feelings towards Tania from her.

'It's of Tania and I, on the sofa at my, Imran and Johnny's house,' I say.

The colours are as bright as they would have been when the picture was first developed. The photo can't have been stored in an album. Tania and I are in animated conversation. I'm laughing and she's gesticulating, as if she's illustrating a story. Her eyes are bright with youth and hilarity. She's strikingly beautiful. Next to her I look like a spotty, embarrassing blast from the nineties past.

'Pass it round, mate,' asks Johnny and, my heart rate speeding up, I reach over the table and give it to him as if we were playing a simple game of pass the parcel.

Guilt clenches in my stomach. I think about what I would have done if we hadn't been interrupted. Even though mine and Johnny's friendship had been seriously strained that year to say the least, outwardly we were still acting friendly. I'm not the type to steal someone else's girlfriend, even though Tania had been mine first. For goodness' sake, why am I so bloody moral? Most other men wouldn't care less. For a moment I have a flashback of me at age four and my dad leaving us for another woman. Him leading Mum on, dangling her on a string that he pulled now and then whenever suited him, hooking her with the bait that he might return, getting her pregnant with my younger brother but staying put with his new woman who came round and threatened to beat Mum up if she ever saw Dad again.

Mum never had the choice. Dad had hardly spent any time with me since he'd left, and after the other woman's warning he never came back. Coward. Not even to visit his new son. My brother has never met his dad. Perhaps it's easier for him that way. He never felt abandoned because Dad was never there in the first place. But he abandoned *me*. I tried to be the man of the family, comfort Mum, look after my little brother. For hours when it got dark I'd sit by the windowsill looking through a crack in the curtains, on guard in case that nasty woman came back and tried to hurt my mum. I heard all of it when she came round. The whole street probably did, she shouted so loudly.

I swore I wouldn't be like my father. I'd never be cruel, hurt a woman, be unkind or cheat. I've seen the long-lasting pain it caused my mum. I think Dad enjoyed it, having power over her, exploiting her love. It made me wary of approaching girls, not wanting to say or do the wrong thing. At school I had a few female friends but nothing more than that. I was tall, skinny, not one of the athletic or indie types they seemed to go for. I didn't have the confidence to ask a girl out.

That's why I stayed single until Tania made it abundantly clear that she wanted us to be together. It was like all my Christmases had come at once.

'Good photo, thanks, Jeannie,' I say, studying her and Johnny's faces for signs of any reaction, remembering the photo shoved under my door, and that it could have been from either one of them. Am I giving anything away?

It's getting hot in here. My shirt is damp under my armpits. Do they know I wasn't as moral as I thought I was? The memories I'd buried start to leak into my head. My being convinced that Tania wanted us to get back together. Me engineering hanging around where I thought I might get to talk to her on her own. The flowers I gave her when I finally managed it, with a card inside imploring her to meet me to talk one evening, just the two of us. The letter I wrote a couple of days later declaring my love after she didn't get in touch, putting it into her hands when I saw her, after a couple of hours' waiting, walking up the street to her house alone. The phone calls I made to her house hoping she'd answer, putting down the phone when it was Keren, Saira or Jeannie. The time it wasn't and Tania told me I was mistaken, that she was my friend but anything else was firmly in the past. Me hanging up in distress, fixated on those final words of hers: 'You've got to move on, Adam. I did years ago and I'm with Johnny.' The anger I felt when I realised that Tania had teased me, wanting to know she could have had me if she chose.

But she didn't and back then I briefly flipped to the other side of the love/hate coin, loathing her for it.

Shame envelops me. I use needing the loo as an excuse to leave the table. I push my chair back brutally. Johnny and Jeannie carry on talking about the photo while I walk out of the room, but I'm so deep in thought I'm not listening to what they're saying. I close the dining room door behind me. There's a click as the lock mechanism falls into place. For a moment I stand with my back against the door, savouring being out of the room and on my own, away from the tension, yet still I'm on edge. The corridor's low lighting doesn't help, shadows from the furniture project on the floor ahead. It's hardly less creepy than the dining room when the lights went off. I hope the fuse is not going to blow again. I would have thought the hotel would have rooms on separate systems so if one light fused they all wouldn't.

The gents' is the third door on the right. My footsteps are silent on the plush carpet, so when there's a loud creak I spring round in the direction where it came from. Don't be stupid, Adam, it's probably one of the kitchen staff clearing up in a back room.

I think the noise came from a door on the left about ten metres ahead of me. There isn't a sign on the door and once again the corridor is silent. Instead of the metal levers on the other doors this one has a knob. I turn it right, then try left, but nothing happens. It's stuck, locked maybe. Shoving the door doesn't work either. The creak can't have come from there. Maybe it was the pipes or someone walking around upstairs? After the drinks I've had, I can't be totally sure where the sound came from.

I turn and make my way to the loo, the need for it creeping up on me. Psychosomatic probably. There are two cubicles in there plus a urinal. I pick the cubicle on the left and hurriedly relieve myself. Just as I'm zipping myself up there's another loud creak piercing the silence. Damn, I nearly catch myself in the trouser zip.

'Hello? Is anyone there?' I say, adrenaline starting to pump through my body, triggering my fight or flight reaction. I'm in the gents' in a hotel. Surely nothing to fear, but was there someone in the corridor earlier and were they following me?

With muscles clenched I slowly open the door and walk into the corridor.

'Only me.'

'Jesus, Johnny, you scared me.'

Does he know? Did Tania tell him? I'd assumed she hadn't because he'd never mentioned it during those miserable days after Tania's death. Maybe he did know and wants to confront me. Is that why he's followed me? It must have been him in the corridor a few minutes ago. But hang on, the noise I heard was ahead of me, and I left the dining room before Johnny.

'Sorry, mate, didn't mean to. I wanted a quick chat on our own. Turning out to be a right train wreck of an evening, isn't it?'

I wipe a sheen of perspiration off my forehead with the back of my hand. 'I don't think it's what Jeannie wanted,' I reply, testing the water. Maybe, when Keren has slept her hangover off tomorrow, I'll suggest going home early. We can always say the kids are missing us. We've done our bit turning up, best not dig up the past any further.

Johnny tries the handle of the door opposite us and it slowly opens. He looks in and switches on a light. It's a smallish linen cupboard with standing space in front of the shelves. 'Want to come in here? It's more private than the gents,' he says. Briefly the thought that he might be luring me in to beat me up flashes in my mind before I dismiss it as ridiculous. Throwing his fists around never was his style, and his expression is conciliatory.

When we're both inside, he quietly shuts the door before starting to speak. 'I saw the look on your face when you opened the photo of you and Tania. I know what you were thinking.'

I gulp, my thoughts grasping for a way to explain.

'It was a long time ago,' I reply, hedging my bets. My muscles brace themselves in case of danger. But if Johnny is going to hurt me why does he look so contrite?

'You and Tania. I didn't know if you knew, I thought you might have done. I should have said something, or rather I shouldn't have listened to her in the first place. Tania thought you might have guessed, you'd been weird with both of us since I said I wasn't going to lend you the money to stay on at uni.'

I'm bewildered. What's he on about? Knew what?

'Then I walked in the night that photo was taken and saw you both happily chatting on your own after having eaten all the pizza. I thought if you'd known then you'd forgiven her, maybe you'd discussed it. I asked Tania later and she said you hadn't talked about it but things were back to normal between you two so you must have gotten over it. She could be very persuasive, couldn't she?'

So he doesn't know. This isn't about me trying to get back with Tania at all. 'I'm not sure I know what you're talking about,' I reply confusedly. Behind my back my hands stop shaking.

Johnny sighs and holds his palms up in the way he always used to when he admitted defeat at a snooker or pool game.

'I saw your face fall, you looked angry for a moment when you opened the envelope. You did know, didn't you? I really am sorry, mate. I was going to lend you the money but then Tania said that it's not a good idea to lend money to friends, that I didn't know if you'd be able to pay me back and you needed to stand on your own two feet. I let Tania's words get into my head and was worried that it could eventually lead to spoiling our friendship. I shouldn't have listened, I should have kept my promise to you. I know you'd have paid me back; you always did what you said you would, and you're a hard worker. I mean look at you, you're doing really well for yourself!'

I hold on to a wooden shelf to steady myself for a moment, letting his words sink in.

'You mean it was Tania who told you not to lend me the money to finish my degree?'

'Oh hell. You didn't know then?'

'No.'

'She thought you'd figured it out.'

'No, I hadn't.'

That night on the sofa, when Tania said she wished I could have stayed on to finish my degree, it was all a load of rubbish. She told me what I wanted to hear, maybe was fishing to see if I knew. I slam my fist into freshly laundered and ironed pile of tablecloths. I'd been a grade-A fool. It wasn't Johnny who betrayed me, it was her. She hadn't still cared about me at all.

'Steady on!'

I curse under my breath. Tania was never going to get back with me. Why did she tell Johnny not to give me the loan? What was it to her? Did she enjoy having the power to interfere or did she want to irrevocably destroy my friendship with Johnny so she had him all to herself? Divide and conquer.

'I'm sorry, I really am,' Johnny goes on. 'I know you'd liked Tania before I did. If it makes you feel any better, we nearly split up before our finals, as well as rowing the night before she crashed my car. I was fed up with her flirting with other men. She said she was just being friendly but I wanted her to tell them to fuck off. We had a big row. If we're clearing the air, being completely honest with each other, turns out I'm a complete screw-up now, single, jobless and broke. I envy you actually.'

My eyes open wide in astonishment. I look at Johnny's smart, tailored trousers and designer shirt, his Rolex watch peeking out from under the left-hand cuff. He'd had us all assume he was wealthy and successful. Johnny sees me staring and raises his arm.

'The Rolex? It's on borrowed time. I'm probably going to have to sell it to pay Olivia's maintenance,' he adds quietly.

Suddenly I feel exhausted. The tension, the wine, the revelation ... I sink down and sit on the floor, legs crossed with my back against the rear shelves. In the bulb light Johnny looks lined but puffy around his red cheeks, and I can tell something is weighing him down. My old warmth towards him comes gushing back. He'd always been loyal to me, it was Tania who wasn't and I'd blamed him for it. When you were captivated by her it was very hard to deny her what she wanted.

'What happened?' I ask kindly.

Johnny's knee clicks as he gets down on the floor beside me. There's just enough room for the two of us to sit side by side if we bend our knees.

'I should explain first that I deliberately didn't say anything tonight, that I wanted you all to think I was still doing well, because I was too embarrassed to tell the truth: that I was made redundant, can't find another job, my wife kicked me out and divorced me, I'm living in a bedsit and hardly ever see my daughters. Not where I thought I'd be in my forties.'

The Johnny next to me now is the one I remember from our uni days. Honest, open with me, if not with everyone.

'Really? What about the Range Rover in the car park?'

'It's being repossessed on Monday.'

Johnny starts to chuckle and it's infectious. We both end up belly laughing despite his situation not being funny in the slightest.

'Well, I'll take that and I'll raise you with me hating my job and having the boss from hell. I'd be dancing on the table at being made redundant with a decent pay-off. I wish!'

Our laughter breaks up any lingering awkwardness.

'Ah, I can do better than that, I'll raise you with me being diabetic. Diagnosed a year ago when I when I was thirsty and going to the lav all the time. Not long after my darling ex took me to the cleaners.'

'Christ. Is it under control?' I ask. There's so much about his life I don't know. Keren was right, I *have* ended up in a better position than him, but my concern for Johnny overrides any joy in one-upmanship.

'Have to inject myself twice a day. Supposed to be getting a pad thing to go on my arm sometime that's connected to a smartphone but I keep putting the appointment off. Not that I've got much else to do with my days other than fruitlessly look for work.'

We're not laughing now. 'That's hard. I'm sorry. And don't worry about the loan. That was years ago. I shouldn't have let it ruin our friendship. I should have made more effort to keep in touch.'

'I did try to contact you. I sent a letter for you to your mum's house, about a year or so after graduation, but the line was dead. After that, well, life got in the way, and I've never been good with the social media thing. Got an account but hardly ever look at it. Only saw about this weekend because I'd logged on to see what my eldest had posted on her account. Despite me disagreeing, Olivia let her have one when she turned thirteen.'

My old mate Johnny. Today hasn't been a total disaster. If anything good has come out of this evening's shit show it's reconnecting with him again. We chat for a few minutes, quickly filling each other in on what we've been up to since St Mark's.

'You really hate your job? What does Keren say?' Johnny asks.

'Haven't told her. My salary is good but life's expensive. I can't see how we can afford for me to leave unless she works more hours and goes back teaching full time. I've had a look around at jobs and I'm not going to get one that pays as well as this. Besides, I'm sick of sales.'

'What would you like to do instead?'

It doesn't take me long to answer. 'Retrain. Do something more practical where I'm outside and solving things. Set up my own company maybe.' A smile creeps on to my face as I think of this pipe dream. The thought gives me a warm and fuzzy feeling that I haven't experienced in a long time.

'I heard of a franchise offer a few weeks ago. A former colleague told me about it. It's an organic lawn care service, mowing, de-weeding, treating, that sort of thing. He thought I might be interested,' Johnny says animatedly.

'Are you?'

'I dismissed it because I'm looking for another banking job. But now you come to mention it, the only thing I liked about banking in the end was the prestige, and the bonus, which Olivia always figuratively spent before it hit my bank account. Banking is a cut-throat business. I worked for all those years and then was out of the door, no loyalty, and since the financial crash everybody hates a banker.'

'You used to like being outdoors at uni. Going on walks, sports and things. Maybe you should think about it, see if the numbers add up. Sounds great to be your own boss, doing some manual labour and then going home and switching off. Never being on out-of-hours call. At least if you're fixing people's lawns you're doing some good, not like selling stuff people don't really need ... or banking,' I tell him.

Johnny turns to face me, an excited look flashing over his face. 'Why don't we go into it together? We both live in London. You'd have the sales and marketing side covered and I know finance and accounting. When you take up the franchise they train you on how to do lawn care. It'd be a fresh start for both of us.'

God, it sounds tempting. A new start. What's past is past and can stay there unmentioned. I picture myself walking into Helena's office and telling her what I really think of her. Plus, once I'm away from the firm, Keren will forget all about me supposedly being beaten by Helena for the MD job. If the business is successful, we might even be able to afford the kitchen extension.

'I've got to work three months' notice.'

'Fine. I can be doing all the groundwork while you work it. If you've got some holiday time you're owed you could take it to do the training with me.'

Despite the fact that I'm sitting on the floor in a linen cupboard I feel more positive than I have done in a long time. Could I do this?

'How much is it to buy into the franchise? I'd have to speak to Keren. I'd likely need to use the kids' savings to help cover costs until we get into profit. What sort of money could we make?'

'I'm trying to remember. I think they do a loan scheme where you pay back the cost of the training and equipment once your franchise is up and running, and then you pay a certain amount each month to the founders based on your profits. My colleague told me about it because he knew I don't have any spare cash to invest upfront. I'll give him a call when I get home. Can't do it here can I with the stupid phone ban.'

'It's been so nice not fielding calls and emails from my boss all the time. My phone can stay in Jeannie's locked drawer as far as I'm concerned.'

Maybe this could solve my problems. A new career path.

I look at my watch. We've been here twenty minutes. 'We'd better get back. Hopefully Jeannie's had enough and will call it a night.'

I jump up on my feet but Johnny holds on to a shelf to ease himself up. Another knee click. 'You head on,' he says, 'I'm just going to take a leak in the gents.'

'OK, mate. And yes, let me know about the franchise. It's certainly worth looking into. I've got a business card in my wallet upstairs. I'll give it to you before we leave the hotel.'

'Great. I'm really pleased we've had this talk,' Johnny says, beaming.

I'm about to leave when I change my mind about my destination.

'Actually, I'm going to hit the hay. Check on Keren, see that she's

OK. Can you make my excuses for me please?'

Johnny nods and I walk into the corridor. Once again it's deathly quiet. There's no noise coming from the dining room either, and the door's still shut. With Johnny and I gone for so long, perhaps Jeannie decided to call it a night too.

It's second nature to me to tiptoe up the stairs like I do at home so as not to wake the kids, even though they're not here. I flinch when the movement sensor light switches on and grasp on to the banister to right my balance.

I'm still buoyed with hope when I quietly open our bedroom door with the key card. I can't see a thing. Keren has forgotten to leave a sidelight on for me. Never mind. I slink into the bathroom by feeling where I'm going and turn on the small pull light above the mirror because if I switched the main light on, the fan might wake Keren up. Then again, the amount she drank she's probably out for the count. It doesn't take me long to brush my teeth and undress to my boxers.

There's just enough light for me to climb into bed next to Keren without stumbling into the desk or chair. She's snoring slightly, and she's tucked the duvet under her chin, like she does to our children when she puts them to bed. A rush of love comes over me. She might have put her foot in it tonight but she's a good woman and mother. I love her and am lucky to have her.

Keren doesn't stir when I lie on my side and put my arm around her. My eyes close quickly and I start to drift off. Then I remember the photo that was put under our door earlier on. The brief happiness I'd felt just ten minutes ago dissipates into the darkness.

My last thought before I fall asleep is, if Jeannie didn't put it under the door, then who did?

Part Two

The Aftermath

Chapter 12

Jeannie

The grandfather clock in the dining room chimes midnight. I'm now officially a Cinderella who has turned into a big fat pumpkin after a disastrous evening. Saira and Keren have gone to bed, Adam seems to have either disappeared down the loo or gone straight to bed without saying goodnight, and goodness knows where Johnny is. Perhaps he's gone to bed too. A smouldering part of me hopes he hasn't, despite his crass comment about the starter Eerik made. Earlier, when he held my hand, I grasped on to it in a way I wouldn't have done twenty-eight years ago when I first met him. Not that he had any interest in me then, I was just his best friend's girlfriend's mate, at the time Tania and Adam were hooking up. I'd longed for him to notice me but if he had, I would have been startled off like a bird that had been told to shoo. It didn't stop me wanting to be in his vicinity though, something Tania noticed with amusement, promising to put a good word in for me. She never did, or maybe she spared my feelings by not telling me he wasn't interested. Of course he wasn't. After Tania split up with Adam, Johnny picked her instead and she'd seemingly forgotten my crush on him.

I'll wait a little bit longer. Like a good hotel manager, I've been hanging around to see if any of them come back and then I'll take a last walk around the corridors to check everything's running smoothly and go to bed myself. Eerik will have gone to his room in the staff quarters after cleaning the kitchen in readiness for tomorrow and Grant drove home after we finished fixing the damn fuse box. Thank goodness they were here and knew what to do. In my nervous state, away from the sight of guests, I was all fingers and thumbs. If the fuses trip again then there's only me to sort it out unless I wake Eerik, which I'm loath to do – it wouldn't be professional this late. Grant has the weekend off. There's only Eerik and me to look after our four guests. We'll be running on a shoestring but I thought it'd be like a private house party with us all getting along merrily and me being the jolly hostess serving the meals and the drinks.

Between the arguments and the things that were said, the whole evening is playing a constant loop in my mind, shattering everything I fondly remembered about my three years at uni. Tears well up in my eyes but I squeeze my knees until they hurt and force myself not to cry until I'm in the privacy of my own room. I wanted so much for it to go well tonight, to honour my best friend.

I'm not even sure if she was anymore.

A minute past midnight now. How much longer should I wait? I've already tided up the room and all that's left on the table is an envelope with Jo on the front and my, Johnny and Adam's half-drunk glasses of wine alongside a couple of bottles with only the dregs at the bottom. They managed to get through a lot more than I was expecting, but I didn't want to stint on my hospitality. I'm footing the bill for their rooms, food and drink. It's a discounted rate because I'm the manager but still, it's all adding up. I thought they might not come if they had to pay for themselves. Everything was supposed to go perfectly to honour Tania.

Despite it being June it's getting chilly in here now. Summer Yorkshire nights are cooler than I thought they'd be. I go and shut the two small windows I opened earlier to let the fresh air in then sit back down at the table and rest my chin under a closed fist.

I'd thought I'd planned tonight so well. Private dining for us in the Selby Room, my favourite because it's intimate and beautifully furnished, with the velvet drapes open to let the evening sunshine reflect off the gleaming silverware I polished this morning on the table. Most of the hotel's decor was modernised in the refurbishment but in here the designers deliberately fashioned an Edwardian country house feel, a place where the gentlemen of the house may retire to on a rainy Sunday afternoon to relax or dine. Landscape pictures in gilt frames adorn the walls. There's a marble fireplace in which we light huge smokeless fuel fires in the winter. It's a special room for tonight's extra-special event, or at least that's what it should have been.

Eerik excelled himself with tonight's dinner. I chose the menu especially to suit our fresh Yorkshire produce with low carbon footprint and a quick farm-to-fork journey, remembering that Saira is vegetarian. All the elements were in place for the five of us to bond, talk about the good times we had at St Mark's and our wonderful memories of Tania. If she could have seen how the evening turned out, all the sniping and accusations, she'd probably be turning in her grave.

It's my fault that things started to go wrong. I've never been good at reading how other people will react in social situations. I shouldn't have bought that cardboard cut-out of Tania and put it here without warning. While it had seemed like a great idea at the time, it set everything off to a bad start.

Looking over to the side of the room I see that someone has turned her around so all we can see is the brown cardboard back, as if a teacher has told her off for misbehaving and made her stand looking at the wall for punishment.

I groan inwardly at the memory of the others' reactions when they saw it. How could I get it so wrong? When I looked through the packs of photos from university that I'd assiduously kept, alongside the negatives, in a couple of shoeboxes, I thought that that one of Tania, looking so happy and carefree, really encapsulated how I remembered her. It wasn't easy finding a place that could make the life-size cardboard image from an old negative, but when I did, and the finished product arrived in a box so huge that Grant had to help me carry it to my room, I honestly thought I'd done well. A lovely surprise to recall our memories and have her with us again, even if it could only be as an image captured in a split second twenty-five years ago.

The photo game was supposed to have the same effect. I chose a picture for each of us that I'd imagined showed a special personal memory. Instead the others stamped all over mine, trying to destroy my treasured remembrances of Tania, and Johnny didn't even look at his. Surely Tania didn't do all those things they claim she did. They didn't know her like I did – never were true friends of hers in the first place, it seems. Doubt and guilt wriggle snake-like into my brain. I did try hard to be a good friend, didn't I? Even though I got the cardboard cut-out very wrong?

Unease spreads over me. Or did I get Tania wrong all along too? I remember the hurt I felt when she went out with Johnny and didn't consider my feelings, even though she knew I liked him. Have I never really had a proper friend at all?

I stand up and walk over to Tania's image and with two hands I turn her around so she's facing me, smiling. I look into her eyes. She'd have had something to say about their behaviour tonight, would have called them idiots like those in our first term at St Mark's who thought they were so special and wanted to cause trouble. I think back to one of my favourite moments with her, when she told me I was her best friend and if she had to choose between us all in the gang she'd pick me. It was in the final term of the first year when the subject of finding somewhere to live for the next academic year came up. In the first term she and I had pledged to live together and find a two-bed flat to rent. I knew it would be a bit more expensive than a big house share, but it meant we didn't have to move in with strangers because neither of us wanted that. After Christmas Tania returned with a new hairstyle and clothes and started acting differently in front of other people, out of nowhere becoming the life and soul of the party. She made other friends and Saira, Keren, Adam and Johnny were often around. I made the effort to be nice to them because they were Tania's friends but I never felt I really fitted in. Unlike when it was just Tania and I in our old routine, going to the refectory, watching a film, or chatting then quietly working together in one of our rooms for the company.

When the others started talking about house shares I feared that Tania would change her mind and I'd be left on my own. One evening over dinner, our favourite, fish and chips, I broached the subject nervously. I shouldn't have worried. Tania said that of course she wanted to live with me next year, and suggested Keren and Saira join us, saying it was easier to find four-bed houses and they were cheaper to rent per person.

I was elated that Tania still wanted to live with me, even if it did involve Keren and Saira as well. I'd feared that I'd might lose her to the others. I can still remember what she said that day, 'I'm looking forward to living with you again, Jeannie. You know that you'll always come first before the others.'

The tick of the clock pulls me back from my thoughts. I'll wait until ten past and then head off. I need to be up in the morning to help Eerik prepare breakfast.

I doubt Keren and Saira will make it to breakfast though, considering the way they both stumbled to bed tonight. I wonder if they'll even remember anything they said this evening. Whatever happens I will be professional as befits my job as the manager. I shouldn't have got cross tonight, that was a mistake. I never usually let anything get to me when I'm in uniform. I invited the group to stay until Sunday and, even though tonight was a complete fiasco, I don't want them leaving with any negative thoughts about the hotel or our service. I have a corporate standard and reputation to maintain. At least I still have that. It means everything to me.

Looking at my watch I do a quick calculation. I can fit in six hours' sleep and be up to clean this room and anything that needs doing before breakfast. Usually I make sure everything is ready before I go to bed because I wouldn't be able to sleep knowing everything isn't pristine, but right now I'm too emotionally and physically drained and want the respite that unconsciousness brings.

The clock carries on ticking. It's ten past twelve. My cut-off point. I walk to the door and reach for the handle to open it only for it to violently swing in my direction, causing me to leap back a few steps out of the way.

'Watch out!' I cry.

'Sorry! I didn't know if you'd still be here.' Johnny's sheepish-looking face appears around the side of the door. 'Are you OK? I didn't hit you with the door, did I?'

My heart pounds with the unexpected shock. I chose to keep full wooden doors for these private rooms to give guests privacy, whereas the doors to the bar and breakfast area have glass panels in them, meaning a situation like this wouldn't happen.

'Don't worry, I got out of the way in time.' Looking at him, my heart carries on thumping like a prize-winning boxer.

'Ah, good. Sorry I've been so long, Adam and I were catching up. He's gone to bed now, sends his regards and thanks for the evening.'

'Thank you. I was about to head upstairs myself.'

Johnny walks up to the dinner table. He doesn't look like he's intending to go to bed just yet.

'Before you do, why don't you join me for a nightcap? I think you can probably do with one after tonight. You looked rather upset earlier. I'm sorry all those things were said. Keren went too far. I should probably have kept my lips buttoned too. I know you put a lot of effort into this weekend.'

He reaches over the table and picks up the envelope with Jo written on it. 'There's this to open too.'

I should go to bed but if a guest wants to stay up for a drink then it's my duty to serve them. I'm touched too that Johnny is trying to make an effort. He's been kind to me tonight. A little less sleep won't hurt.

'OK, just the one. Why don't we go to the bar, it's comfier there and the bottles in here are empty.'

'Lead on, Macduff,' he says brightly and he follows me out of the room, down along the corridor, across the entrance hall and into the bar where I switch on a couple of standing lamps for a cosy atmosphere. It's strange being in here so late with only one other person. The bar shuts at 11 p.m.

'It's a cracking hotel, Jeannie. I can picture myself as a landed country gentleman in this room.'

I open the bar counter flap and head behind. 'Yes, can you imagine having this whole place to yourself? It used to be owned by a London family who came up here for the shooting season up until the Second World War when it was requisitioned as a base for army training. After that its use was changed to a hotel. Now, what can I get you?' I hide my trembling hand under the counter.

'A port would go down very well, thank you. And yourself?'

I shouldn't really have anything more to drink. It would, however, be rude not to join Johnny for one and being with him alone is intoxicating in itself. Despite the exhaustion that's seeping into my bones I plaster on my best smile, willing myself not to mess this up. 'Good choice. I'll join you.'

I pour the glasses and put them and the bottle on the bar. Johnny swiftly picks them all up, deftly managing to carry the two glasses in one hand and the bottle in the other and walks over to a couple of comfy armchairs at the side of the room with a small table in between. He's obviously done that before, I note wryly.

The bar flap creaks loudly as I open it up to get out and Johnny starts to chuckle.

'The ghost of the house's butler. Hope he doesn't wake the guests!' he jokes.

Despite my nervousness a real smile takes over my face. I walk over the plush carpet, one I had specifically designed to capture the spirit of this room and sit down next to him.

Johnny raises his glass to me. 'A toast. To all the hard work you've put in this weekend, and to Tania, whom we could never ever forget.'

There's a chink as our glasses touch.

'I think you'll like your photo,' I tell him, warming to his kindness. Or is there another feeling behind the courtesy? I daren't hope so.

He carefully opens the envelope and pulls out a picture of him and Tania standing together, burgers in hand, in the park near our student houses. We all went there for a barbecue in the late spring on the first day it was warm enough to do so. Tania loved barbecues. She'd told me her and her father often had them at home in the summer. It was about the only thing her dad knew how to cook.

The sun is twinkling on Tania's light blonde hair and she's smiling at the camera. Johnny's jovially pretending to take a mouthful of burger. Happy days.

'Thanks, Jeannie. Is it OK if I keep this? I don't think I've seen this photo before,' Johnny asks.

'Of course. All the photos I gave everyone today are copies.'

Johnny's voice sounds wistful. 'She had so much to look forward to, her whole life ahead of her. We were going to get a flat in London, me starting my banking traineeship and her looking for a job in the museum sector. She saw herself planning big exhibitions like the ones she loved visiting as a young girl. You never know, she could have been running the V&A by now.'

I frown slightly in confusion. 'No, she was going to find a place with me. I didn't know what job I wanted to do but thought it would be quite easy to find something in London.' Tania had said she didn't want to move there on her own and when Johnny got knocked back after several interviews she asked me to go with her.

Johnny takes a swig of his port. 'Is that what she said to you?'
'Yes.'

'Ah. It sounds like she was hedging her bets. We nearly split up, you know, a few times around our exams and for a while I didn't have any luck bagging a job. I thought about applying for places in Scotland or even Europe, but then I got a phone call from one of the companies that turned me down after the second interview. They said I'd only just been pipped to the post, another vacancy had come up and they offered it to me.'

The past breaks up and re-forms in a different, bewildering shape in my head. 'When did she say she wanted to live with you?'

Johnny ruffles his brow quizzically.

'It was when we'd finished our finals. I'd been offered the job, she'd promised me she'd settle down and wouldn't flirt with other men, and we were back on, strong again.'

So Tania was never going to flat hunt with me, I think. I wonder when she was planning on breaking the news? In the end I didn't go to London, I went back home to my parents and did a few dead-end jobs before I got a marginally better one in a large hotel as a receptionist and then got a place on the chain's management trainee scheme.

'I suppose, after what I've heard tonight, it shouldn't surprise me,' I admit sadly. 'She never invited me to her house in Devon, she always said her dad didn't like her having friends round, and yet before our finals Keren went to stay with her there for a week to revise. That stung a bit, but she said it'd be her last chance to spend time with Keren before we all left St Mark's and that she and I would have loads of time together when we lived in London.'

'They were both on the same course, remember. Tania always did prefer to revise with other people around. She didn't invite me either you know, she stayed with me and my parents in London but I never went to Devon.'

'Did it bother you?' I ask.

Johnny shrugs his shoulders. 'Sure, I'd have liked to have gone, but that's just the way it was and I accepted it. I knew Tania's dad was very protective. She did value you, you know. She told me once that if it wasn't for you, she might have dropped out of uni. You took her under your wing on the first day. Without you she wouldn't have had a friend in that first term. You were the first proper friend she ever had.'

I remember opening my door and seeing her for the first time.

'I suppose it was the same with me. I didn't find it easy to make friends at school but with Tania it came naturally.' I clutch my palm over my mouth to stop myself talking. I've never admitted that to anyone before.

Johnny reaches to the table and refills our glasses.

'I wish I'd been better at getting to know you more at uni,' he says. 'You would have been a good friend. I mean you were a friend but I didn't spend any time with you on our own, did I?'

'Ah, we were living different lives back then,' I reply before daring to add, 'but I always secretly loved the idea of spending more time together, before you and Tania were an item, of course.' Holding my breath, I daren't look at him to see how he reacts.

'Maybe we can make up for our past mistakes. I'm sorry again about how the night turned out. I wasn't on my best behaviour either. To tell you the truth I'm in somewhat of a pickle and the stress of it all was likely getting to me. You see, I got made redundant, my wife divorced me and I'm living in a bedsit.'

For a split second I wonder if he's joking. Johnny always seemed so self-assured, the sort of person that strides easily through life, and his family were loaded.

I look up, shocked. 'No! I'm sorry.'

'I'll claw my way back to gainful employment and a decent place to live somehow. My ex though, well she can remain that way. Those bridges are well and truly burnt,' he says before raising his glass again. 'Here's to the future. I know this night was a bit of a lead balloon but one funny thing came out of it. Did you know Keren's real name is Agatha?'

I shake my head and then a snort of laughter escapes through my nose. Here, in the low light, chatting easily with Johnny, I feel relaxed, almost comfortable in my own skin. It suddenly seems hilarious to me that Keren's been going by her alias for so long.

'I didn't! I can't believe it. She doesn't look like an Agatha. I don't know what an Agatha is supposed to look like, mind you, perhaps the matriarch of this house in 1902.'

Johnny throws his head back and laughs. 'And calling herself after a member of Bananarama, that's priceless.'

'She could have had her pick of eighties pop star names. We might have spent the last few decades calling her Tina, Annie or Bonnie.'

'Or Madonna!' he adds, which sets us both off in fits of laughter.

We carry on talking and I begin to feel happier than I have in a long time. With a bong, the clock strikes 1 a.m.

'It's late, we probably should go to bed now,' I say, standing up to clear away the drinks. I take our empty glasses behind the bar and walk back to the table, when Johnny clears his throat and starts to speak.

'I've enjoyed spending time with you, Jeannie. Can you spare a few more minutes? What you said earlier, I didn't know you'd wanted to spend time with me at St Mark's, before I got together with Tania. You have a very beautiful smile,' he tells me, leaning so close towards me that the intoxicating scent of his aftershave envelops my skin. My heart booms in my chest. I look at my watch, undecided, but the way Johnny is gazing at me makes my mind up.

I sit back down next to him, saying, 'Thank you. You have a lovely smile too. A few more minutes won't hurt . . .' Our eyes lock in a moment of delicious awkwardness.

'May I kiss you?' he asks.

I close the gap and press my lips to his and we kiss tentatively, feeling our way while his hand explores my back and then slowly makes its way towards my breast. I gasp with pleasure, a heady rush with finally getting what I wanted after all these years. His tongue starts to explore my mouth and I pull back, my worry that he doesn't really mean it overcoming me.

'You OK? I'll stop if you want me to,' Johnny says with tender concern that melts away my insecurity.

'No, I don't want to stop,' I say, and pull myself close to him, letting my body respond as it wants to and my hand slither up his taut thigh. His lips once again meet mine and we kiss like hormonal teenagers, our hands gingerly going further and further in exploration of each other's bodies.

When we pull apart for a breath, he asks me if I want to go to his room. This time I don't hesitate to say yes. Johnny takes my hand and we quietly tiptoe up the stairs so ask not to wake the others.

With a swift key card in the slot he opens his bedroom door. In nervous anticipation we walk over to the bed then slowly savour the pleasure of removing each other's clothes. I shed my inhibitions as well as my underwear. He takes the lead and we kiss and caress, crying out as quietly as we can with pleasure until our energy is spent and we fall into a deep sleep.

Cramp in my arm where Johnny is lying on it wakes me up. Faint daylight is glancing through the curtains. Outside, I hear a chorus of birds welcoming the new day. A different call of nature overtakes me and, naked, I creep to the bathroom to answer it.

When I return, Johnny is sitting up in bed watching me move with a lascivious look on his face. Usually I'd dash for something to cover up with but this morning I'm still high from the night's delights.

'Now this is turning out to be a *very* good morning. What a view to start the day,' he says.

I jump on the bed and hit him playfully with my pillow. He pulls me into his arms and reaches down with his hand, causing me to gasp with pleasure.

Ten minutes later we both lie back on the bed, exhausted. Every nerve in my body feels alive, as if they've come out of hibernation into the summer's dazzling rays. The world has spun on its axis and I am not alone.

Then, like a knock on the door from a bailiff, reality kicks in.

I sit up straight in panic. 'What's the time?' I look down at my watch that I forgot I had on; I usually take it off each night before I go to bed. It's 5.36 a.m.

'Damn it, I've got to sort the dining room out and get everything ready for breakfast.'

Johnny strokes his fingers through my hair, lingering when they reach a sensitive point on my neck. 'Breakfast starts at seven thirty, doesn't it? Don't worry, you've got loads of time.'

I lie back, nestling into the crook of his outstretched arm, but then my stomach churns with dread as the doubting Thomas voice in my head tells me that Johnny's going to say last night was a mistake or that he's not actually divorced at all. Sleeping with a guest is totally unprofessional. No one can know.

My concern must have shown on my face. 'I hope we can do this again,' he says. 'I'm not really a one-night stand kind of chap.' I exhale with relief. He hasn't used me for sex. Jeannie, the easy one because she doesn't get many offers.

'I hope so too,' I say quietly, 'but is it OK if we don't let the others know? Or the staff. I don't want to lose their respect.'

'Whatever you want. Let me help you organise whatever you've got planned for today. Forget last night's dinner. Why don't we all start again fresh, hey?' He kisses my forehead tenderly and I curl in towards him like the cat who's licked the top of the milk.

'Would you? I thought maybe a picnic or a walk this afternoon if Saira can manage it. I didn't know she had walking difficulties when I was trying to think up activities. I can always take her in my car. How about we ask them at breakfast what sort of thing they'd like to do? It might be best if I don't suggest any more Tania-themed activities.'

Johnny murmurs in agreement. 'I think you're right. I'm not sure the others will make it up in time for breakfast though. I certainly don't intend to.'

'*I* have to, I manage the place,' I retort. 'I really wanted this weekend to be perfect, you know, not just for Tania but also for me. I think the others look down on me, I've never felt like I really was a part of the group.'

'Well, I only look down on you because I'm slightly taller than you,' Johnny quips. 'I don't think Saira, Keren and Adam do and they certainly won't when they get to know you better again today.'

I consider a point that's just occurred to me. 'I suppose we've all changed a lot since St Mark's, but I want them to think the best of me. They always seemed, well, so put together, unlike how I feel.'

Johnny removes his arm, sits straight up with his back against the headboard in bed and looks me directly in the eyes. 'Jeannie, no one's perfect. Everyone's covering something up. Look at Saira, not telling Keren the real reason why her wife left her. We all want to show our best sides to the world and hide our worst.'

'What are you covering up then?' I tease. 'Apart from the redundancy, divorce and housing situation?'

'Isn't that enough?' He smiles. I feel for his hand and squeeze it.

'Actually, if you want full disclosure, there is something I haven't told you,' he says.

I search Johnny's face to see if he is being serious. He is.

'What is it?' I ask gently, before wondering if it's something about Tania I wouldn't want to know.

'I'm diabetic. I skipped my injection last night because I didn't want to break the mood, and you and I had much better things to be getting on with.'

I realise I don't know much about diabetes at all other than it's something to do with blood sugar.

'Do you feel all right? Is there anything I can do?'

'No, it's fine. I stashed my insulin in your kitchen fridge, I'll get it when I go downstairs later on. It's type 1. I was diagnosed not that long ago. It's all fine, I just look like a junkie with all the needles I get through,' he jokes.

I tense involuntarily at the word needle. Like a knife it can draw blood.

'Let me know if you need anything,' I say, trying to be empathetic. Another useful phrase I've learned over the years.

'I can think of something that I'd like,' he says, caressing my right breast with deft fingertips.

It takes a lot of willpower for me to move his hand away.

'I'll write you an IOU for that one. I've really got to get up now, we're very short-staffed this weekend and the responsibility stops with me.'

I get up and reach for my rumpled clothes, putting them on quickly. Outside I hear the moo of a cow. It's this part of Yorkshire's morning alarm clock.

'I do like your boss woman outfit, very sexy,' Johnny says.

I smile. 'I'm going to run upstairs and hope nobody sees me. I'll have a quick shower and put a clean suit on. This one's only fit for the dry cleaner's.'

'See you later.' Johnny smiles as I sneak out of the doorway, looking left and right first to check no one's there.

Although I've hardly had any sleep I'm wide awake and quickly achieve all the things I have to do before I help Eerik getting breakfast ready. I never would have thought at midnight that seven hours later I'd have a huge, natural grin on my face. Every now and then I force the corners of my mouth downwards in case he suspects something's up.

By mid-morning no one has yet come down for breakfast. The others are missing a beautiful morning. The sun is streaming through the windows. It's going to be a hot day.

I power walk through to the kitchen where Eerik is chopping some mushrooms in preparation for dinner tonight.

Through the open window a bird sings as happily as I feel. My mouth starts to salivate at the scent of freshly brewed coffee that's coming from Eerik's mug. When I've got a minute, I'll pour a cup for myself.

Eerik turns to me with a concerned look on his face.

'Jeannie, have you taken a knife from the kitchen?' he asks.

Abruptly, the bird outside ceases singing. A cold shiver makes me twitch involuntarily.

'No. Why, is one missing?'

'Yes, a medium-size serrated one from the block. When I went to get the knife to slice the mushrooms, I saw it was missing. I've looked all around but it's not there. I always put knives away carefully as soon as I've washed them.'

'I know you do,' I reply. He's very fastidious about his kitchen tools, it's one of the reasons why he's such a good employee.

'When did you last see it?'

'I'm sure it was there last night. When I leave the kitchen last thing, I do a quick check to make sure everything is ready to use the next day.'

It's strange to see Eerik looking worried. He's usually so happy-go-lucky. My heart beats faster with trepidation.

There's an unsheathed knife on the loose in this hotel, my idea of a horror film scenario. Fear floods into my mind as I ask him, 'If neither of us has removed the knife then who else could have, and why?'

Chapter 13

Keren

Ouch. My head hurts. A lot. My brain feels like it's pulsating like a Belisha beacon against the bones in my skull. I'm hot and sweaty with lots of cloth entwined round my legs.

Where am I? I open my eyes gingerly. There's some light filtering through a small gap between the curtains. I don't recognise the floral pattern and they're on the wrong side of the room. It takes a second before I register where I am, why I'm here, and what happened last night comes flooding back to me.

Looking down, I'm still wearing last night's dress, now ridden up to my stomach and creased. The only thing it looks like I managed was to take off my shoes. Glancing around I see them kicked off randomly on the other side of the room. My stomach churns and I stumble to the en suite, switching the light on and trying to shut the door behind me quietly so as not to wake Adam.

Immediately, I squint. The light is too bright and the noise of the fan sounds like a jumbo jet taking off. My throat feels like woodchip wallpaper and my breath stinks of booze, leaving a rank taste in my mouth.

While sitting on the loo I look at my watch. Seven a.m., not too far off the time I usually get up at. What time did I go to bed? It's been at least a decade since I've had a hangover like this. Why did I drink all that wine? Probably because it was such an awful evening. Adam and I were supposed to be retiring early for a night of child-free sex. I hope he'll forgive me. What a wasted opportunity.

I wince as I remember in a flashback getting annoyed with Adam when he advised me to drink water and pouring more wine for myself instead.

After finishing up, I wash my hands and down a couple of glasses of water from the tap that I've poured into the small glass by the sink. I look up and staring back at me in the mirror are bloodshot eyes with huge dark saddlebags. It'll take half a stick of concealer to cover those up. And then I see it. A piece of white paper nestled under my washbag. I wrack my brains to remember what happened when I came to the room the night before. Yes, that's it, there was a note under the door. I picked it up and brought it into the bathroom with me before I took my contact lenses out, went to the loo and then passed out in bed. For the life of me I can't remember if I read it, what it said or who it was from.

With shaking hands – I'm in need of a fatty cooked breakfast and a black coffee to steady them – I pull out the paper and open it up. Before me is spidery black writing on a piece of this hotel's branded notepaper. There's a pad of it on the desk in our room alongside a free biro I was going to take home for the kids. They're always losing them.

It doesn't take me long to read the note, although it's hard to decipher. The writer must have been pretty drunk. I manage to make out:

Keren, I really need to talk to you alone. Can you meet me at 7.30 a.m. in the car park before breakfast? I want to explain. Saira x

More snippets of memories from last night start to come back to me. Saira telling us all she cheated on Hannah. Me getting cross and mouthy. The cardboard cut-out of Tania, and the photos that spawned a row rather than happy memories.

I throw my body into the shower to try and kick-start myself awake. There's no point trying to go back to sleep now, my body clock is too used to being up at this time. I wonder if maybe I can have a nap this afternoon, before remembering I can't because I'd said we'd visit the nearby waterfall.

I get myself ready for the day, as quietly as possible, checking up on Adam every now and again to make sure I've not woken him. As I'm about to head out, he's still sound asleep, curled up on his side. I look over at him fondly. We both rarely have a chance for a lie-in. I'll leave him to it. I also don't want to wake him up and put him in a bad mood if he's feeling annoyed with me about last night. I vow to make it up to him later. No booze, an early night and the chance for some alone time as promised.

I hope I haven't upset Saira. I am still a bit peeved that she didn't tell me the truth in the first place but now that I've sobered up, I'd like to give her the chance to explain why. Something that Adam said last night pops up in my head, that it can't have been easy for her. I suppose not, although that's not an excuse to seek the comfort of another woman's arms. I suppose I'm old fashioned. You wouldn't catch me in an open marriage. If Adam cheated on me I'd react like Hannah did, but I know he never would, that's one of the things I love about him. He hated his dad for leaving them and leading his mum on.

On the way out of the door I grab a cardigan from the wardrobe to wear on top of my clean T-shirt and jeans. Although it's sunny outside the temperature hasn't started to rise yet and the little hairs on my arms are spiking up. With the light cotton cropped cardigan on (a charity shop bargain last year) I'm just right.

Thankfully, I manage to close our bedroom door quietly enough to not kick-start my headache. In the corridor I rifle through my handbag and find a half-used strip of paracetamol at the bottom. I pop a couple in my mouth and swallow them without water, feeling them slowly make their way down my throat. Yuck. They'd better do the trick.

According to my watch – I reached for my phone at first to check the time and thought I'd lost it until I remembered Jeannie's confiscated it – it's nearly 7.30 a.m. The staircase seems far less creepy in the morning light. I look through the glass door to the breakfast room to see if Saira's in there. She isn't. Back in the hall I stroll to the front door and push it open, taking in a deep breath of fresh air.

My eyes have become accustomed to the light now and I've got to admit it's a beautiful morning. Beyond the driveway there's a fence and behind that is a field with some sort of crop undulating in the slight breeze. To the left of that field is one that's home to a number of cows and huge trees dotted around, looking like an image that an eighteenth-century landscape painter could have captured in oils. It's certainly not the bumper-to-bumper parked cars and nearly identical semis you get when you walk outside our front door at home.

The gravel crunches under my feet as I walk round the side of the hotel to the car park. Our car's there where we left it, next to Saira's, but she's nowhere to be seen. I bend down and peer in the driver's window to see if it looks like she's been in there. No sign of her. I hope she's OK.

I stand around, shifting my weight from one foot to the other for a minute then make my way to sit on a wooden bench at the side of the car park that's strategically placed for hotel residents to make the most of the neighbouring view. The wood is quite hard under my bum but I lift my head back to the sky, shut my eyes and bask in the sun's early rays. I reckon it's going to be a glorious day later, hotter than yesterday.

My hands don't quite know what to do with themselves. Usually I'd pass the time by checking my social media, seeing if anyone has texted me and scrolling through the celebrity news. If I'm honest I feel a bit bereft without it. How daft is that? I'm always telling the kids to get off the internet.

Still no sign of Saira. I look out at the view and take some more deep breaths. I can feel my head starting to clear, the fresh air and paracetamol are working hand in hand. My mind wanders to what to have for breakfast when I go back in. Lots of coffee certainly, and thick buttered toast. I'm not quite sure if my queasy stomach can manage a full English quite just yet, even if the fat might do me some good.

Breakfast. Jeannie will be there. I'll have to face her after embarrassing myself last night and upsetting her. She never saw fault in Tania, even after hearing the hard truths I delivered. The thought of slinking off in the car is rather appealing but I can't. I always tell the kids to own up to their mistakes, so I'm going to have to practise what I preach.

Where is Saira? I look again at my watch: 8 a.m. I bet she's not woken up yet. With everything she drank last night she's probably still snoring away like Adam. Maybe she forgot she put the note under my door.

It's so quiet here. You can't hear the nearest road. The only sounds are from nature: the cows, the birds, the swish of grass when there's a slight gust of wind. I don't know if I could ever get used to it. It makes me feel like I'm in one of those horror films where there's no one to hear you scream.

I'm sick of waiting and decide to go inside for breakfast. As I walk into the breakfast room, Jeannie greets me formally.

'Keren, good morning,'

'Morning, Jeannie,' I reply, then grasp the nettle. 'About last night, sorry again.'

I'm not sure what else to add.

'All forgotten. We've got a lovely day ahead of us. Did you sleep well?'

'Yes thanks, and you?'

Jeannie's cheeks start to flush and a smile, not the fake one she treated us to yesterday, takes over her face.

'Yes. Can I get you some breakfast?'

She leads me to a table and I order coffee and toast. Jeannie certainly seems very chirpy. I'm relieved she's not holding last night against me. She's about to go into the kitchen to tell the cook my order when I suddenly remember what I wanted to ask her.

'Has Saira been down this morning?'

Jeannie turns round. 'No, you're the first,' she replies and wanders off through the double doors.

The toast and butter satisfy my carbs craving and I ask for another pot of coffee. When the caffeine kicks in I feel much better and my headache is relegated from the front row to the back seats. There's no sign of Saira, Johnny or my husband.

Climbing back up the stairs, I'm still a bit annoyed at being stood up and decide not to knock on Saira's door. She'll have slept in. Me waking her up won't do any good. No doubt she'll come and find me when she's ready.

In our room I'm surprised to find Adam still out for the count. He's rolled over onto this front and is snoring lightly with regular breaths.

I'm not sure what to do now he's still asleep. Without a phone or TV, the only option to pass the time while I wait for Adam to wake up is the novel I packed in my suitcase. My mum bought me it for Christmas and I've only read a chapter; I hardly ever get time to myself to sit down and read. Decision made then, I'll fill the water bottle I brought with me and take my book outside. I think there's an outdoor seating area somewhere in the garden that I didn't get a chance to explore yesterday.

Back in the entrance hall downstairs Jeannie is standing behind the reception desk fiddling with some paperwork.

I ask her the way to the garden and she points me in the right direction, waxing lyrical about a hammock and a swinging seat covered by a canopy they bought last month to enhance the guests' experience, and offers to bring me out a jug of iced water. She tells me we all have free time until this afternoon when she has an idea for a group outing. Goodness knows where that's going to be. Now I'm more alert than I was earlier, I want to go to the waterfall.

'Thanks. No Saira or Johnny yet?' I say.

At the mention of Johnny's name she jumps slightly. That smile comes back on her face, and it occurs to me that she's acting slightly suspiciously.

'No, just you, so far,' she replies and I could swear she looks away to avoid my gaze.

It can't be.

Did they?

Surely not.

Oh. My. God.

I think Johnny and Jeannie might have got it on last night. How on earth did that happen? I start to chuckle to myself at the incongruous thought.

Crikey, stranger things happen at sea.

Then another thought hits me. I wonder what Tania would have thought about her self-appointed best friend and her boyfriend hooking up? Ah Jeannie, not so butter wouldn't melt in your mouth now are you? Were you after your self-professed best friend's boyfriend all along?

Chapter 14

Jeannie

Alone once again after Keren left for the gardens, offering me a half-hearted apology, and with Eerik prepping food, I allow my smile to beam all over my face again. I could run upstairs and see Johnny for ten minutes. No one else is around. I'm sorely tempted, it's like there's an invisible thread pulling me in that direction, but my head overrides my heart. Adam and Saira could come down any minute wanting breakfast, there's still an hour to go before breakfast time officially ends. I've got to be here holding the fort and answering any calls that might come in. It'd be Sod's Law that one of them would spot me going in or out of Johnny's room.

I've only had a few snatched minutes to try and look for the missing knife. Whenever I think of it being at large somewhere in the hotel it's like an electric shock goes through me, pumping my every nerve with anxiety and foreboding. I like everything to be in its proper place and can't relax when it isn't.

I've got to find it or I won't be able to rest. In one of the reception desk's drawers is a laminated card telling visitors to ring the bell for attention. I pull it out and place it next to our antique brass bell that you push down on like they do in TV game shows. It's loud enough for me to hear in the kitchen if I leave the doors slightly ajar.

When I walk the short distance to the kitchen I hope that Eerik will say that he's found the knife, that it was put back in the wrong drawer or hiding under a chopping board. My hopes are dashed when I walk in and see his face.

'Still missing?' I ask.

'Yes. I have no idea where it is. It doesn't make sense.' Natural, positive Eerik starts to shine through. 'I'm sure it will turn up and we'll be saying, "Oh no, why didn't we think of looking there?"' he adds with a smile.

'It's got to be in this kitchen. We never take any equipment out of here.'

'Who could have taken it out?' he asks. There's the sweet smell of sugar in vanilla in the air. Eerik is baking a couple of pound cakes for afternoon tea.

I try to think. 'I don't know. You didn't, I didn't. Grant had no reason to and he's not working this weekend. You didn't see him in the kitchen yesterday, did you?'

Eerik shakes his head and starts to wipe down the worktop with a clean cloth.

'No, but I did see one of the guests come in.'

I react with surprise. 'Why would a guest come into the kitchen? Who was it?'

Eerik looks up. 'One of your group. The man with the shaved head. He had some medication to store in the fridge. I thought you wouldn't mind.'

It all makes sense now, Johnny and his insulin.

'I know about that, it's fine,' I reply. Johnny wouldn't have taken the knife. Why would he? A flicker of doubt comes into my mind. He deliberately hid his current life situation from us. Could he be hiding the knife too? I swat the thought away like an intrusive buzzing fly.

'What about your other friends?' Eerik asks.

'They wouldn't either and, besides, they were with me all night in the dining room. Did you ever leave the kitchen unattended?'

'A couple of times but not for very long. I went to the toilet and once I went to the storeroom to fill up the ingredients jars ready for today.'

Knives don't just vanish into thin air. It has to be here somewhere.

'I've got five minutes to have a good look around. We're more likely to find it with two pairs of eyes.' The knife block still has one empty black slit in it. I search through all the drawers, double-check the dishwasher, go through the stack of baking trays and roasting tins to see if its nestling inside one of those and even get down on my hands and knees to look under the appliances standing on small feet. Nothing. Our cleaning is so thorough that I don't even find a stray potato peel.

My secret phone vibrates and I go to a quiet place to see what it is. Head office has sent through some more bookings they've taken along with any special requests.

I go back to reception and log them in our old-school large diary. They're on the computer in my office as well but, seeing as we're a digital-detox establishment, we try to never show any modern gadgets in public areas. When we first reopened after the refurbishment I had an iPad at reception and I caught one guest trying to use it when I walked away to talk to someone else. It was password protected of course but having phones and computers on display here is like waving a bottle of vodka in the face of an alcoholic.

'Good morning, Jeannie, and may I say what a very good morning this is,' a newly familiar voice says above me. I turn round, and Johnny moves towards me cheekily. I check to see if anyone's there and, as we're alone, let him kiss me fully on the lips. He tries to pull me towards him for a longer one, but I giggle and playfully push him away, mindful that Saira or Adam could follow him down the stairs at any moment. Or, if they used the lift, they'd appear from the other side.

'Back in a minute,' he says with a wink. I pretend to be sorting through today's post but really I'm reliving my memories of us together earlier this morning until I decide I must switch to thinking about the management report I have to write instead because I'm getting far too hot and bothered.

When Johnny comes back worry lines criss-cross his forehead. 'Jeannie, have you moved my insulin? It was in an orange plastic bag in the fridge.'

Not something else missing.

'No, is it not there?'

Johnny shakes his head. 'Your chef says he hasn't seen the bag today. He thought I'd come by already and taken it.'

'And you didn't?'

'No, I was going to inject myself now.'

This is starting to get really weird. One thing to go missing is an innocent misplacement. But two? Now that's no coincidence. I'm the manager and the buck stops with me. Has Saira, Keren or Johnny taken the knife and insulin to cause me trouble somehow? Are they trying to get back at me for something? Someone said last night that I'd been used. Is one of them taking out their resentment towards Tania on me because I wouldn't believe them?

Surely not. They wouldn't, would they?

Johnny follows me through to the kitchen where Eerik is taking everything he can out of the fridge to see if any of the medication slipped out of the bag.

'It's not here,' he says as we walk in.

'Are you sure you didn't move it somewhere else? Maybe you wanted to make room to put something in the fridge?' Johnny asks. His face is slightly flushed and he's tapping his foot anxiously on the floor.

'No, I didn't,' Eerik says. He looks mournful. Eerik's an open book and has never lied to me. I can't imagine him being able to. It'd be far too obvious because he hasn't got an ounce of deceit in him.

'Will you be all right? When did you last take it?' I ask Johnny.

'Um, yesterday morning before I set off driving. I skipped it last night. I'll be OK but I need to take some soon.'

'Do you need some sugar? Can I make you a cup of tea or coffee with a few spoonfuls of sugar in?' Eerik asks pensively.

'Tea please. I could murder a bacon sandwich too. I don't suppose you have any?' Johnny grins. I can tell he's putting a brave face on it.

'Of course. I'll make one now.'

'Thanks, mate,' Johnny replies with a cheeriness that belies the expression on his face. I haven't got a clue what the risks are if he doesn't take his insulin soon. I resolve to google it and see, to check that Johnny isn't downplaying his situation so as not to cause a fuss.

While Eerik is grilling bacon and making a pot of tea I take Johnny through to the seats in the breakfast room, to a table next to a huge window that I notice a bird has pooed on since earlier today. My skin prickles at the glass not being pristine and I resist the urge to run outside and clean it until it gleams. Instead, we sit down, me deliberately sitting with my back to it.

Think, Jeannie, think. You're in charge. What to do? I know.

'I've got an idea. You probably can get insulin on an emergency prescription. I'll give the nearest pharmacy a call. It's about twenty miles away but I can drive you there when you've finished breakfast. The others can occupy themselves until we get back.'

Johnny sighs with relief. 'Why didn't I think of that? You're brilliant.' Underneath the table he squeezes my knee and I slide my hand briefly up his thigh, before breaking off to say, 'I'll go and give them a call.'

This time I don't bother with any pretence that I don't have a working phone. Behind the reception desk I pull my mobile out from its place hidden in my side pocket to search for the pharmacy number.

There's no internet connection, just an error message.

Annoyed, I turn it on and off again, stabbing at the buttons in a hurry. Still nothing. I try and think of a Plan B. There must still be a phone number you can ring for directory enquiries? I wrack my brains to recall the TV advert that used to be on all the time a decade or so ago with an earworm jingle that was their number. What was it? I hum the tune and it comes back to me. Quickly I punch it in. Nothing happens. A sheen of moisture forms on my brow and I wipe it off with the back of my hand. The temperature is rising, the sun's rays are beaming through the windows. For goodness' sake I don't need another technical fail now.

With my key card I let myself into the back office where our router is. We're so remote here that there isn't a landline. Phone calls all go through the internet. I make a beeline for the line of plugs under a table next to the filing cabinet. Photocopier, printer, travel kettle. One plug is missing. I freeze with shock.

The router is gone. It's not on the table's lower shelf where it normally lives. Someone must have moved it. But who would want to? I scan the office frantically to try and find it. Did Bethan move it somewhere else in the room? I check all the plug sockets and then every drawer in the office. It's not there.

I dash back to the breakfast room where Johnny is tucking into a bacon sandwich. It's such a lovely sunny day, how can all this be happening? The knife, the insulin and now the router. Who is behind it, and why? I tremble involuntarily at the thought of a hunter out there, wanting to track me down like a lion waiting for the right moment to pounce and tear the throat of a gazelle. Surely no one in the hotel could be out to cause harm. But what if there's someone here I can't trust?

Johnny finishes his last mouthful and swallows, causing me to realise I'm overreacting. There must be a simple explanation.

'All sorted?' he asks with a smile.

I shake my head and bend down close to his ear, lowering my voice but trying to keep my burgeoning anxiety out of it.

'The phone and the internet aren't working I'm afraid, but don't worry, I'll drive you to the pharmacy. We'll get it sorted.'

Johnny turns to face me, this time failing to keep the worry from his expression, and brings his sandwich straight back up.

Chapter 15

Saira

Midday. I can't believe I slept this long. The curtains in this room are blackout ones and, not realising, I drew them firmly shut last night. Not even a chink of light could get through. I'm an owl not a lark and one of those people who need daylight to wake up. I'm terrible in the winter when my alarm goes off in the dark, it feels like I've been knocked over by an ice breaker. Hannah bought me one of those lamps that mimic natural light to gradually wake me up, which helped a lot. Without it, whenever I wake up and it's dark my body reacts like it's two o'clock in the morning and wants to go straight back to sleep.

Although I've slept, I don't feel very rested. My dreams were fitful, me screaming at Tania for her leading me on. My throat feels hoarse as if I had really been shouting and crying. My head isn't too bad, I've dodged a bullet there, but my joints are aching. It feels like I've done two rounds in a boxing ring. I sit up in bed and stretch to try and get myself moving, rubbing my knees to will them back into life. I'm absolutely ravenous and reach into my handbag, which I'd left on the end of the bed when I got in last night, for a snack. There's a biscuit in a plastic wrapper in there somewhere. Found it.

I'll have long missed breakfast. I wonder if the others all made it down, sitting there talking about me and what I did. The thought of them gossiping about my adultery is awful. It's none of their business. Oh hell, there's all the stuff we said about Tania too. Jeannie, she seemed pretty upset. My heart lurches. I'm not sure I remember everything. My memory from last night is hazy. I vaguely recall taking the lift upstairs and stopping outside Keren and Adam's room. Maybe I got confused and thought it was mine. I hope I didn't try to get in. I'll have to face them all sometime very soon, particularly Keren. I really don't want her to think badly of me. I'll try and talk to her on our own and explain why I didn't tell her the whole truth about me and Hannah.

A wave of loneliness engulfs me, mentally knocking me sideways, leaving me scrabbling in the sand on the shoreline. I wish I were back in my old home with my wife and Emily, a family again. I brought it all on myself I know, but haven't I paid the price? I never wanted Hannah and I to split up. It was her decision to kick me out. All I can do is carry on making the best of it and focus on Emily, as I have been.

I swivel round on my bottom and gingerly stand up, reaching for my stick that thankfully I left beside my bed last night.

The cardboard cut-out of Tania, and it setting me off in tears, jumps to the forefront of my memory. Seeing her again, it reminded me of her rejection and me pretending nothing was wrong but trying to avoid her, until our final confrontation alone.

That's not something I want to think about – it's long over. Looking back, of course she wasn't interested in me, I'd been stupid to think there might have been something between us. Even so, digging those memories up again still hurt like an aftershock following the main earthquake. Especially after what I did.

It doesn't take me too long to wash and dress. I might as well face the music sooner rather than later. I take the lift downstairs to spare my knees. As the doors slide open on the ground floor I can hear raised voices. Jeannie, I think, and another man's voice.

'What can I do to help?' the man says.

'Get him a glass of water and a bring a wet dishcloth. Hurry.'

The voices are coming from the breakfast room where the door is ajar. I walk through a bit slower than I usually do, leaning on my stick to minimise the pain in my left knee with each step.

'What's going on?' I ask, my trepidation about seeing them again fading away, replaced with curiosity. Johnny is sitting back in a chair, groaning, and Jeannie is holding him upright, cupping her hand to the side of his face in what could either be a caress or an attempt to keep him conscious.

A man runs in carrying a glass of water and a damp tea towel. Jeannie grabs it and wipes Johnny's face with it then presses what I hope is the clean side on his forehead. In front of Johnny on the table is a pile of vomit on a plate. The man, I think he's the chef we were introduced to last night, lifts up the tablecloth, pulls the ends up like a knapsack, and carries it all away.

Jeannie looks round at me. She seems concerned. 'Johnny's not very well.'

Well, he did drink as much as Keren and me, I think. He obviously can't hack it now we're middle aged. Who knows how much he put away after I went to bed?

'What's happened?' I ask.

Johnny stirs and starts to speak. 'Sorry about all this. No need to make a fuss, how embarrassing. I'm OK now, Jeannie. Saira, I have diabetes. My insulin has disappeared and I felt a little under the weather.'

'Have a sip of water. I need to take you to the pharmacy. Do you think you're going to be sick again?' Jeannie asks him kindly.

'No, there's really no need for a fuss.'

'Can't you ring for an ambulance or something?' I suggest.

'Our wireless router has gone and I can't phone out,' replies Jeannie, still watching Johnny like a hawk. He takes a few swallows of water.

Something about Jeannie's expression, her furrowed eyebrows, clenched jaw, and the way she's hovering around Johnny as if he's been in a road traffic accident or the like makes me think this is more serious than she's letting on.

'Have you tried our mobiles? You can use mine if you like.'

'They won't work here,' she says straight back.

It occurs to me that there's one thing I can do to help. 'I'll drive Johnny to a pharmacy if you tell me where to go and give me the postcode for my satnav. As you're the manager you probably ought to stay here,' I suggest.

Jeannie looks thoughtful, torn between the two choices. 'Are you safe to drive? You did drink a lot last night.'

'It'll be out of my system by now. I feel fine.'

'Thanks, Saira, that's a good idea,' Johnny says. 'Good of you to offer.'

The sound of footsteps makes us all turn round. Keren walks in.

'There you are. I couldn't find you earlier,' she says to me.

I wonder why she was looking for me, whether that is a good or bad omen. Her expression isn't giving anything away.

'I had a lie-in. Johnny's not well. I'm going to drive him to a pharmacy.'

I turn to Johnny and tell him that I'll go out and get rid of the rubbish from the passenger seat to make room for him.

'I'll walk out with you,' Keren offers.

The warmth hits me as soon as I walk out of the door. I've always imagined it to be cold in Yorkshire but today it feels hotter than a summer day in London. I reach in my bag and put my sunglasses on to shade my eyes.

'What was it you wanted to talk to me about? Is it Hannah?' Keren asks as we slowly walk around the corner to the car park. I can't tell if she's annoyed or not – her voice is neutral.

'Sorry?' I ask.

'The note you wrote me. I came out here at seven thirty like you asked me to but you didn't show up. It's all right, you must have really needed the sleep. Adam's still snoring away too.'

Note? I stop and turn to Keren. 'I didn't write you a note.'

'Yes you did, I've got it here.' Keren pulls a piece of paper out of her handbag and shows it to me. The writing is barely legible but even so I can tell it's not mine, and surely I wouldn't have forgotten writing it? I think back. No, I don't even remember contemplating writing a letter for Keren, never mind actually doing it.

'That's strange. It wasn't me, I know that, for sure.'

'You really didn't write it?' Keren asks me.

'I swear on Emily's life I didn't. Weird. But I'm glad I've got you now. I did want to apologise for not telling you the truth about Hannah and me. I know I should have done. Please forgive me.'

Keren opens her arms wide and encircles me with them, being careful not to knock me off balance. I lean into her with relief.

'I'm sorry too. I shouldn't have judged,' she tells me. 'I'm so daft. I thought you were going to confess something about Tania. I wondered, you know, if you two had something going on around exam time. Silly of me.'

Thankfully, as my face is over her shoulder, Keren can't see the shock that hits me when she says that. I quickly compose myself, pull away and keep my mouth firmly shut while we carry on walking to my car. There, I unlock the driver's door, get in and pick up the litter in the footwell of the passenger seat that's been accumulating there for a month or so. Crisp packets, a free newspaper and a few things Emily left behind. The rubbish goes in my handbag to take to the bin and I throw the rest into the back seat.

'What's wrong with Johnny?' Keren asks me.

'He needs insulin he says. The internet's down in the hotel and they can't ring out.'

'I didn't know that he's got diabetes,' Keren replies.

'Neither did I. No reason why we should, he didn't know I have RA,' I say, thinking back to last night. 'I'll be glad to get away from this hotel for a few hours. It's giving me the creeps to be honest. The cardboard Tania, the power cut and now Johnny getting ill.'

I get out of the car and shut the door.

'I know what you mean. I felt like I was being watched yesterday when I went exploring around the hotel on my own,' says Keren. 'I didn't mention it to Adam because he'd probably think I was being daft.'

'When you first knocked on my door yesterday evening it made me jump, that's when I knocked over my wine glass. When you kept banging on a few minutes later I was glad to see it was you and not some random ghost,' I confess, trying to make a joke out of it.

'What do you mean? I only knocked on your door after I heard a smash.' Keren sounds confused.

Despite the heat in the sun's rays, my skin turns cold and clammy. I'm about to say that I've no idea who it was then, when I look down at my car tyre, and I see it's flat. I walk round my car and see that all the tyres are the same. Holding on to the side of the car to keep my balance, I bend down. There's a slit that looks as if it has been made by a pen knife.

'Someone's slashed my car tyres,' I cry, my heart hammering in my chest.

Keren's mouth opens wide in shock. She turns to her and Adam's car, next to mine and runs all the way round it. 'Same here,' she shouts from the other side. 'Oh my God! Who's done this?'

How am I going to get home? I've got work on Monday and it's my turn to have Emily to stay for the week. I've only got one spare tyre and I can't say I've ever checked it. With the hotel's phone not working I can't even ring a breakdown company to come out either.

There are only three other cars in the car park. Keren goes to check them. 'They're all flat!' she shouts back at me.

I'm trembling, which makes my knee start to throb. What's going on? Then I remember why I'm out here. I said I'd take Johnny to a pharmacy to get the insulin he needs. Now I can't, none of us can, nor can we ring out for an ambulance or the police.

Someone's done this deliberately. Someone who wants to hurt Johnny. But why? He might put his foot in it sometimes but he's harmless, isn't he?

Keren takes my other arm for support and helps me walk back inside the hotel because I'm still trembling and feel like I could easily lose my balance. When we walk into the entrance hall, Johnny is sitting on one of the easy chairs waiting for me, with Jeannie standing over him like a sentinel on guard. She knows something is wrong as soon as she sees us.

'What is it?' she asks, her voice wavering.

'All the tyres on the cars in the car park have been slashed. Someone has done it deliberately. Somebody in this hotel wants to harm Johnny,' Keren says forthrightly.

'What? Who'd want to hurt me? You mean we can't drive anywhere? What about my car?' says Johnny.

'Your tyres have been slashed too,' I say. There's been no discrimination between my old banger and his expensive motor.

Jeannie rushes out the front door, I assume to go and see it with her own eyes. I take her place on the seat next to Johnny. 'I'm up the creek here,' he says to us. 'I haven't done anything. Why would anyone want to hurt me?'

'It wasn't me,' I tell him, as does Keren, who says that Adam wouldn't either, adding, 'It's got to be someone who is in this hotel right now. There were five cars in the car park, mine and Adam's, Saira's, yours and I assume Jeannie's. I don't know who the other one belongs to but their tyres were slashed too.'

I say what flashes into my head without thinking.

'Could Jeannie have done it? She bought that cardboard cut-out of Tania and frightened us all to death last night. We're all here because she offered us a free weekend. Is this all part of some sort of twisted plan to scare us, to make her feel in control? Or maybe she thinks that you, Johnny, are responsible for Tania's death, because it was your car she was driving when the accident happened?'

Is that a flash of remorse that appears momentarily in Johnny's expression? 'No, Jeannie wouldn't want to hurt me,' he replies.

'How do *you* know?' Karen challenges him.

'Last night, well, she stayed in my room. She didn't want to hurt me, quite the opposite,' he says sheepishly.

Well, well, Johnny and Jeannie? I'd never have put them together in a million years.

'I thought something might have gone on,' Keren points out. 'Jeannie kept blushing every time your name was mentioned this morning.'

On cue, Jeannie dashes back in, the front door closing with a bang behind her in a sudden breeze. Concern lines are etched all over her face.

'Jeannie, whose is the car in the car park that's not one of ours?' Keren asks.'

'Eerik's, our chef.'

'Then it must have been him who did it, if it wasn't any of us.'

Jeannie jumps to her employee's defence. 'No. Why would he have slashed his own car tyres?'

'To deflect attention from himself probably.'

'Why would he want to hurt a guest he barely even knows? He wouldn't have done it. Did any of you go in the car park this morning?'

'I did,' Keren says. 'I waited for Saira there from about half seven until eight. I didn't notice anything wrong then, but then again I wasn't exactly staring at all the tyres.'

'Then it can't have been Eerik. He's been in the kitchen all morning. I've either been with him, in the office or in the entrance hall. I'd have noticed if he went out the front door.'

'What about a back way?' suggests Johnny.

'There's a back door to the garden and the bin store but a high fence separates that and the car park. The only way out to the car park is through the front door.'

'I hate to ask but, was it you, Jeannie?' Keren pointedly says to her. I hold my breath.

'No! How could you say such a thing? I invited you all here, I run this hotel, I'm proud of it, I wanted everything to go well for Tania's sake.' Her eyes redden up and she blinks rapidly.

Johnny takes her hand kindly. 'I know it's not you.' Jeannie doesn't pull away.

'If it's none of us, and not the chef, then who slashed the tyres? Is someone outside lurking in the bushes?' I say. The thought sends shivers down my spine. We're in a hotel with no communications. If there is a person out there who wants to hurt us, we're sitting ducks.

'Where's Adam? I haven't seen him today,' Johnny asks Keren with an underlying tone of concern.

I remember the awkwardness between Johnny and Adam last night. Adam clearly hadn't forgiven Johnny for not loaning him the money to stay on at St Mark's and finish his degree. He wouldn't have wanted revenge on him, would he? Adam's a family man, he's not got a bad bone in him. Or so I thought. You know what they say about the quiet ones . . . I keep my thoughts to myself in front of Keren.

'He was still sleeping when I left him. He's been exhausted recently with long hours at work so I left him to rest. How far is it to walk to the nearest village, Jeannie?'

'Well over an hour.'

'If all else fails then Adam and I will go. We might be able to flag down a car on the way. I'll go and get him.'

Just after Keren leaves the room Johnny utters a loud groan.

'Are you OK?' Jeannie asks him.

'Feeling a bit sick again to be honest and a headache has come on.'

'I'll take you back to your room for some rest. I'll sort all this out, I promise.'

Johnny doesn't argue. Jeannie takes his arm and leads him tentatively to the lift. He walks like an old man, small steps, shuffling one foot in front of the other in stark contrast to his energy last night.

There's silence after the lift's doors have closed. I'm alone. What if whoever slashed the tyres walks in through the front door? I clutch my bag closely to my chest. I need to stay here to wait for Keren and Adam to come down. I realise I can't walk with them, I'd slow them down and there's no way I could manage that distance. I try to calm myself. When Jeannie comes back I'm sticking with her. I don't want to be on my own.

Footsteps speeding down the stairs break up my thoughts. It's Keren.

'I can't wake Adam up. I think something's wrong,' she screams.

Chapter 16

Keren

Right now I want my mum, someone, anyone, to take control or to slap me in the face and tell me I'm having a nightmare that I can wake up from.

When I went back to our room Adam was lying down in bed where I left him. I thought he was still asleep but his breathing was softer, not deep like it normally is.

I walked to the side of the bed where he was curled up facing the wall.

'Adam, wake up, it's after midday,' I said, shaking him gently on the shoulder. His skin was wet. I patted the sheet and the duvet around him. It was damp. A sheen of sweat glistened on his face.

'Adam, wake up, this isn't funny.' I shook him harder. His eyes opened and he tried to look at me but couldn't seem to focus, then he mumbled something incoherent.

Something was very wrong. This wasn't a hangover or him being slow to wake up. In desperation, I rubbed his cheek roughly to try and bring him round.

'Adam, please, what's happened?' I shouted in a panic. His mouth opened but nothing came out and his beautiful eyes looked at me in confusion while he tried with his hands to push the duvet away from him. I folded it back but his eyes closed again and his arm dropped down onto the bed. Nothing I did could rouse him. I bent my ear to his mouth. He was still breathing. His chest rose up and down, slippery with sweat.

My first instinct was to reach for my mobile to call an ambulance but it's in that locked drawer downstairs not in my handbag and I remembered it won't work anyway – the internet is down and there's no way to call out.

I'm sure my heart rate has doubled. It's thudding in my chest as fast as it can. I didn't know what to do so in terror I ran downstairs as quickly as I could to get help. There's only Saira here.

'I can't wake Adam up. I think something's wrong,' I shout.

'Why? Has he had an accident?' she asks, a look of fear sweeping onto her face.

'I don't think so. I can't wake him up. He's all sweaty. He did open his eyes for a bit but he couldn't talk or focus.'

Saira stands up and hugs me. I want to shut my eyes and for all this to go away, for it to be a story on TV and not my actual reality. Adam can't die. The children and I need him. I love him. Has someone hurt him? With the things that have happened today it's too much of a coincidence for this to be some bug that's going round. He was fine last night.

'Please help me,' I say. 'He needs a doctor.'

Saira lets me go and starts walking with her stick towards the lift. 'Jeannie took Johnny back to his room. Let's go and find them.'

With my mind blank of any other ideas I blindly follow her. Johnny's room is a floor above mine. Neither of us know which room number it is so Saira knocks on the three doors until someone opens one. Jeannie appears from the other side.

'Adam's ill. We need to go to him,' she says.

'Please, urgently,' I shout behind her.

Jeannie looks as if she doesn't know what has hit her. She freezes for a moment, her eyes flitting left and right as if she's thinking hard.

Johnny walks up to the door and sounds anxious. 'Did you say Adam's ill? What's happened?'

'I don't know! He's unconscious. Hurry, he needs help,' I reply impatiently. There's no time to waste.

The four of us make our way down a floor, Jeannie and I using the stairs and Saira and Johnny in the lift. I get to the room first and fumble with the key card. The red light keeps flashing and then I drop it in my haste.

'I'll do it,' says Jeannie. She picks up the key card, slides it into the slot and we're straight in. Adam hasn't moved since I saw him a few minutes ago. His breathing is still shallow. I rush over to him and cradle his head in my arms.

'Adam, it's Jeannie. Are you awake?' Jeannie says in a raised voice from across the room.

'Of course he's not bloody awake. I told you he's unconscious!' I snap. 'Does he look awake to you?'

'Sorry,' Jeannie says. She opens the curtains and light floods into the room. In the sunlight I can see that Adam's face is flushed pink, as if someone's turned up the heat, bringing him to the boil.

Saira and Johnny come in. From behind I feel Saria's palm on my shoulder to comfort me.

'Let me look at him please,' Johnny says. I don't want to move but Saira gently leads me out of the way so Johnny can take my place.

'Mate, it's Johnny,' he says to my husband. He shakes him on his shoulder like I did before. Adam's eyes flick open, he groans, and then his lids close firmly shut.

Johnny rolls him onto his back.

'What are you doing? Be careful!' I cry.

'I want to see if he's got a rash or anything that might give us a clue as to what's wrong with him,' he says. Johnny's face is the same colour as my husband's, he's sweating too.

Johnny looks at Adam's torso and then examines his arms, first the left, then the right, then the left again, peering closer.

'There, can you see that?' he asks us.

'What?'

He points at a place a couple of centimetres from Adam's shoulder. 'There's a little red bump. A mark. There isn't one anywhere else on his arms. It's not a spot.'

I push him out of the way and look myself. The mark is small, it looks innocuous.

'A goosebump?'

Johnny bites his lip, his face more red and more furrowed than ever.

'I think it might be a mark from an injection. I should know, I often get them.'

'Injection? Why would he have had an injection?' I cry. None of this makes sense.

'I don't know for sure but I think someone might have injected him with my insulin. I didn't take a great deal of notice at the time about everything my doctor told me when I was diagnosed but he did stress the importance of taking the right amount and not overdosing. Gave me a leaflet. Adam's got the symptoms: sweaty, tired, confused. I might be wrong though. I hope I am.'

My knees buckle and I sink down to the carpet.

'Insulin overdose? Oh my God. We've got to get him to hospital. Is it life threatening?'

Johnny lowers his faltering voice as if Adam might be able to hear him.

'It can be, yes. Jeannie, we need to call an ambulance.'

'I know,' she says. 'Where's that damned router?'

'It's all your fault, Jeannie!' I shout. 'This is your hotel and it's a complete shit shambles. A hotel with no working phone and no internet? You're responsible for this. If anything happens to Adam then I'm blaming you.'

Saira reaches for my hand and squeezes it, trying in vain to comfort me.

'I didn't do it. I'm sorry! I'm as much in the dark as you are. I'll think of something,' Jeannie squeals.

I turn my rage on Johnny. 'Who knew where your insulin was? We didn't know you are diabetic.'

He sits on the edge of bed and sighs. 'The chef saw me put it in the kitchen fridge. I told Jeannie about it this morning.'

'There you go. It's that chef. He's the one who knew about it. You said he couldn't have gone outside to slash the tyres, Jeannie, without you noticing but there's no way you could keep a close eye on him all the time. Have you got CCTV so you can see who went in and out of the front door?'

'Yes, I can check it,' Jeannie says, 'but I know Eerik. I really don't think it's him.'

'How could he have got in here to inject Adam in the first place?' Saira says.

The pieces start to fit together. I stand up and sit next to Adam on the bed, cradling him in my arms. He doesn't stir. I start to feel a bit faint with fear.

'The note under my door to meet you outside in the car park at 7.30 a.m. You said you didn't put it there. Whoever did must have wanted me out of the way.'

'And there's a universal key card behind the desk that can open all the rooms. I remember you telling us that, Jeannie, when we arrived,' adds Saira.

'I keep it hidden!' Jeannie exclaims.

'Hardly! *We* all knew where it was,' I cry.

I don't know if I'm imagining it but Adam's breaths seem shallower now. I hold him close to me and look at Saira, Johnny then Jeannie, scrutinising their faces. One of them, or the chef, did this to my husband. Can I really trust any of them? Yes, they all look worried and concerned but I'm convinced that one of them must know something. I'm not leaving Adam. That chef is downstairs somewhere, God knows what he could be doing.

'I'll go down and check on Eerik and check the CCTV. The only option is for me to run to the nearest village and hope that I pass a car to stop for help. I'll take my mobile with me, I might be able to get a signal somewhere further away from here.'

After Jeannie rushes out, the three of us sit in silence for I don't know how long. Every second seems like an hour as I cradle Adam and will him to get better. Saira brings a wet flannel from the bathroom and gently wipes his forehead with it. Johnny sits quietly on the chair by the desk.

Ten minutes later the door opens abruptly with a jolt. Two people come in, Jeannie and the chef.

'Don't let him in here!' I shout, clinging on harder to Adam.

'I've asked him. He didn't take the insulin,' Jeannie says. 'We all have to stick together. I checked the footage, the CCTV camera has been moved to point away from the door.'

Saira bursts into tears. 'What? Why aren't you out running to get help?'

'The front and back doors are locked and we can't open them.' Jeannie's voice is rising higher, shrill now. She's scared, I know it. She's totally incompetent. There's no way I can rely on her to get help for Adam.

The awful chef has the gall to look concerned and worried. 'The fire exit too. They've all been chained and padlocked. We can't get out.'

'What, not even from a window?' Saira howls.

'No. We changed them all to safety windows in the refurbishment. They only open wide enough to let fresh air in,' Jeannie admits.

Bile rises up into my mouth and the room starts to spin. Johnny runs into the bathroom and I hear retching noises.

The last thing I'm aware of is a thump before everything goes black.

Chapter 17

Johnny

The flannel on my forehead feels welcomingly cool but my mouth is as dry as the Kalahari. I'm back in my room. After I collapsed in Keren and Adam's bathroom I passed out for a couple of minutes. It feels like someone's whacked my hip with a sledgehammer and my chin is smarting. I think I bashed it on the sink when I fell. There'll be a big bruise there soon. The chef Eerik helped me up to sit on the toilet while I got my breath back. There was lots of arguing that I tried to tune out because it made my headache worse. Eventually they must have agreed that Eerik should take me to my room and stay with me. Keren seems to think he's the devil incarnate but he seems all right to me and there's no one else to help. I'll have to trust him. Anyone who went into the kitchen could have seen my insulin in the fridge. Why would Eerik want to steal it and inject Adam, if that is what's happened? He doesn't know us from Adam, excuse the poor pun, and has nothing to gain.

'Do you want some water?' he asks. Eerik has been sitting by my bedside manning the fort while I dozed for a little while. I don't want to panic the others but I'm really starting to feel rough. Those information leaflets they gave me at the hospital, there was a bit in them about DKA, something that could happen if I didn't have enough insulin or stopped treatment. I've played a bit fast and loose a few times in the past when I've forgotten my injection or was in a situation like last night when I didn't want to break away and go and shoot up. It's always been fine, but now, if I don't have some insulin soon, I know I'm in big trouble.

160

'Thanks, mate,' I reply and drain the whole glass he passes me in one go.

A memory comes back to me. 'Is Keren OK now? I heard someone saying she fainted.'

'She did. Your female friend looked after her. She's OK now I think but very worried about her husband. She's in their room with him.' He sighs anxiously. 'I am so sorry. Nothing like this has happened here before. This is a lovely, friendly hotel. Can I do anything for you?'

I look over. His shoulders are bunched up, nearly reaching his ears and, with the concern on his face furrowing premature lines between his eyes and on his brow, he looks nearly as bad as I feel. Which is rough. Very rough.

'Some insulin would go down well,' I joke. Black humour. My trademark.

'I hope your friend will be all right. I didn't talk to him but he seemed like a nice man.'

'Yes, he is. He used to be my best friend. We talked last night about going into business together. Organic lawn treatment. There's a lot of demand for it right now.' I'm gabbling, I know. It's on purpose. I can't think about leaving my children, or Adam leaving his. Something has got to come right. Jeannie's gone downstairs to try and find the router. It'll turn up, it has to. The alternative is something I refuse to think about. A guilty thought comes in my head that this is karma, payback for it being my long-overdue-a-service car that caused Tania's crash, but my brain can't concentrate and almost as soon as it popped up it's washed away by wooziness.

'That is good! I walked past the dining room last night and heard arguing. I was worried about Jeannie, I know she wanted for you all to have a special time.'

What he says barely registers because my eyes flick towards the bathroom door and I freeze at the sight of Tania staring back at me. After one blink she disappears. Bloody hell, am I hallucinating? I think of what I just saw and it's the image of last night's cardboard cut-out of her. Yesterday evening seems so long ago now. The photo game and us sniping over who knew what about Tania and what she'd said and done. All so trivial, so unimportant. I close my eyes for a second and cast my mind back to the night of our first anniversary meal out at a local curry house with a bring-your-own bottle of champagne I pulled out of my sports bag to surprise Tania. How we held hands and talked about our hopes, dreams and where we wanted to travel in our future that stretched so long in front of us. Welcoming in a new year in Thailand. Backpacking round Australia. Yes, I'll think about that now. Tiredness is creeping over me like a summer tide drawing in towards the shore. Think about good things, when I was happy. Like this morning with Jeannie. A chance for a new start.

I relax my aching muscles and let the mattress take the strain. My mind drifts. Sleep calls me towards it with a soft, tempting voice.

Voices now, pulling me back. A man's first, then a woman's, hysterical.

'What is it?'

'Adam's dead. It's all my fault.'

My heart races. Sobbing sounds swirl in the distance and then sleep takes me in its arms and gently pulls me towards unconsciousness. I try and push back. Adam, my old best friend. It can't be true, my mind is playing tricks. I have to get up and help him, but the tide pulling me into unconsciousness is too strong, taking me out far into the gently lapping waves of the ocean under the hot sun.

I'll sleep for a while and when I wake up all will be well.

Chapter 18

Jeannie

There's a small pile of mobile phones before me that I've taken out of the safe. In vain I switch them all on and dial 999, praying that somehow a miracle will happen and they'll work.

They don't. Nothing. For the first time in my life I want to shout as loudly as I can with fear and anger, vocalise the terror and guilt that's pulsating through my veins.

It's all my fault. I'm the manager here. I'm in charge and have let my friends down in the worst way possible. I invited them here. It was my job to keep them safe and I haven't. Someone is stalking us, baiting us, picking us off like ripe apples from a tree. I don't know who, or – and as I think this my body begins to involuntarily shake even more – if there's more than one person, or the reason why. Why have they locked us in? Eerik and I tried to find something to break the padlocked chains keeping the doors shut. I stood far back with my eyes closed in trepidation as Eerik tried to chop one with the meat cleaver. It only made a dent. The chains are thick. We need bolt cutters but we don't have any. Whoever put them there thought this through. Despite what I said to the others, I did start to doubt Eerik earlier. He knew where the insulin was and the universal key card. I studied his face as I told him what had happened. It occurred to me that he could have taken the knife and hidden it somewhere outside of the kitchen. But why? He loves this job. And he didn't lock the doors, he was with Johnny. The worry on his face, the concern for me and the guests is genuine.

I bang one of the phones down on the reception desk in frustration. It's a fancy one, Johnny's. I even for a second wondered if he might be double bluffing. Did he take the insulin himself and sneak in Adam's room when Keren was outside waiting for Saira? Was it him who wrote the note? No, that doesn't make sense either. He cared about Adam and anyway he went to bed after Keren, therefore he couldn't have pushed the note under her door because he was in the dining room with us. And he looks really ill. If he'd have skipped taking his insulin to give himself an alibi he'd surely have taken some by now. He's very poorly. You can't fake that kind of illness. An extra shiver of guilt runs through me. How can I be doubting him? He was so kind to me last night. Earlier I dared to think that this might be the start of something great between us.

Saira. Could she be lying about not writing the note? I didn't see her this morning but there's no way of finding out if she left her room or slept in like she said she did. We don't keep records of when the room key cards are used. Did she steal the insulin before she went to bed and this morning inject Adam with it? But why? Surely he'd have woken up if she tried. The insulin wouldn't have worked that quickly. He could easily have overpowered her and shouted for help. Could she have injected him with something else as well to knock him out? If so, how could she have got that close to him without him realising and struggling? No, it must have been a man who did it, someone strong enough to hold Adam down while he injected him, maybe even staying there, watching, until Adam passed out.

Keren wouldn't have hurt her own husband. I suppose she could have written the note herself but why? Last night they seemed in love – though they did bicker a little at dinner – I was even a little envious. I've had a few short relationships but not one where I had a love like theirs.

That leaves Adam. Could he have killed himself? But why? He and Keren seemed so happy together last night, talking about their home life with big smiles on their faces. Keren would have had an inkling if her husband was suicidal. She would have mentioned it to us by now. It can't be that.

The horror of seeing him not long ago in his bed rises up again. I'd gone in to check on him and Keren. She was crying, urging him to wake up for her and the children, telling him how much they loved him. I went over to him even though Keren didn't want me to. I had to see how he was. He was barely breathing and his pulse was as faint as invisible ink that you can only detect by heating up the page. I suggested trying CPR but Keren wouldn't let me near him, screaming at me to stay away, that I'd done enough damage. Then Adam's breathing stopped.

All my senses are on alert. What's going to happen next? Next to me is a rolling pin I took from the kitchen to arm myself with, not that I'm very strong. I couldn't bear to take a knife and am acutely aware that whatever I have could be ripped out of my hands and turned on me.

Who is doing this? Is there a gang wanting to rob the hotel? If there is then why didn't they storm in and take what we have? It doesn't add up. What's happened has been pre-planned, feels targeted even. I've got to pull myself together and think of some way out. The windows are triple glazed. The glass is tough, particularly in the downstairs windows, to prevent an intruder smashing them and breaking in. I wonder whether I can use the fire extinguisher to throw at one. If I can break it, I can climb out and run for help, but even if that works it could be an hour at least before I come across someone else or get a phone signal.

Johnny's seriously unwell. Can he spare an hour?

Saira comes back in after a quick trip to the downstairs loo opposite, having instructed me to keep an eye on the door at all times in case the intruder tries to follow her.

Creak. I jump as I hear a noise, too wound up in thought to work out where it came from.

'Did you hear that?' Saira cries. She's sticking with me, afraid to be on her own for very long, and is constantly looking around on alert, clutching her bag like a safety blanket.

'Yes,' I say, digging my nails into my palms with tension.

'This place is creepy. When I get out of here I'm never coming back,' she says.

'Saira, get Keren, Johnny and Eerik, and bring them downstairs. We need to all stick together. There's strength in numbers.'

I jump as I hear the sound of a door shutting with a bang. Saira screams, its pitch piercing my eardrums. 'No way am I going upstairs on my own!'

'Quiet!' I hush. I hold my breath to try and work out where the noise came from and tiptoe from behind the reception desk.

I pick up the phone and call Keren's room, telling her to get down here now. Next, I call Johnny's room and Eerik answers, saying that Johnny is sleeping. 'If you can move him, wrap him up in a duvet and bring him downstairs. Carry him if you have to. We all need to be in the same place for safety.' I don't add that if we're all together then it's less likely that whoever is doing this will attack one of us. If we're all apart, well, it's a lot easier to pick us off one by one. I've heard about the horror films where this happens, even if I haven't watched them.

Saira tries to stifle the sound of her tears but she's not doing a very good job. I try to work out which door I heard bang. I can see the bar door and breakfast room doors and they are shut. It could have been the kitchen door or the one leading to the corridor that has the private dining room at the end. Keren, Johnny and Eerik were upstairs when I called them.

I don't know whether to be relieved or terrified that the bang must mean there's an intruder behind all this.

'Are they coming down?' Saira sniffles.

I nod. We both wait silently, on tenterhooks, until Keren bounds down the stairs with her car keys in her hand, poised as a weapon, and the ping of the lift and its opening doors announces the arrival of Eerik, holding up a half-asleep Johnny. I rush towards them and help support Johnny's weight as we half drag him, wrapped in the throw I chose to decorate the bottom of each guest bed, to an armchair and sit him down in it. His eyes can barely focus on me now.

'Where am I?' he asks, trying to raise his head.

'The hallway. We're all together for safety,' I say, attempting to sound far more confident than I am. 'Keep awake, Johnny, please,' I urge him.

'Why have you brought us all down here? Adam's on his own up there. I should be with him,' Keren accuses me.

'I think there's an intruder in the hotel,' I reply quietly. 'We're safer together.'

'I'd be better off barricaded in my room with Adam. How do I know it's not one of you who killed him?' Keren shivers. I think she's in shock. I pass her my work jacket that's hanging on the back of my chair behind the desk.

'Here, put this on,' I say. She does so and pulls it round herself. Saira stands up and leads Keren to the chair next to hers and grasps her hand tightly.

It's my job to protect them all. This is my hotel. The buck stops with me, even though I'm only five foot three and every cell in my body is terrified. I walk into the middle of the room, all of my senses straining to work at peak performance to try and pinpoint where the intruder is, even though my primeval instinct tells me to run and hide.

Hide.

Why didn't I think of it before?

'Saira,' I whisper. She looks up. I point my head in the direction of the office behind the bar. 'You and Keren go into the office. Eerik, carry Johnny there. There's a bolt on the other side of the door. Lock yourselves in. Barricade the door.'

Saira nods, now-silent tears streaming down her face. With the help of her stick she pushes herself up and takes a step forward. Eerik hovers over Johnny as if trying to work out the best way to lift him up. Johnny probably shouldn't be moved but he'll be safer in the locked office.

Click. Another door shuts, quieter this time. I've been so busy concentrating for a few seconds on the others that I've taken my eye off the ball. I twist my body in the direction of the sound. This time it was much nearer. The breakfast room door is shut and in front of it I see with horror that there's a person holding a can of something in their left hand and pointing a gun in our direction with their right.

Saira screams again. My blood runs cold.

It can't be.

The person speaks.
'Now where do you think you're all going?'
My jaw drops. A bolt of recognition strikes me.
'Tania?'

Part Three

Tania's Story

Chapter 19

Twenty-eight years ago

My suitcase is full. So full that it's bursting at the seams. It was the addition of the long, boho dress that tipped the balance but the dress is non-negotiable, despite Mamie's sartorial advice during the weeks I spent in Nice with her this last balmy summer between the end of A level exams and results day. Dad was working, as per usual, and so sent me to what I call Granny day care behind Mamie's back. He's done it every summer apart from a week or two off when we've holidayed at home, making the most of our private beach, or Dad took me to London to see the sights and go to the theatre. When I became interested in history at school I wanted to scour all the important places from the past, the Tower of London, Westminster Abbey, St Paul's Cathedral, the V&A museum. You don't get those in Nice.

Mind you, having said that, there could have been worse things than spending every summer holiday with Mamie, even though when I arrived back in Devon at the beginning of September each year I could tell Dad was scrutinising me, checking what I'd been up to *en France*. God forbid a few weeks should prompt me to follow in the path of my dead mother. No boys, no booze, no drugs allowed. Still, he can't have been too concerned that I'd turn into the mum I barely remember since he never took the summer off work to spend the time with me. He obviously hoped I take more after his side of the family: sensible, reliable, British.

'Don't follow fashion, *ma joie*, and certainly not English fashion. Make your own timeless style like French women do,' Mamie lectured me when she took me shopping in the boutiques that catered to both locals and tourists. In my suitcase the straight leg jeans, soft T-shirts and jumpers, a blazer, blouse and skirt she bought me still have their store tags on. It had been too hot to wear them in the French July heat, where I stuck to a pair of old jeans I'd cut the legs off to make shorts, and a rotation of T-shirts. Back home the clothes look out of place. Not me at all.

I've got to hurry up. On my bedroom floor is the cardboard box full of toiletries and books I want to take with me. There's no room in there for anything more. If I want to be able to shut the suitcase I'll have to get rid of something.

'Ten minutes, Tania. We need to avoid rush hour traffic on the M5. Be downstairs in five minutes with your bags so I can pack the car. Do you want help carrying them downstairs?'

Dad's calling from the bottom of the stairs. He's not quite shouting, he never does that, but his voice is raised enough for me to tell he's checking his watch impatiently.

There's something about Dad's voice that's always unsettled me. What's his tone, is he annoyed or pleased with me? His word is law and he's the only parent I've got left, or ever really known, other than a distant memory, a figure in an old photograph.

Thanks to doing well in my A levels – three As and a B – and getting my place at St Mark's University to study history, I'm no longer the disappointment to him that I was when I was expelled from boarding school three years ago. I'll never forget the look on his face and him quietly saying I'd let him down but let myself down more. It was only after that he got round to asking me why I did it. My crime, according to the school, was sneaking out and hitchhiking to Dover to catch a ferry to France and go to Mamie. The police found me at the terminal. My real crime though was being unhappy at the swanky, expensive boarding school I didn't fit in at and having the audacity to do something about it. Dad found an independent school locally for me to finish my GCSEs and do A levels, keeping an eye on me at all times. If he had to go away for work he booked me in to the school's dormitory overnight until he returned, not wanting me to be at home on my own. I spent weekends ambling around this large house, reading on the beach or swimming in the sea, always on my own or with Dad. I didn't have any friends, not ones I'd want to spend time with out of school anyway, and besides, bringing someone back to the house and them meeting Dad would be far too embarrassing. If that friend was a boy, not that I met any at my girls' only school, it would have been unthinkable. Mum had surrounded herself with men and even though Dad was one of them, he hated any sign that I might be taking after my mother.

'I'm OK, thanks, Dad. I'll be down in a minute,' I call back.

I look at my watch. Why is time going by so quickly? I've got to get a move on, this case has to close. Only one thing for it. I pull the T-shirt I'm wearing off over my head and shimmy out of the jogging bottoms, then reach for the flowery dress. If I take a couple of the French outfits out of the case, it might close. I sit on the top to force everything down then tug at the zip, which easily meanders its way all around.

Success! Job done. Shame about the mess on the floor. I quickly scoop up all the things I've chosen not to take and shove them into a couple of drawers, then straighten my duvet cover in an attempt to tidy up, although no doubt our cleaner Cathy will come in and strip the bed when I'm gone.

I take a deep breath, savour the scent of the Devon air through my bedroom window before I shut it, and take took a last look round at my haven. I don't remember living anywhere else other than that school from Hades. On my bedroom walls are art posters, gifts from Mamie, who despises posters of pop stars on teenage bedroom walls (one thing she's got in common with her son-in-law). Sitting on top of my pillow is the teddy bear I've had since I was a toddler, my one-eyed furless best friend that the girls at boarding school laughed at me for having and threw out of the dorm window.

When I was younger the rose wallpaper here used to make me feel as if I were I was sleeping in a garden, like a nymph in *A Midsummer Night's Dream*. On my bedside table is a photo of me aged about three with Mum hugging me and laughing, looking like a goddess with long blonde hair, tanned skin, beautiful bone structure and full lips that were rosy without lipstick.

'Bye, Mum,' I whisper, blowing a kiss at the photograph. I've decided that she is staying here. This is a new start for me and I've got to do it on my own, without teddy, Mum or the past creeping in.

I wheel my suitcase out onto the landing then come back for the cardboard box, which proves to be far heavier than it looks. Dad's footsteps echo downstairs on the wooden hall floor. After carrying the suitcase downstairs, holding onto the banister to steady myself, I run back up, two steps at a time, for the box. When I bend to pick it up I feel an invisible pull back into my bedroom. The photo of Mum and I. I look at Mum's eyes smiling out at me. What harm would it do to take it? I pick it up and sandwich it safely in the box between two hardbacks on my course reading list.

Mum can come with me – I'll keep her out of sight, in a drawer for good luck. That way no one will ask me questions I don't want to answer.

Eight minutes later, Dad's car is packed with my suitcase, boxes containing snacks, coffee and a kettle, books, my portable CD/radio player, and some CDs.

I fasten my seat belt in the passenger seat next to Dad and take a last look at my seaside home. Suddenly I feel the urge to throw the car door open and run back inside, back to safety. What will St Mark's be like? What if it's a rerun of the hell of boarding school? I sit on my hands to stop myself.

'Time to go,' Dad says.

I won't let fear stop me. I'm an adult now, it's time to live my life the way I, and not Dad and Mamie, want.

'Ready?' he asks, as if he's sensing my second thoughts. I nod. Dad turns on the car engine, takes off the handbrake and puts his foot on the accelerator. I hear the familiar crackle of the driveway's gravel beneath us. We drive slowly to the main road, passing the oak trees and green shrubs that mark our territory, all that is familiar and comfortable fading into the distance behind us.

Dad's not one for listening to music on the radio. We don't talk much on the journey, or rather Dad talks but I say little, trying to swallow down queasy unease. Dad tells me what a great time I'll have at university, how it could turn out to be the best three years of my life, but then switches to a list of what I'm not to do, namely anything he wouldn't approve of. I nod. The only thing I've ever done that he didn't approve of was running away from boarding school.

When he's finished his speech he switches on Radio 4 for the news headlines and then, as soon as they're over, switches the radio off and we continue on our way in silence. Perhaps it's as hard for him to have me leave as it is for me to take the chance and do so. But if I had run back into the house and decided to stay in Devon, what would be my future? There aren't any jobs locally, other than seasonal ones in hotels or cafes, and those aren't things I'd want to do, and probably would be no good at anyway, even if Dad let me give it a try. I had daydreamed about moving to France to live with Mamie and perhaps teaching English, but that would only be swapping one parental figure for another, far older one. No, it has to be university. That's my ticket to freedom, whoever I may be (not that I know at the moment), away from Dad's expectations, the lingering shadow of my dead mother, and the family fear that I'll turn out to be like my her: highly strung, unfaithful and suicidal to boot. Dad's always drummed into me: no drink, no drugs, no boys and I'll be safe.

It's a Sunday. Freshers' week starts tomorrow. The thought of going to a big party where I don't know anyone makes me feel even more sick. I leave my suitcase with Dad and join the queue for a table where keys and information are being handed out. Finally, it's my turn. The tall, skinny boy in front of me heads off with his suitcase and a bag along a path towards one of the student residences, briefly looking me in the eye and smiling as he goes.

The smiley woman behind the desk gives me an envelope with my room key for The Orchards Hall, a welcome pack and information about activities for freshers' week. I follow her directions to the hall, followed by Dad, summoning up my courage.

'You have to speak to people, Tania, if you want to make friends and be sociable. Sometimes you'll need to make the effort first,' Dad follows on from his speech in the car.

'Yes, Dad.' I hope the corridor is empty and we won't come across anyone else for him to embarrass me in front of. He never went to university. He built his business from scratch after school and has never experienced anything like this.

Behind the thick wooden fire doors, the halls corridor is like a ghost town. Number six is my room and I put my key in the lock, trying to conceal my shaking hand from Dad, and turn it.

The room is bare and functional, with pale blue painted walls. On the right is a door to an en-suite bathroom, something Dad insisted on me having because he didn't want me sharing a loo or shower with boys and the halls are unisex. The brochure said that the communal room for socialising, including a bar, is in the refectory. The single bed is covered with sheets, a blanket and a darker blue bedspread.

'Cosy,' Dad says.

My suitcase, bags and boxes take up most of the floor space.

Dad stands in front of me, looking like he doesn't want to leave me, but also that he doesn't want to say so. He reaches to give me hug, something that startles me because it doesn't happen very often but is very welcome. I lean into him, breathing in his familiar scent, then force myself to let go.

After he's gone, I unpack, keeping an ear out for signs of anyone else. The fire door in the corridor bangs twice but aside from that there are no signs of life elsewhere. My stomach churns. I can't stay in this room forever. I walk into the corridor. A couple of doors have name tags stuck on them, but there's no sound behind them as I walk up and down the corridor like a cat burglar.

'Hello? Is anyone in?' I ask, feeling distinctively foolish and wanting to run straight back into number six and lock myself in. I'm about to do just that when the door of number eight opens with a squeak. From behind it pops a head, a girl with shoulder-length mouse-brown hair in a centre parting and wearing tortoiseshell glasses. Thank goodness, a girl. I really hope I can make a friend here and not have to go to the refectory on my own, but what if she's like those girls at boarding school and doesn't accept me?

'Hi. Have you just moved in?' the girl says.

'Yes,' I reply, wondering what else to say. I think on my feet. 'I'm Tania.'

'I'm Jeannie. Do you want to come in my room? I don't think anyone else is in.'

I step inside Jeannie's room, which is identical to mine except for a sea blue cushion on the bed and postcards of a couple of classical sculptures I recognise on the pinboard. Michelangelo? Jeannie motions for me to sit on the chair and offers me a biscuit from an open pack on the bedside table. Ooh, chocolate digestives.

We make small talk about A level grades, courses and what we've packed for university. I begin to relax. She seems nice, at least not like she'd throw my metaphorical teddy out of the window.

My stomach starts to rumble and I remember Dad's words about taking the initiative. I try to stop my voice from trembling when I ask, 'Do you want to come to the refectory with me? I'm getting hungry and haven't been there yet.'

I hold my breath for Jeannie's reaction and breathe out when she nods her head. 'Yes, sounds good. I've already eaten there so I can show you the way. The food's OK, better than I thought it would be.'

'Thanks,' I say, beaming gratefully, then broach the subject of the others in the corridor. What if Jeannie's already made friends and won't want to stick with me very long?

'I thought there'd be more people around. Have you met the others on the corridor yet?'

Jeannie nods again. 'I did yesterday. You're the only one to arrive today. There are a couple of international students who have already been on campus a week and know each other, a couple of third years who went out to meet their friends, and a couple of boys, Tommy and Nathan, who went out together last night to, and I quote, "hunt for skirt". I think it goes without saying that they didn't invite me to go with them, not that I would have done.'

My mouth opens wide in shock and we both laugh in solidarity at the situation.

'They woke me up at 1 a.m. making a racket coming into the corridor,' Jeannie continues.

'Were they alone?'

'What do you reckon? Of course!' Jeannie replies. We both collapse into fits of giggles at Tommy and Nathan's lack of hunting skirt success.

My stomach starts to rumble again. I self-consciously cover it with my palms and suggest, 'Shall we head off for some food now?'

'Good idea. I'll just grab a jumper.' Jeannie reaches into her wardrobe for a knitted sweater to put on over her T-shirt. A faint scent of menthol hits my nostrils.

'I'm so glad you came. It's good to have another first year girl in the corridor. We can stick together,' Jeannie says to me.

'Great.'

'Perhaps we can explore the campus after dinner? I'll point out Tommy if I see him terrorising some girl!' Jeannie replies, and we both burst out laughing again. Relief washes over me. I've finally made a friend and the novelty feels good. Jeannie seems to like me and she doesn't already have plans with other students. I don't have to spend this evening on my own. Dad will be pleased with me.

For the first time in my life I'm liked for who I am by someone other than Dad or Mamie. From that evening on, we settle into a routine that lasts for the whole term, sticking together: we go for our meals in the refectory, spend the evenings studying, chatting and drinking tea in each other's room, or watching films at the cinema society, and avoid the others in the corridor, clinging to each other as if to a life raft when overboard at sea.

That is until I meet the rest of my gang.

Chapter 20

Ten weeks later

It's the last night of the first term at St Mark's and tomorrow will be my first trip home since I arrived. Dad's coming to pick me up in the morning. I didn't go back to Devon for reading week because I preferred to study and write essays in the library with Jeannie instead of rattling around home on my own while Dad worked long hours in his study. I'm looking forward to the Christmas break though. Mamie is coming over and I've missed my own bed, the beach, and even Dad.

Tonight there's a Christmas party at the students' union. Something for me to avoid like the plague. I'd have preferred for Dad to pick me up today after my afternoon seminar but he had a meeting and it makes more sense for him to drive to get me in the daytime tomorrow.

Tommy and Nathan have Sellotaped mistletoe to their room doors in the hope of getting a free kiss. Idiots. Jeannie and I have got into the habit of peeking out of our doors to see if the coast is clear before we leave. I suppose we needn't bother because they pay us zero attention anyway, other than once drunkenly speculating whether they would get off with Jeannie and me if we were the last two girls on earth.

In the day the students' union is bearable, it smells of greasy food, has a couple of cafes, a few bars, a room for club nights and a shop selling books and stationery. A few weeks ago, Jeannie and I went in the evening to see what it's like – loud, busy, sweaty and sticky. Everyone seemed either pissed or confident, and I'm neither. I'm not interested in getting drunk. Mum was when she walked out on Dad and drove her car into a tree. I don't want to go down that road. As for dancing, I don't mind in the privacy of my own room but there's no way I want other people watching me. My skin prickles at the thought of it. They'd comment on how I don't fit in, how I stick out like a sore thumb. I don't want boys ogling my body, like men ogled my mum.

Dad's always drummed into me to not follow in her footsteps and even Mamie, who I think silently blames Dad for some of what happened, has told me not to follow in Mum's footsteps. Every so often I take my photo of Mum out from where I keep it in my T-shirt drawer and stare at the face of the woman I can barely remember. A scent, a feeling, an accent, that's all that remains – rather like having a blurred negative instead of a colour video. Mum had undoubtedly been pretty, far more than I am, but from the things Dad and Mamie have told me she also knew how to leverage her attractiveness and loved the attention it brought her. Perhaps her beauty was her downfall and if she had been average looking then Delphine Armstrong-Jones wouldn't have had or wanted other men going after her and could have settled down into everyday life as a mother, still being here for me to phone every week, eagerly wanting to hear how I'm getting on. Because if Dad and I were enough for Mum, then she wouldn't have killed herself, would she?

We have to vacate our rooms over Christmas because the uni rents them out to people coming to conferences. I've nearly finished my packing. My room is nearly back to the blank canvas it was when I moved in. I got another cardboard box from the local supermarket to put in the books, folders and papers I've accumulated over the last ten weeks. Only my toiletries, pyjamas, clean underwear for tomorrow, kettle, spoon and a pack of tea bags, now perilously close to empty, to go. Without a fridge in the room, I've come to enjoy black tea. Its lingering scent makes me feel at home whenever I come back to my room.

Knock, knock. It'll be Jeannie calling on me to go for dinner, because no one else ever comes to see me. A few times I've been to the cafe after seminars and lectures with people on my course to show willingness, but I haven't struck up any friendships. The others all seem to have their own friendship groups, either from their halls or people they knew from home.

Friday night in the refectory is my favourite. It's usually fish and chips, but tonight Christmas dinner with crackers thrown in has bounced it off the menu. I tie my hair back with a piece of silver tinsel in a nod to the festive season. Last weekend I bought Jeannie a pair of Father Christmas earrings for a laugh. When I open the door I'm pleased to see she's wearing them, along with her usual jeans and jumper, but she seems subdued.

Jeannie doesn't say much as we walk to the refectory and head for the quiet table in the corner with a wonky leg that has become our usual spot. The smell of roast potatoes and turkey is delicious.

Someone has decorated the room with paper garlands, and a fake Christmas tree with multicoloured baubles and lights has stood at the entrance since the end of November. Its boughs are rather depleted now as some idiots think it's hilarious to nick a bauble and see if they can get away with it.

'Anything wrong?' I ask Jeannie as we put our coats on the table to reserve it before we go up to the canteen counter to choose our dinner.

'I'm going to miss you,' Jeannie says, her face looking glum. She pulls her glasses off the end of her nose and rubs the lenses with the sleeve of her jumper before putting them back on again, covering her sad eyes.

'It'll be a long month back home with my parents. I don't really have any friends back home.'

'Neither do I,' I confide.

'You could come and visit if you like?' Jeannie asks, her face lighting up at the idea. I sense she's been building up to asking.

'I'm sorry, my dad wants me home for Christmas with him and Mamie, and she's staying for New Year. Besides, Devon to your place must be a long way on the train?'

Going to stay in a house with people I don't know, even though it's Jeannie's family, doesn't sound very appealing, although I'm careful not to tell her that. She doesn't exactly wax lyrical about her parents and like me she's an only child.

Jeannie's face falls. 'I guess so,' she says.

There's an awkward pause. It occurs to me that she's waiting to

181

see if I'll invite her to stay with me instead, so I add that my dad doesn't like me having friends to visit. Her shoulders slump and she looks even glummer. I feel bad. She's been my best, and only, friend this term.

We queue up for food and I pile my plate high with turkey, the full trimmings, roast potatoes, parsnips, sprouts, carrots, peas, and gravy, and a fill a separate bowl full of steaming Christmas pudding with custard. Back at the table, we pull our crackers together and tuck into our food, while wearing our paper hats. Jeannie's earrings tinkle when she moves her head, causing us both to giggle. We're back to normal. It's nice to see her smile again.

I chew a parsnip and roll my eyes at her, pointing out a group two tables away that's being rowdy and laughing, playing catch with a hard sprout. She raises her eyebrows and laughs in acknowledgement of what annoying idiots they are being.

I glance over at them again. One of the party, a girl, sitting at the end of the table, wearing a glittery top, looks familiar. I don't usually take much notice of who else is in the dining hall, there are hundreds of students at St Mark's, but I'm sure I know her. I think hard, then it comes to me. She's Caroline, studying history and politics. She once sat next to me in a lecture and borrowed a pen from me when hers stopped working.

Jeannie shakes her head. 'They're really trying to show everyone that they they're having the best fun, aren't they? Like throwing a sprout around is so cool, not something a toddler would do. Idiots.'

I start to agree with her but then look at Caroline again. In lectures she's quiet and not show-offish at all. Seeing her now, howling with laughter and clearly a part of, not apart from the group, a stab of envy pierces my thoughts. She and I are quite similar, so how come Caroline is accepted into a group she's so clearly relishing and I'm not, even though they are chucking a sprout around? I wish I had her confidence instead of always feeling on edge and not good enough.

I like spending time with Jeannie. She's really nice. It's the first time I've ever had a good friend I can rely on, but am I missing out by only hanging around with her? Could those students not be show-off idiots but instead a bunch of happy friends having fun in a way I haven't learned to? I've never been in a group like that. I don't know what having fun in a gang is like.

For a few seconds I want to be in that group, accepted, making everyone laugh, being the life and soul of the party they all gravitate around and look up to.

I'm staring too long, my envy building as I watch Caroline chatting happily. Suddenly, she turns her head and sees me. Before I can quickly turn away, she waves at me and raises her glass of orange juice in our direction.

'Do you know her?' Jeannie asks between mouthfuls of turkey.

'Yes, she's Caroline. She's in some of my lectures.'

'You haven't mentioned her before.'

'Nothing to say,' I reply. 'Have you finished your packing?'

Jeannie shakes her head. 'No, I got side-tracked planning an essay I have to write over the holidays. I'll do it after dinner. You said you're having an early night, didn't you, to be ready for when your dad arrives. I'll knock on your door for breakfast. Nine a.m.?'

I'm not really concentrating on what she's saying, I'm too busy scanning the other tables to see what they're doing. I sort of recognise nearly all of the students from all the breakfasts, lunches and dinners I've been to here, but only know a few of their names. I might say hi to someone to be polite if we're next to each other in the queue or cross paths on campus, but I realise that I've never had a conversation with any of them that goes beyond what's on the menu or a polite enquiry as to how they are, that usually goes along the lines of 'Fine thanks, you?' or 'Busy, got an essay deadline.' I haven't had the courage to.

Jeannie waves a hand in front of my face. 'Earth to Tania. Would you prefer eight o'clock?'

'Nine's great,' I say to her. We're both usually relatively early-risers. If we go to breakfast at nine, rather than at our usual eight, I can have a bath and get the rest of my packing done beforehand. I had been looking forward to going home but now an unexpected gloom washes over me like fog creeping over the shoreline on our private beach at home.

The Christmas pudding is lovely and we both finish it quickly. Jeannie goes up to the counter to get us a free non-alcoholic mulled wine ladled out from a large pot into a pottery mug to celebrate the end of term.

I'm so deep in thought that I don't hear or notice Caroline's heavy-booted footsteps on the lino floor coming towards me until she's standing right by our table.

'Tania, hi, how are you? Enjoying the Christmas dinner?' she asks, smiling at me in a friendly manner.

'It was delicious. How are you? I've not seen you in here before.'

Without being asked, Caroline sits down on the empty chair next to me.

'I'm in Meadowview Halls and usually eat in the refectory there but my friends invited me over here this evening. The uni lets you do it on special occasions because our canteen is too small to offer Christmas dinner. We're having a farewell get-together. Can you believe the term has gone so quickly?'

'It's flown by.' I try and think of something else to talk about. Ah yes. 'How are you getting on with the course?'

'I'm really enjoying it, but it's a lot harder than A levels, isn't it?' replies Caroline. 'It'd be great to talk with you about it sometime, the essay questions and all that for the history modules. I never see you out and about.'

'I suppose I spend a lot of time studying. I'm not really one for parties,' I say. I'm embarrassed to admit it to her. I don't want her to think I'm an odd one out.

'I know what you mean, I don't like drinking loads, it's not my thing, but it's great to sit in the bar with a shandy and chat with my friends. I'm guessing you're not going to the Christmas disco at the union?'

I smile. My revelation hasn't sent her scuttling away. 'You guessed right.'

'Well, a few of us are going to a quiet bar for goodbye drinks, not a big group, a couple from my halls and a friend from our course. Want to come? I'd love you to join us.'

Her kind words blow my gloom away. She wants to include me. People don't usually ask me to join in with things. Only Jeannie does.

I see Jeannie walking back to our table carrying two steaming mugs. I'd planned on finishing a novel I'm enjoying later tonight in my room, not on making small talk in a bar with people I hardly know.

'Just come for one if you want to. I can introduce you to the others, and I'd really like to know what you thought of the last lecture. I struggled to make heads or tails of it!'

Suddenly I feel very self-conscious. 'Is what I'm wearing OK? I'm not dressed for a party.'

'Of course, it's not a party anyway, no one cares what you've got on. That's a yes then?'

My stomach starts to churn at the thought of putting myself forward, but then I remember the fun Caroline's group appear to be having, and that Dad told me to make an effort with people.

'Yes!'

I buzz with pleasure at my new-found bravery. I hope I don't regret it.

'Yes to what?' asks Jeannie, who sits down and pushes a mug in front of me on the table, looking at me and then to Caroline with unease.

'I'm going to have a drink with Caroline after dinner.'

Am I imagining it, or does Jeannie look upset? Her face has fallen as far as it did before when I turned down her invitation to visit in the Christmas break.

'I thought you said you were having an early night,' she replies, frowning slightly. Her fingers tighten around her mug, forcing her knuckles to jut out like mini mountain peaks.

'I am, I'm only going for a quick one.' I smile at Jeannie to placate her. I suppose I ought to ask her along with us but I doubt she'd would enjoy it and anyway, Caroline said she wants to talk to me. Bringing someone else along would be rude.

'Lovely,' Jeannie says, smiling fakely. She stares down at her mug, as if the liquid inside it is the most interesting thing on earth, and says nothing more.

Caroline's gaze flicks from Jeannie to me with a questioning look.

I speak to break up the prickling awkwardness of this situation. 'See you in about twenty minutes?'

'Great! Meet you at the refectory door?'

'OK.'

'See you then,' Caroline says and she stands up and walks back to the noisy table where they are now tucking into Christmas pudding. Jeannie doesn't look up or acknowledge Caroline's departure. Perhaps I should have introduced her properly but, well, Jeannie is being a bit off. I drink my mulled wine quickly and put the mug down on the table with a slightly passive-aggressive bang, which causes Jeannie look up.

'You going already?' she asks.

'Yeah, I'm going to put a dress on, I've been in these clothes all day.'

'There'll probably just be a bunch of sprout-throwing idiots there. Hardly worth making an effort for.'

'I'm not making an effort for them, I'm making one for myself. See you tomorrow for breakfast,' I reply curtly and pick up my dirty dishes to carry to the trolley from where the staff wheel them to the kitchen to be washed.

Walking away, I can feel Jeannie's eyes watching me. Have I upset her? We've never had a cross word before. It's always been just the two of us doing everything together. Maybe I should turn back, say something like she's right, they'll be idiots, and I'll probably only stay for half an hour, and I'll tell her all about how awful it was tomorrow. Stop her feeling left out. But then, passing the noisy table, I see a boy who looks vaguely familiar, laughing with the group, proper belly-laughing and not the sort of mirth that comes from sarcasm or being polite. There's something about him that intrigues me. Perhaps he'll be at the drinks too. I don't know why but I hope so.

I've never been part of a group. Watching them earlier I'd felt as if they were specimens in a fish tank and I was observing them, outside the glass, unable to join in. A different species. Now I realise it's the other way round. It's not them but me who is the odd one out. I'm the creature in the fish tank that swims around in a small space with only one other fish for company. That's suited me fine, but now I feel an urge to break through the glass wall and venture outside the tank. I want to see where I can swim to. Reefs, coral, the wide ocean maybe.

What I don't want to do, even though it would be the easiest choice and my usual one, is turn back, so I put one foot in front of the other and carry on walking away.

Thirty minutes later, I nearly do a U-turn. I've changed into my trusty long floral dress that I've quickly retrieved from my suitcase and have sprayed on some Chanel No. 5, which Mamie bought for me earlier in the year at the same time as the clothes. Caroline had said that it was a small group meeting for drinks but the bar on campus she's led me to is packed, heaving with sweaty, intoxicated bodies. My shoes stick to the floor because of all the spilt beer and I can hardly hear a thing over the cacophony of voices competing with each other to be heard; raucous laughter and a Christmas song blaring out of a speaker nearby, the one about wishing it would be Christmas every day that you can't escape in December.

I usually avoid places like this like the plague.

'They're over there,' says a grinning Caroline, pointing at a table in the corner with two boys and a girl sitting at it. They've put coats over two spare seats to stop others taking them. A warm glow comes over me when I see that one of the boys is the one I vaguely recognised in the refectory.

'Everyone this is Tania. Tania, this is Imran, Keren and Adam,' Caroline says jollily as we reach the table before leaving to push her way through the crowds to the bar.

'Hi, Tania. I'm sure I've seen you before,' says Adam, the refectory boy, in a deep voice with a slight townie accent. My heart flutters and I smile back nervously.

'Of course you've seen her before, she lives on campus. We're like rats in a lab, we all pass each other every day!' laughs, the girl, Keren. 'Tania, we're on the same course, I think. I've seen you in lectures. How's it going?'

Pieces of the jigsaw start to fall into place. I usually keep my head down at lectures, sitting by myself near the front unless it's a busy lecture shared between a few courses, and someone comes and sits next to me. I concentrate on the tutor rather than on the others around me. Keren is slightly dumpy, has long mid-brown hair tied back in a ponytail and looks totally at ease in her own skin, wearing jeans and a navy and burgundy striped sweatshirt. I think she's in one of my seminar groups. She always seems to have something to say, not like me who is too timid to speak up.

'Good thanks. Yes, I recognise you. That's how you know Caroline then, is it, through history?'

'Yeah, but Caroline is doing joint history and politics and she's thinking of dropping the history next term to stick to politics.'

'I'm studying chemistry, I'm in the same hall as Caroline and Adam,' Imran says, offering his hand across the table for me to shake. Sitting on the table in front of him is a half-drunk pint of Coke. Beneath the table I wipe my still clammy hand on my leg and will myself not to accidentally knock his drink over when I shake his hand.

'Hi.' I don't know what else to say and desperately try to think of something vaguely witty. I'm relieved that Imran's drink remains upright.

Adam chimes in. 'I've got it! The day I arrived you were behind me in the queue for room keys. I've got a good memory for faces.'

'I thought you looked familiar,' I reply, sneaking a chance to look at him, take in his sparkly grey eyes, the hint of stubble appearing on his chin, and his angular cheekbones. Not conventionally handsome but *interesting*, arresting, rather than loud and overconfident like the boys here who scare me off.

As the others chat, Adam draws me into conversation, asking me where I'm from and what I like doing at St Mark's, looking into my eyes and holding my gaze. I start to relax and, after a short feeling of awkwardness, I find him easy to talk to. He really does seem to be interested rather than just making polite conversation. We talk about books and music and he smiles with pleasure when I ask him about himself. I get the feeling that, like me, he's not used to people caring about what he thinks.

My leg starts to get pins and needles and I flex my knee, accidentally brushing his leg with my calf. 'Sorry,' I say straightaway, startled by the electric shock I felt touching him. He must think I'm an idiot.

'That's OK!' he says with a reassuring smile, and the others draw him into a group conversation, recounting funny stories of things that happened that term.

Although I don't have much to add to the conversation they are careful to include me, which I'm grateful for. It's wonderful to feel part of a group, wanted and accepted.

For the rest of the evening I don't have a chance to talk to Adam alone again but he keeps looking over and smiling. I'm drawn to him, a feeling new, fizzy, exciting yet unsettling for me. Boarding school and Devon were single sex only and sapphism had never held any appeal. There'd been a couple of boys in France who'd shown an interest, but I certainly didn't reciprocate. Dad's words popped up in my head, *they're like dogs on heat*. It was just because I'm English and a novelty, I know, someone different to have a crack at, like Tommy and Nathan on their skirt hunt. Besides, look what happened to Mum when she craved love. Men, maybe even including my own dad, flocked to her for her body but didn't want to fully embrace the actual person inside the packaging.

Sitting here, being part of the group, is a new and welcome experience I want more of.

'Tania? What do you reckon?'

Jolted from my reverie I look to see who asked me a question. It was Caroline.

'Do you want to come to my nineteenth birthday party?'

'Going to be a banger!' laughs Imran.

'When is it?'

'The first Saturday after we get back in January. This lot will all be there. Thought we could go out for a pizza and then to a bar.'

Adam will be there. My cheeks flush brighter at the thought of a valid reason to be in his presence again, and my chance to be part of this group. Caroline can't have thought I was boring tonight or she wouldn't have invited me.

'Sounds good. Thanks.'

'Brilliant. Last year of my teens. Got to start it off in style!'

That night, feeling giddy, buzzing and a bit queasy, I struggle to sleep. Is it the alcohol I'm not used to, although isn't that supposed to render you comatose? Thoughts about the evening compete with each other in my head and I can't drift off. After lying there for what seems like ages I switch on the bedside lamp and see my clothes strewn on the floor: the flowery dress I cast off when I got in and changed into my pyjamas, and the garments I pulled out of my suitcase earlier to find the dress beneath and left on the carpet in my hurry.

There's five weeks to go to Caroline's party. Five weeks before another chance to be with Adam and to be wanted as part of the group. The shadow the lamp casts on the floor feels like the dim hole in my heart, the darkness where the light of Mum's love should have been. I wish I could ask her what to do.

I lean over and pull open my T-shirt drawer, put my hand in and feel around for the cool metal of the photograph frame. Under the light of the lamp Mum smiles back at me, her eyes dancing in faded colour. When she chose to, from what Dad and Mamie have told me, Mum had been the life and soul of the party. She knew how to get people to want to be around her and men to desire her. What elusive quality did she have that enabled her to do that? Yes, she was pretty, but she wasn't extraordinarily stunning like a model. Mum was intelligent rather than academically gifted. Yet, in the photo in front of my face, and in her presence in my dim and distant memories, there'd been something about Mum that demanded attention. If she was a bee in a hive she would have been the queen. Until, that is, she was assassinated by her successor, or in her case caused her own downfall.

Five weeks.

Thirty-five days.

Could it be possible? That's all the time I've got to transform myself into the person I want to be for them all to want me.

Chapter 21

Two weeks later

It's misty here in Devon. Curled wisps are floating on top of the sea's peaked crests as I look out of the conservatory window at the back of the house, the doors firmly shut to keep out the December chill.

I sit back down on the sofa, wrapping a knitted throw around my knees, thinking of how envious I am of Caroline finding it so easy to make friends, and wondering what the magic ingredient is I need to find. The conservatory is lovely in summer but in winter cold draughts sneak through any crack they can.

I've spent the morning looking through photo albums and packs of prints still lying untouched in the developer's envelope that I found in a cupboard in Dad's study. He's out at a meeting and won't be back until six o'clock.

There are three photos of Mum on display in this house. The one I have of her and me, which is now back in its usual place in my bedroom; one posed portrait taken on Mum and Dad's wedding day, which Dad keeps on his desk; and a picture of the three of us with Mamie at my christening when I was a baby. For as long as I can remember it has held pride of place in a silver frame on the mantelpiece in the sitting room. When I think of Mum it's one of those three images that springs to mind, but now I'm hungry for more. What did she look like every day? What did she wear? How did she manage to draw so many people into her spell?

In the albums are pictures of Mum I'm not sure I've seen before. In the three photos on display, Mum had longish hair, down past her shoulders, but in some of these new ones, which must have been taken before I was born, she has a stunning pixie cut, feathery around her ears with a short fringe, and her eyes are lined above with black flicked liner, making them pop out, wide-eyed and arresting. She looks so happy.

I think of my long hair, now tied back in a ponytail, and wonder what it would be like to chop it off like Mum. It would certainly get me noticed, but am I brave enough?

In another slightly grainy photo of Mum and Dad posing arm in arm I recognise the place. They're somewhere on the Promenade des Anglais, probably during a visit to Mamie.

History is a funny thing, which is one of the reasons I love to study it. We are born knowing nothing before we start to lay down our first memories, yet so many things happened before we were here. Generations upon generations of people lived their lives not knowing what was coming, but we now can look in a history book and see how everything pieced together. I run my forefinger over Mum's smiling face on one photo, caressing it. She didn't know what was to come. Tears spring to my eyes because I do.

The clock in the hall chimes five. I place the two albums back into the carrier bag I'd discovered them in and carefully open the envelope containing the loose photos, then put them back where I found them. I'm deep in thought about how attractive my mum was, when there's a knock on the front door and I go to open it.

'*Bonjour, ma petite.*'

To my delight, it's Mamie. I kiss her in the traditional way on both cheeks. 'You're early! I thought you were coming tomorrow?'

'Ah, I caught an earlier ferry as I wanted to surprise you and spend an extra day with *ma petite fille.*'

I hug her, noticing with a hint of concern that she feels a bit bonier than usual. When we draw back I can see her collar bones are jutting out, but I say nothing.

'Come on in. In fact there's something I really want to ask you before Dad gets home.'

A few minutes later, we're in the kitchen sitting on padded chairs around the large wooden table. I've made coffee and steam is rising from our cups.

'What is it, *ma petite*?' Mamie asks. 'If you don't want to say it in front of your father then I imagine it's about your mother, *oui*?'

'*Oui*. I've been thinking about her a lot recently, what with going to St Mark's and being away from home. From what you and Dad have told me, Mum was so lively, the sort of person everybody wanted to be friends with. How did she get people to like her? I don't find it easy to make friends.'

Mamie takes a thoughtful sip from her coffee cup. 'You are perfect the way you are, *ma cherie*. Just be yourself. Smile, have confidence.'

'I wish I'd inherited it from my mum,' I confess sadly.

Mamie reaches out and places her hand on top of mine.

'Your mother was one of a kind, special, delicate. Yes, her fire burned brightly and she drew people towards her wherever she went, but she needed so much love and attention and could move so quickly from happiness to despair. Delphine gave her heart too freely. I'm glad you didn't inherit that, Tania.'

I think back to what happened to Mum. How after a heartbreak in France she moved to Devon to teach English and met my dad. They married, had me, and she died a few years later in a car crash.

Mamie and I sit in contemplative silence for a moment. I look at the clock. Nearly time for Dad to arrive home. I turn on the oven to cook the coq au vin I prepared this morning. The potatoes I peeled and cut into pieces to make mash are in a pan of cold water on the hob, which I turn on. I'm about to ask Mamie to tell me more about why my mum became so unhappy in England, a subject that Dad has always avoided, when he arrives home.

Later that night, after we've eaten dinner, which I accompany with a glass of red wine in celebration of Mamie's early arrival, and we've all caught up on each other's news, I go upstairs to the spare room that is Mamie's when she stays over. We have three spare bedrooms and the one at the back right-hand side with a sea view is the one she prefers.

I knock on the door quietly in case she's already gone to sleep.

'*Entrez*,' she calls.

Mamie's bedside light is on. She's in her nightclothes and is in bed reading a book.

I lower my voice even though Dad is downstairs watching *Newsnight*.

'Would you mind telling me more about Mum? The stuff Dad never talks about. You know, the reason why she was unhappy,' I ask her hesitantly, concerned that her inclination to open up to me may have passed.

Mamie pats the bed beside her, indicating for me to sit down.

'This novel isn't very good anyway. It has been a long day with the ferry and the train but yes, I can spare a few minutes, *ma petite*, before I go to sleep.'

I hold my breath briefly then let it all out. 'I know that when I was very young, Mum started drinking and going out with other men. The night she died she'd had an argument with Dad, walked out and drove his car into a tree. But why did she do that? Wasn't I enough to make her happy?'

'Oh, *ma cherie*, your mother loved you very much. This is a painful subject to talk about for both of us. Only Delphine can truly know what was in her mind. All I can tell you is what I think.'

I take Mamie's hand and hold it. 'And what's that?'

'The inquest gave a verdict of suicide. They said your mother meant to drive into the tree at high speed and kill herself. I don't believe it. My daughter, like I said, was delicate. She loved you dearly but still needed love and attention herself. Your father, what with you and his business, didn't have the time to devote to Delphine like when they first met. He didn't understand she needed him to. Your mother became unhappy. She was lonely. When your father got home from work, she'd sometimes hand you over to him and go out drinking, meeting male admirers. The night she died, your father said he had begged her to stay in but she'd arranged to meet someone and went out anyway, getting a taxi back three hours later. Your father had put you to bed. At the inquest he said he'd told Delphine that they couldn't carry on like this and that she had to stop the men and the drinking. They argued. She picked up his car keys and drove off.'

I shudder at the thought that my parents' final argument happened under this roof while I, so young, slept soundly, knowing nothing about it, unable to appeal to my mum.

'I don't think your mother meant to kill herself. I know my daughter, she loved you so much, she would never have left you motherless. your father thought she didn't love him anymore but, well, I think it was the opposite. She loved him too much and needed constant reassurance that he also still loved her. Her self-esteem depended on it. When she climbed into his car I think she meant only to crash and hurt herself a little, to scare your father, for Jeremy to realise how much he did love her. It was a cry for help that went wrong. She was drunker than she thought she was, her driving reactions were slow, her tears blurred her vision and she lost control of the car. The inquest said that she knew she had drunk too much to drive and that's why earlier she'd hired a taxi to come home from the bar. The man she met said he'd invited Delphine to go back with him to his house but she turned him down, telling him she had a child at home, and called for a taxi. I think she wanted to come home to you and stop herself doing something that could irrevocably damage her marriage. It doesn't make sense to me that she would then deliberately take her own life.'

We sit there for a while holding hands, Mamie missing her daughter, me mourning the mother I didn't get to know.

Christmas and New Year celebrations pass quickly. In between them I struggle to concentrate on the essays I have to write because all I can think about is what I'd learned about my mother. I vow to never feel alone again, like my mother did. I would transform myself into someone likeable, lovable and popular.

I pore through the fashion and women's magazines I'd bought, trying to learn about makeup, clothes, what bands were cool, which were the in places to go out, which celebrities were on trend and styles that were fashionable.

A few days into the new year I borrow Dad's car and drive to Exeter to spend the cash he'd given me for Christmas. The sales are on and, with knowledge gained from the magazines, I know what I want to buy. I come home with bags of clothes; a case of makeup including thick black eyeliner; posters for my room at St Mark's; and a short, pixie cut bleached blonde haircut. The reflection that stared back at me in the mirror was a beautiful, striking young woman.

* * *

In the first week back at university I join the RAG society to meet new people, which is where I meet Saira. At their social event I practise my new image and persona, smiling brightly, asking people about themselves, properly listening when they reply, and amusing them with stories I'd gleaned from the magazines. I force myself to talk to the other students in my modules, compliment them, join in after-lecture coffee shop visits, where some of them think I am a late starter, having never taken any notice of me before.

In our first lecture back I spot Caroline and go and sit with her. 'Wow, I love your hair, I wish I had the courage to go for the chop! You look amazing,' she says and a few other people I barely know say the same thing. When the lecture finishes Caroline asks me to go to the coffee shop with her and Keren, and reminds me about her birthday party. Jeannie sounds a bit deflated when she mentions the regular Friday film night at the union we went to last term and I tell her I can't go because I'm going to a party. For a moment I feel guilt for letting her down, for the schism that I'm causing, but then I think of Adam and how much I want to be a part of Caroline's group again.

On Friday, I'm the last to arrive at the bus stop, having waited around a corner nearby until the others arrived just in case plans had changed and they didn't show up.

Adam's there. 'Tania, wow, I like your hair!' he says as I walk over. Caroline pulls me into a welcome hug, then I smile, look into Adam's eyes, hold his gaze a fraction longer than people normally do, and look down demurely as a magazine article I read suggested.

At the restaurant I engineer sitting next to him, plucking up the courage to ask him questions and tell a couple of pre-prepared anecdotes that have the group roaring with laughter. With my new hair and clothes, I start to feel like someone else, a more confident me, a more attractive and desirable version of myself – a caterpillar that's metamorphosed into the butterfly it's meant to be.

The evening passes quickly in an exciting, intoxicating blur. When the bus drops us off at campus, Adam lingers with me and asks if I'd like a coffee in his room. Caroline raises her eyebrows and giggles, then tactfully links her arm through Keren's and pulls her ahead.

Adam's hall is a very short walk away from mine and, although it's a slightly older building than where I live, the rooms are pretty similar, just a bit more chipped and faded. Sitting on his bed I feel dizzy with anticipation as he plugs in his travel kettle, pulls out two mugs, some instant coffee and dried milk powder, and makes our drinks. After a few sips we put our mugs down and he tentatively moves in to kiss me, his lips soft against mine, and my heart leaps as we enjoy a lengthy snog. We only pull apart because of a Morse code-style knock on door.

Adam stands up quickly. 'Sorry, that's my best mate, Johnny. His room is a few doors down. He does that knock so I know it's him.'

'It's OK, I don't mind if you answer it,' I say, intrigued to meet the boy that Adam had mentioned a few times.

He pads to the door and opens it.

'Mate, you're back! How was the meal? It was a cracking night with the football lads. We went out to a new bar in Bristol, I've got to take you there sometime. Cheap beer and loads of pool tables,' the voice behind the door says rather merrily.

'I've got company, mate,' Adam replies, and I wonder if it's accompanied by a wink I can't see.

Johnny walks in nosily and his eyes meet mine, causing a huge grin to shine across his face. I'm not experienced at all with this kind of thing but the way he's looking at me, and the flicker of electricity that passes between us, I think this tall, athletic, square-jawed, very handsome boy likes what he sees.

'Johnny, meet Tania. Tania, meet Johnny,' Adam says.

Johnny continues smiling at me before saying, 'Good to meet you, Tania. I'll leave you two to it. I hope to see you again.' He walks out of the room and Adam shuts the door behind him.

Even when I continue kissing Adam, it occurs to me that I hope to see Johnny again too. Life is really looking up.

Chapter 22

Twenty-five years ago

On the doorstep of our student house is a big bunch of roses with my name handwritten on an attached card. My annoyance with Johnny, and his flirting last night, melts away. He must have come round to make up and get his car back. I pick them up and take them and my bags into the lounge, calling out to see if anyone's home. My voice is met with silence apart from the background hum of the fridge in the kitchen. The ancient plumbing is quiet – the absence of creaking and spluttering coming from the boiler me tells that no one is in the bath or having a shower.

I drop my carrier bags on the floor and flop back into the brightly patterned cushions on the sofa which, along with a purple throw, disguise its curry and wine stains. After a couple of hours shopping, spending the money Dad had put into my bank account so I could buy a stylish suit and some smart clothes suitable for London interviews and workwear, it's good to be off my newly designer-trainer-clad feet.

Thinking back, I probably shouldn't have driven off last night and left Johnny at the party. It's not that long since we nearly broke up and I don't want to go through that again. Things will be different when we're living together in London. I promised him I wouldn't encourage any other men. I only flirted last night after those two hangers-on – girls with their boobs nearly hanging out their dresses – pulled him away and he left me on my own. He said he was just being friendly. Well, if he can 'just be friendly', then why can't I?

The roses are beautiful. I inhale their scent, touched that Johnny has bought me my favourites that he usually buys me for my birthday. I do love him. I pull open the card to read his conciliatory apology, but reading the words, my heart sinks and I rip it up then put it in the bin with the roses.

The flowers aren't from Johnny, they're from Adam. Another message to try and persuade me to meet with him alone. I thought I'd made it perfectly clear when he followed me in the street that I'm not interested in getting back together. I groan. Johnny hasn't apologised at all. He might not have forgiven me after our argument. I don't want to let it fester and hope that he'll have calmed down by now. After I've eaten, I'll take his car back and hopefully everything will be OK. I'll stop off at the supermarket on the way and take him a packet of his favourite sweets that he's loved since he was a child and I tease him for.

Keren is probably out at her regular exercise class but I've no idea where Saira is. She's avoiding me after she bawled me out the other day about our kiss, calling me a bitch and a user. I've never seen her like that before, she's usually so easy-going. At one point I even wondered if she was going to hit me when she walked up close to me and screamed in my face. The whole thing was very distressing and she didn't want to hear my apology. I suppose I deserve it, although I never set out to hurt her. I hope she's finally forgiven me and we can put it all behind us. I'd got carried away with the flirting and attention she paid me during the intensity of our revision sessions. It was exciting being on the edge, pushing the boundaries, being desired in a way that Johnny hasn't made me feel lately because of the rough patch we've been going through. I didn't plan on anything actually happening between us but when she kissed me it was nice for a minute or two, something I never before thought I'd like. It was exhilarating trying out a new identity. Until she kept carrying on and I didn't know how to stop without offending her. Thoughts of Johnny flashed into my mind, how I'd much rather I was doing this with him. Things were so rocky between us that I knew he would end it permanently if he found out. That's why I asked her not to tell him.

It was days after I'd tried to let her down gently that she let rip at me, red-faced, spitting her venom, telling me to drop dead, catching me by surprise as I thought she'd accepted that the kiss was a silly mistake between friends. Saira had made sure she had her say when we were alone in the house. She can't have wanted Jeannie and Keren to know what happened, which suits me fine. The more people who know, the more likely it is that it'll get back to Johnny. We've been together over two years now and he understands me. With him I usually never feel alone, and I never want to be.

When we're around others Saira acts normally, but we haven't been alone since. I'm avoiding her too until she cools off. Yesterday she asked Keren and me if we had an idea how much our next telephone bill will be because she's planning on packing up and going back to her parents in a day's time and wants to settle up before she goes. I gave a sigh of relief when I heard that. I want to leave here too but Dad can't pick me up until next weekend. I can't really take Johnny's car back to Devon, can I? Dad's promised me my own for a graduation present. He didn't want me to have one before, probably because of what happened to Mum, but he knows that I'll need a car in London, particularly to get back to Devon whenever I want to. The train services in our area are useless.

The atmosphere in this house is tense now. Our gang is falling apart at the seams. I wonder what I can do to bring us all back together like I usually do. The only person who seems to like having me around is Jeannie, but even she sulked after I invited Keren home to Devon to revise and not her. Keren had been a bit wired all week and grumpy when I asked her to help me with the bits of our course I'm not so strong on. We've revised together loads and though she's made a few comments that it's easier for me to study because I don't have to have a student job in my spare time to pay my way, she's never seemed annoyed before. When we got back Keren stayed out all hours before our exams. It was all a bit odd. The night before our second to last exam I heard her come in and went into her room without knocking to ask her what was wrong, not wanting to fall out with her over something I had no idea about. On her bed was a packet of pills with some missing from the plastic pockets.

She looked up at me in guilty horror and stuffed the pack under her duvet. 'Get out! What are you doing barging in without knocking?' she shouted angrily.

'You've been acting really strangely. I wanted to see if you were OK. What are those pills?'

'Oh, I thought you only wanted to spend time with me when you needed help revising the work you never bothered to do!' she snapped.

I strode over to the bed and threw back the duvet cover, wrestling with her to see what the pills were.

'Give them back, it's none of your business,' Keren snapped, trying to take them back off me. I looked at the packet. It was prescription medication for ADHD.

'Why have you got these?'

'It's not like you've never taken drugs. You're always smoking dope with Johnny.'

'I'm not taking someone else's prescription drugs. You haven't got ADHD, have you? Keren, you're my friend, I'm worried about you.'

She slumped back on her pillows and sighed. 'I bought them off another student. They help me stay awake and concentrate for the exams. I haven't had much time to revise because I can't afford to give up my bar job. I'm struggling. It's all right for you, if you fail you've got your dad's cash to fall back on. I've got to do well to be accepted on the PGCE course. I need a job, a career. My parents can't keep supporting me back home.'

I couldn't believe I'd missed this. How long had she been taking them? Had she been using them in Devon?

'I get it, Keren, but you're smart, you've studied hard, you don't need these. They're on prescription for a reason, you don't know what harm they could be doing to your body.'

She looked at me wide eyed, with a hint of desperation in her voice.

'Please, Tania, just give them back to me and don't tell anyone. I promise I'll stop taking them after my last exam.'

I looked at her and then the blister strip in my hand, a resolution forming in my mind.

'No, I'm going to flush these down the loo. You don't need drugs to pass your exams, it's cheating. You'll always feel guilty if you know you only did well because you took them.'

'Tania, please!' she begged, but I raced out of the room and popped the pills in the toilet basin, pulling the flush before she could come in and stop me.

She's hardly said two words to me since she shouted 'Bitch!' and slammed her bedroom door in my face.

I pick up the TV remote and flick through the channels, hopping from one evening news bulletin to another. All depressing so I switch it off quickly.

My stomach starts to growl. It's a long time since breakfast. I swapped lunch for a chocolate bar because I was too busy shopping and besides, I hate sitting down to eat in a cafe on my own. People stare and probably think I've been stood up.

A car horn beeps repeatedly in the road outside. It took me a long while to get used to urban noise after the peace and quiet of Devon. I walk to the kitchen at the back of the house and switch Radio 1 on to drown it out. What shall I eat? I open the fridge and there's hardly anything in there other than half a pack of Cheddar. I take it out and look in the bread bin where there are a few slices left. Bingo. Cheese toasties it is.

While I'm waiting for the cheese to bubble under the grill something on the side of the fridge catches my eye. It's an electricity bill one of the others has pinned to the fridge with one of the many magnets that adorn it. I'll sort that out later. Then I see that the alphabet magnets are spelling out a new message. Months ago Keren's mum rang up and Saira answered but she didn't have a pen to hand and instead used the alphabet fridge magnets to leave a message. Since then it's become a house tradition that Adam and Johnny take part in as well. Johnny has a key and they both come round sometimes, letting themselves in. We mix the letters back up when we know the right person has received the message.

The toastie smells delicious. I slide it from under the grill onto a plate and take a bite, the cheese oozing deliciously into my mouth. When I've wolfed it down, I put my plate in the sink and go to read the message to see if it's for me. It is.

T meet me at Dark Horse 7.30 tonight

That grungy pub? We don't usually go there, it sells cheap drinks but attracts a rough crowd. The only couple of times I've been in it is when they've had a band on. There must be one on tonight. I wonder who left the message. It can only be one of the five others.

I was out shopping for a good few hours. The message says meet me, not meet us.

I smile with happiness at the thought that things are getting back to normal and my friends want me again. Has Johnny been round to see me today after all? Hopefully Saira and Keren have stopped being pissed off with me too. Given time Adam will move on after our near sofa kiss like I've told him to, stop following me around like a lovesick puppy and all will be back to normal. It's not like I can avoid seeing him again, because he's friends with Johnny. When I told him that evening that I wondered if I'd chosen the right man, I only said it to give him an ego boost because he'd been so miserable-looking since he dropped out of uni and, well, he doesn't know that it was me who advised Johnny not to give him the loan, so I suppose I felt a bit guilty.

I think hard. The message could be from any of them. None of us have a mobile phone to get in touch. Saira, Keren and Adam can't afford one and Johnny says he doesn't want his dad to be able to contact him anytime. I didn't think there was any point in getting one if my friends didn't have one but I'm definitely going to sign up for one before I move to London. Most people there will probably have them.

I've got loads of time to get ready before I need to head off and I make the most of a long leisurely bath with bubbles in and a book. Bliss. With the others being out I don't have to worry about using all the hot water, although I half expect Saira or Keren to come home and knock on the bathroom door. We only shut it when someone's in there, otherwise we leave it open so we know when it's free. It's a code we dreamed up not long after we moved in because there's no lock and Johnny had an embarrassing moment walking in when Saira was on the loo.

When I get out of the bath there's still no sign of any of the girls. That means I can't whittle down my list of five who might have left the message. Is it another attempt from Adam to get me on my own? I hope not. Or could Keren be wanting to talk about the drugs in private, perhaps needing some help to stay off them? Has Saira calmed down and asked me to meet her to smooth things over? Did

Johnny leave the message as a peace offering, or perhaps Jeannie's noticed all the tension in the house and wants to talk to me about it without the others there? I'll go to the pub and find out, then drive to Johnny's if the message wasn't from him.

In my room I decide to wear a cropped top and a pair of combats together with my new trainers that I put on as soon as I bought them earlier. My old, battered pair went straight in the bin.

Although I'm well practised at applying eyeliner, my hand slips and I have to take it all off with lotion then reapply it. By the time I've finished and look at my watch I startle at the time. The bus went five minutes ago. I'll have to skip the booze and take Johnny's car, which is parked a few streets away. I can drive over to his afterwards and make amends. I've left a few toiletries and clean underwear there for when I stay over.

Spraying a touch of perfume before I dash out of the door, I realise that I've grown out of this place now. Soon I'll be in London and hopefully have a career in museums to look forward to. I've applied for a work placement at three in London and am waiting to hear back. When I've got some experience I'd like to do a master's degree in Museum Studies. There's a great course at UCL. I'm sure Dad'll support me and fund my further study.

There isn't much traffic on the road and I arrive at the pub ten minutes early. The car park is at the back, overgrown with weeds. In one space is an overturned supermarket shopping trolley and in another a car without wheels propped up on bricks. I opt for the space nearest the road and head on inside.

Walking up to the bar, the stench of cigarette smoke hits me. I take a second sniff. Hang on a minute, that's not ordinary ciggies. At the bar, I order a lemonade and ask if there's a band on tonight. The barman shakes his head. There isn't one until a week on Saturday.

Just as I don't like eating on my own in cafes I also feel really uncomfortable waiting for people in bars. I should have waited in the car park for ten minutes, but then again, it's not the sort of place you want to hang around in on your own, even if you are inside a locked car.

I choose a seat that isn't in the middle of the pub but from which

I can still see the door. And I wait there, willing whichever one of them it is I'm meeting to hurry up. It's more likely, I think, to be one of the boys. Saira, Keren, Jeannie and I usually go to the pub on the corner of our road if it's just us.

'I recognise you, I do,' says a lilting Welsh voice behind me that doesn't ring a bell. I turn to see who's talking to me. It's a girl about my age, maybe a bit older, wearing jeans and a Take That T-shirt. Her dark brown hair is tied back in a ponytail with a stray wisp hanging down at the side of her face that's free of makeup.

'Sorry, I don't think I know you,' I reply, taking a sip from my lemonade. The fizz goes up my nostrils causing me to cough and she laughs.

'You go to St Mark's, right?' she asks.

'Technically not any more. My finals are all over, thank God,' I reply.

'I've just finished a postgrad there. I've seen you around on campus. Great hair by the way, you certainly stand out in a crowd, that's why I remember you. I'm Flic.' She holds her hand out for me to shake.

'I'm Tania.'

'Mind if I join you for a bit? My boyfriend's popped out to do some business.'

Hmm, business? I wonder what sort of business he's doing after hours.

It feels rude of me to say no though and Flic seems friendly. If she sits down with me at least I won't have the gut-curdling embarrassment of being on my own with nothing to do but stare at the walls.

'I'm meeting a friend but yes, go ahead.'

Flic sits down and chats away while I keep one eye on the door.

Flic is easy company. At one point I smile when I see a tall-ish man with hair down to his shoulders coming in, thinking for a split second that it's Johnny, but then I remember he had his hair cut for job interviews. The man wanders over to join a large group gathered in one corner around the pool table.

'Friend not turned up yet?' Flic asks, seeing me looking. I don't want to look like Billy no mates, so I reply with a small chuckle, 'They're always late. I'm sure they'll be here soon.'

The clock on the wall, above the hideous brown-stained flocked wallpaper, tells me that I've been here almost half an hour now. The group of men, student-age-looking along with a few a bit older, is starting to get a bit rowdy. This isn't the sort of pub that I feel comfortable in with just women, never mind on my own. One man, smallish with short, cropped hair and a beer belly looks over in my direction and I swiftly divert my gaze downwards so as not to attract attention.

The opening bars of Prince's '1999' thumps out of the jukebox drowning them out.

'Don't mind them, they're harmless,' Flic says. 'Regulars. They look a bit rough but they're all right.' She pulls a battered cardboard packet out of her jeans pocket, slides out a white roll-up, then walks over to the group for a light before coming and sitting back down with me.

It's not regular tobacco. As she takes a drag, the sweet, pungent scent hits my nostrils. I look round in surprise to see if anyone is looking. I've been to quite a few parties in other students' houses where joints get passed round, but I've not seen it in a public space. The barman is busy drying some pint glasses and doesn't appear to be paying any attention. None of the other drinkers are, not even the couple of men who are as probably old as Mamie, sitting on their own at a table with a Labrador on a leash.

Prince carries on singing his party anthem. 'Want some?' Flic offers me.

I've smoked dope loads before but have steered clear of coke, E and LSD. Johnny was violently sick one morning after trying an E and when I've been around others on coke or acid they were boring company. At one party a terrified girl thought spiders were crawling over the ceiling and about to drop on her head. That put me off ever trying it. She got so distressed her friend called an ambulance.

'Go on then,' I say and take a drag. No one bats an eyelid. I start to relax.

Flic starts to tell me some funny stories and we pass the joint to and fro until all that's left is the butt. The songs someone put on the jukebox have finished.

I suddenly feel really peckish. 'What we need, my new friend, is crisps!' I laugh.

'And music!' she adds. 'I'll get the munchies, you do the jukebox.'

I saunter over and choose three eclectic songs starting off with Pulp's 'Common People', which always makes me feel like dancing, and I half walk, half shimmy back to the table, singing along.

'Ready salted and cheese and onion,' says Flic, arriving back at the same time as me. She rips open both of the packets so we can share.

'Dunno where my boyfriend's got to and your mate's later than a condom at a baby shower.'

'Ha!' I splutter. 'Never heard that one before!'

Right then there's a loud bang as the main doors burst open, followed by a stampede of footsteps.

'The filth!' someone cries out and I look round, panicking, to see what's happening. Two officers are heading for the pool table and one has the man who looked at me earlier on the floor with his hands forced behind his back. The other is chasing the rest of the group who are swarming away as fast as they can.

I feel like I'm in the middle of a Wild West film set and am rooted to the spot.

'Quick, follow me,' Flic shouts. She grabs my left hand and pulls me up to my feet.

'What's going on?' I ask, trailing behind her as she heads towards the back of the pub.

'Drugs raid,' she wheezes, and scoots ahead of me, pushing open a fire door and running through it.

Instinctively, I look behind me. There seem to be more police now and one is looking in our direction. Fear courses through my veins. I can't be arrested, I only smoked half a joint. What if they think I'm a dealer?

I slam through the fire door and it swings behind me as I race through and see Flic ahead of me. She's making for what looks like an emergency exit at the back that has a long, chrome push bar.

'Stop!' shouts a voice behind me. I keep on running. Flic has disappeared through the door. I'm about to go through too when I trip on an uneven flagstone and topple to the floor. I've never been this scared. There's no time for me to look backwards. I pull myself to

my feet, my ankle painful when I put weight on it, and I half expect
a burly pair of arms to push me back down on the floor.

They don't.

I run through the door follow Flic and dash to Johnny's car. As I
fumble with my keys in the lock, get in and start the engine, I sigh
with relief that the police officer hasn't followed me out.

The engine won't start. Once, twice. 'Start for God's sake!' I
shout, shaking with alarm. Flic is nowhere to be seen – she might
have climbed over the pub car park fence into the warren of streets
behind.

There's a rumble as the engine turns over. I put it into gear and
press my foot down hard on the accelerator when I see an officer,
carrying what looks like a truncheon, running into the car park
through the entrance off the road.

For a split second I'm paralysed with indecision. Do I stop or
do I go? If he catches me I'll be arrested for sure. I can't have a
criminal record. I can't go to prison, but he's seen me now. It'll be
worse if I run. I try to do an emergency stop but the brakes don't
work straightaway – I turn the wheel so as to avoid him but there's
a sickening thump as his body hits metal and the car jolts as tyres
roll over him. Vomit rises in my mouth. What do I do, what do I
do? There aren't any other people watching. Think, Tania, think. I
must get help for him. I drive out on to the street and apart from a
man running away in the distance there's no one to see me carrying
on down the road and speeding away.

In shock, I don't know where I'm heading for, I just need to find
a phone box. The backlights on the van in front of me turn orange
as the vehicle slows down for a major traffic junction and I slam
my foot on the brake, but this time it doesn't work at all. In a split
second I crash headlong into the van then lurch again as another
car shunts me from behind.

Everything goes black. When I come round, I'm on a stretcher in
an ambulance on my way to hospital. I try to flex my muscles. With
relief, it doesn't feel as if I've broken any bones. I'm pretty sure I have
a huge bruise on my forehead and a muscle in my back is hurting
but other than that I think I'm OK.

'Can you tell me your name, sweetheart?' the ambulance woman says to me.

'It's Tania. I need to phone my dad. Please, I've got to ring him.'

At A & E I insist on walking rather than being stretchered in and head straight for the phone box, several thoughts jumbled up in my head.

Who was it that wanted to meet me at the pub?

Have I killed someone?

Fear, shame and horror grasp me with their bony fingers. I dial the one person I know I can trust.

He answers straightaway.

'Dad, please help me. I'm in hospital, in big trouble.'

Part Four

The Reckoning

Chapter 23

Tania

Eeny, meeny, miny, moe. Catch a traitor by its toe. One of my so-called best friends, someone I trusted and thought would always be loyal, stabbed me in the back and twisted the knife for good measure.

I've had a great deal of time to think about the message on the fridge and that night at The Dark Horse. At first, I thought it might have been a coincidence that I was stood up the night the police turned up to do a drugs raid. Then, the more I dwelled on it and replayed the events in my mind, along with the weeks beforehand, I knew it wasn't. I felt it in my gut. None of them came to my funeral. There was no outward display of sorrow or loss. My so-called best friends simply carried on with their sorry little lives as if I'd never even existed.

One of them held a grudge against me. I thought of reasons why it could have been any of them. Someone left the message on the fridge and then called the police, tipping them off about drugs in the pub. They wanted me to be there, to be questioned, arrested even. If it weren't for that message on the fridge I'd have been safely at home, wouldn't have panicked and run when the police stormed in, wouldn't have driven Johnny's car that I later found out was overdue a service or run over the policeman who ended up in a coma, on the edge of death for months until he eventually, against all odds, recovered and was pensioned out of the force on ill health.

When I snuck into Bluebell Lodge on Friday morning, though, I was nearly certain, but still not totally sure. I added everything up. Who had held a grudge against me the longest? I wanted to be totally sure who my enemy was. If they said something that proved me wrong I'd spare them, creep out of the door tomorrow as deftly as I came, in my hire car that's parked a short walk away. If not, then, well, they brought it all on themself, didn't they?

Adam got his just deserts. He'd never forgiven me for choosing Johnny over him, and turning him down in those final few weeks when he told me I was the only one he'd ever wanted and he was still madly in love with me. When he brought up The Dark Horse and the drugs rumour at the meal last night it sealed his fate. He's the only one who knew, because he had set the trap to punish me. They say love can quickly turn into hate.

It's amazing what you can do with little spy bugs bought cheaply off the internet. The hotel was practically deserted on Friday morning before my gang arrived. It was easy to sneak in and put bugs in the breakfast room, reception hall and the private dining room Jeannie had set up with that quite flattering cardboard version of me. At least she chose a good picture. The spy bugs are tiny but they manage to pack in a little camera and microphone that broadcasts to a radio frequency.

Right at the top of the hotel, on a floor where guests aren't allowed to go, there are a few junk rooms with a couple of spare beds and chairs in them. The one at the end of the corridor was perfect for me. Downstairs, the hotel is immaculate but up here it looks like it hasn't seen a duster for at least a few months. I fixed a bug up in the corridor to trigger an alarm on my radio if anyone came up. They didn't. In my tiny roll-up sleeping bag I was quite comfortable listening to what was going on on the ground floor, and when I knew they were all safely in the dining room I sneaked downstairs, wearing all black like a hotel chambermaid might do, in order to trip the fuse switch and plunge them into darkness to spook them. They deserved it after what they said about me. It gave me time, with my torch, to go and plan my revenge.

Twenty-five years ago, when I rang Dad, distraught, he raced up the M5 at dawn to whisk me off to a private hospital in Devon where I was thoroughly checked over before discharging myself. I told him everything. Back in Devon I was amazed when his first thought was not to shout or scream at me for being so stupid but to protect me. We sat in the conservatory looking at waves breaking on the beach, me tucking up my legs on the sofa, terrified of what was going to happen to me. Outside, the wind was whipping up unseasonably for the time of year. Tears started to well up in Dad's eyes. 'I feared this would happen. It's your mother's genes. It's not your fault.'

My eyes were sore and dry from too much crying. 'I didn't mean to do it, Dad. I only smoked half a joint, I promise, and I was going to stop for the policeman. The brakes didn't work properly. It was an accident. When I hit him I was so scared. I know I shouldn't have driven off.'

He sighed and took my smooth hand in his larger, calloused one. 'Perhaps it's best that you did. You'd surely have been arrested and you could be looking at a manslaughter or murder charge.'

The thought of prison was too horrendous. No way could I cope. 'Murder? I can't go to prison, Dad. I know I was wrong but I didn't mean to do it.'

We had no way of finding out what happened to the poor policeman. Local news wasn't online back then. I prayed he'd be OK, that he'd been found in time.

If I could have boarded a spaceship going to outer space forever I would have done it. My body began to shake with fear and Dad had to hold me close, wrapping his warmth around me for five minutes, before I stopped. He kissed me tenderly on the top of my head.

'The police will find you, Tanie,' Dad said sadly.

I wanted to sob but there were no tears left. I clung to Dad to help keep me safe.

'You ran over a police officer. It'll be their top priority, trying to find out who it was. There might be camera footage of the car park. The police will question the people they arrested about who else was in the pub. They're bound to want to speak to you. And if the police officer survives, well, he'll recognise you and testify against you.'

Despite the warmth of the summer day I started to shiver again. I'd no hope. I'd rather die than go to prison and Dad knew that because, between crying, I'd said it in the car when he drove me home.

'You've got two choices,' he told me in a compassionate tone that I didn't deserve. 'One, I drive you to the nearest police station and you confess. That might get you a reduced sentence, and I'll hire a great lawyer.'

'I can't go to prison, Dad, I wouldn't survive,' I moaned, still wrapped in his arms. Everything seemed so surreal. How could I have been out shopping one day, and the next I'm a wanted criminal?

'I know, Tanie, I know. You're delicate like your mother. Then it's Plan B. You'll have to disappear.'

'What?' I cried and broke away to look Dad squarely in the face to see if he was joking.

'I've been thinking. I'll have Johnny's car towed away and crushed so they can't get any forensic evidence. I'll say I looked at it and it wasn't roadworthy and not worth repairing. I've got a friend with a boat whom I can pay to smuggle you over to France.'

I stared at Dad, astonished. 'You know someone who could smuggle me? Where? What would I do?'

'Let's just that say some of the business deals I've made weren't entirely legal. I can get a fake passport to you and arrange for money transfers. You need to go somewhere no one will think of looking for you, certainly not Mamie's.'

Elation and dread hit me at the same time. I sat back on the sofa feeling the familiar smooth velvet under my palms. I could be free, but what would I do? The life I'd planned for myself would disappear into the ether.

'Where would you say I'd gone?'

A solitary tear dropped from Dad's black eyelashes.

'I'd say you'd drowned.'

My eyes opened wide with incredulity. 'How? Everyone knows

I'm a strong swimmer. Would the police believe you?'

'Look outside,' Dad said and pointed to our private beach, home to the happiest times in my life. Playing on the sand, sunbathing, swimming daily when the weather was good enough. In front of me the waves were growing, peaking in white crests then crashing onto the damp sand.

'I'll say I left you resting for a little while and, without me knowing, you went swimming like you usually do. You didn't realise you could be concussed and it might be dangerous. When I saw your towel on the beach and I couldn't find you I called the police.'

'Won't they try and look for me?' I was dumbfounded. Surely this plan couldn't work?

'Yes, but you could be anywhere. They can't dredge the whole of the sea. If anyone asks me about the crash, I'll say you'd told me you'd had an argument with your boyfriend the night before and drove back to your student house in his car. You went out for a drive to clear your head before you took it back to him, but the brakes failed. Johnny must have known his car needed fixing. You didn't tell anyone you were going to the pub, did you?'

'No, Dad.' I thought back with relief that I broke up the alphabet message on the fridge after I saw it. Jeannie, Saira and Keren wouldn't have known it was there – unless any of them were in the house when I was out shopping, or they picked out the letter magnets and put them together to form the note.

'Think carefully. It has to be your decision. If we do this you won't be able to come home,' Dad said seriously. 'It'll be forever, though when everything's settled down I could try and travel to see you. I'm your father. It's my number one job to keep you safe. I didn't manage it with your mother. I won't lose you too.' His voice started to break with emotion, which set me off crying even harder.

I couldn't do it. Leaving my home, my whole life to start a new one on my own under a false identity. I was about to say I'd go to the police station and confess when I thought of a prison documentary I'd seen on TV. The inmates were locked up in their cells twenty-three hours a day. I didn't know which would be worse, being on my own or trapped with someone who was violent, a drug addict or worse. The law would throw the book at me because I'd injured, maybe killed, a policeman. Everyone would hate me. I could be locked up for over ten years. I'd never make it, I'm not strong enough. I'd rather be dead.

If only I could have turned back the clock, but I couldn't.

'I'll go abroad.' I sniffed.

Dad's face turned grey. 'Are you totally sure?'

No, but I nodded.

'I'll go and make some phone calls. Go and pack an old bag. Don't take anything that people might know is missing. Nothing personal. We can't even tell Mamie. Never forget that I love you.'

I watched Dad walk out of the conservatory, probably for the last time. Upstairs I found my old school satchel from when I was about eleven at the back of the wardrobe. It was brown and boring, the reason why I'd ditched it, but that meant it was unidentifiable and wouldn't stand out. I also picked out an old wig I'd bought to wear in a school play years ago. It was a mousy bob. Again, something that'd help me blend into the background. In the bag I threw a few pieces of my oldest underwear and a couple of black pairs of socks, then I changed into a pair of navy leggings that were saggy round the knees and a grey T-shirt. I tied a dark blue unbranded hoodie I used to wear for PE at school around my waist. Off went my new trainers to be replaced by a scuffed pair of black lace-ups. I added in a paperback that was behind another in my bookshelf, a chewed biro and a plain A5 spiral notebook. On my bed I left the clothes I came home in, my watch, and with a pang, the solitaire ring Dad had given me for my eighteenth birthday. I ran into the bathroom and took a spare toothbrush and tube of toothpaste from the medicine cabinet, some tampons and sanitary towels plus a packet of paracetamol, then carried them through to add to the bag. In my wardrobe I found a crumpled pair of jeans, a white T-shirt and a jumper I hardly ever wore. No one had seen me in it or would connect it with me.

The bag buckled up easily. I couldn't believe what I was doing. Mum's eyes in her framed photo by my bed smiled out at me as if it was an ordinary day. I knew I couldn't take the picture with me. The cleaner would know it was missing. Mamie would too. I took one last look and tried to burn an imprint of it on my memory. That would be all I'd have left.

A mental picture of Mamie grieving for me nearly changed my mind but then I imagined her reaction of shock and shame after being told I'd killed a police officer. She might hate me. Perhaps it was kinder for her to think I'd drowned rather than to know the truth. Little did I know she'd die of cancer a year later.

Dad came up and took away my swimming costume to burn.

'Write a note for me saying you're going for a swim and can we ring for a pizza when you get back,' he told me, his voice quivering.

It didn't take me long. The guilt of doing it piled on top of the tsunami of sin that was sweeping me away.

I don't remember much about the rest of the day; fear, panic and loss wiped most of it from my mind. Saying goodbye to Dad is a blur, as is the contents of the ziplock bag he gave me. I know that when it was dark I got into a boat and hid in its bowels. The sailor, whom I'd never seen before, called me up on deck when we reached France and I climbed out, to scramble onto some rocks in what looked like a small, deserted cove. He must have told me where to walk, what to say and how to find a small chambre d'hôtes.

That was the first night of my death that changed my life forever.

Jeannie is staring at me, her mouth wide open as if she was saying 'ah' for the dentist.

I know this weekend was her idea, but really, she's proved she couldn't organise a booze-up in a brewery. Her security precautions are atrocious. Taking the universal key card was like stealing a baby's teddy out of its pram. It was easy for me to move the security camera so it didn't point at the front door. It's not even fixed, it's on a pivot for goodness' sake. She didn't spot the tiny sliver of wood I put under that door to stop the tubular latch clicking in so I could nip in and out without it locking.

By my calculations, Adam's probably dead by now. I saw the guilty look of shock on his face when he spotted the cardboard cut-out of me. As far as I can tell he didn't tell his wife about the photo I put under their door for him to see how he'd react.

Adam liked to play Mr Nice Guy. *Merde*.

It was child's play to go into Adam's room when Keren left. I was hiding around the corner to see when she did. The insulin was in my small shoulder bag and in my hand I held a hankie soaked in black market chloroform that I'd brought with me just in case. A safety precaution. My heart sped up but I needn't have worried. Adam was sleeping like a baby and didn't even wake up. With one hand, I held the handkerchief over his face and with the other I pricked him with the insulin pen. Then refilled it twice and carried on. Finally, I opened his mouth and tipped in 50 ml of morphine liquid for good measure. His swallow reflex still worked fine.

Actions have consequences. Now he knows what it's like to have your future taken away from you like I did.

I do feel a little remorse about Johnny. When I found the insulin in the fridge I planned on putting it back when I got a chance (there was a sticker on it showing it had been dispensed to him) and no one would be any the wiser. Then I think that he let me drive when the brakes didn't work properly. Despite everything being fine the night before when I drove, he must have known his car might be unsafe. He didn't stop me driving home on my own. I could have been killed in the car crash. Johnny deserved to be punished for that. Had he wanted me to get hurt as payback for my flirtations? Could he have possibly known about my kiss with Saira?

'Surprise, surprise!' I say with a grin on my face. 'I thought I'd make a special guest appearance. Are you all pleased to see me?'

Saira has stopped dead in her tracks. Jeannie holds both her palms up facing me as if she's a soldier surrendering. 'Tania? What? How come you're still alive?' she splutters.

'Oh my God. You're not dead. It all makes sense now. You must be the intruder. It was you who killed Adam. Murderer!' shouts Keren at me, jumping up until my outstretched gun teaches her to sit back down.

'I can't say I'm that pleased to see you after the events of last evening. You weren't exactly complimentary. That's right, sit down, Keren. There's plenty of time for me to explain my resurrection. You know I thought it was you who set me up for a while, being a petulant child because I took those drugs off you, until I realised it was your dearest husband. Wasn't so ardently in love with me was he, when he got together with you!'

'Please, Tania, it's good to see you. It really is. But Johnny is very ill. Let Eerik take him back to his room where he can rest,' Jeannie says, holding both her hands up in the air, while gesturing towards the tall blond man.

I look at my ex. His face is grey. A streak of compassion tugs at my heart. I don't know for certain he meant for me to get injured in his car – after all, he didn't know I was going to drive it that evening.

I nod. Eerik stumbles trying to lift a moaning Johnny up from the chair and nearly drops him.

Jeannie lets out a wail. 'Tania, Johnny needs two people to help him. I'm begging you, please let Keren go too to help.'

I nod, but point the gun in Keren's direction in case she tries anything stupid. There's no one else to help, considering that Saira needs a stick now to walk. The only noise that breaks the following tense silence is the shuffle of Johnny's feet as the two of them drag him towards and into the lift. The doors close and the light shows the lift is going up.

I walk a few steps towards Saira, waving the gun between them both.

'Stay back! Don't hurt me!' Saira shouts.

'Why, you told me to drop dead! Remember?' I ask. 'I did wonder if it was you who tried to get back at me for that stupid kiss by setting me up to go to the pub and calling the police on a drugs tip-off.'

'It wasn't me but right now I wish I'd thought of it first,' Saira replies, before yelping when I point the gun directly at her forehead.

Jeannie steps backwards towards the reception desk, still holding her hands up.

'Steady,' I warn in case she's going to retaliate. I don't know what she could do though. I checked and there's no panic button under there. If there was one to alert the police or a security firm she'd have pressed it hours ago.

'It's great to see you, Tania. I've missed you,' Jeannie says in a calm voice. 'I don't know how you did it, but I'm so pleased you're still alive. Thank you for letting Johnny go and lie down. I know that deep down you're a good person.'

I waver just a little. Does she really? Jeannie was always the most loyal of them all, my first friend of the lot of them. Perhaps she's the only one of them I can truly trust.

Or is it all a load of codswallop and she's stalling for time?

A gut feeling passes over me. Why was she so keen to get Johnny away from me? I think back to the way she looked over at him as she spoke. That was more than a concerned hotel manager gaze. They'd spent a long time together last night in the bar. A memory comes back to me of her when she was eighteen admitting she fancied him.

There's a clank in my mind as the penny drops.

'Do you still have feelings for Johnny? How clichéd that you slept with him,' I say.

Jeannie says nothing but the pink swell in her cheeks tells me everything.

'My so-called best friend. You organised this weekend to commemorate my memory then jumped into bed with my boyfriend faster than a gold medal sprinter,' I say.

She takes another stride backwards.

'I thought you were dead. I was upset. I'd wanted the night to be perfect, for us all to honour our friendship with you, and it ended up being a disaster. Johnny was there to comfort me. I'm sorry. I'd never have done anything if I had any idea you were still alive. You always came first with me, Tania. Didn't I always stick by you?'

I hesitate. 'Yes, yes you did – until now,' I admit. My eyes flick wildly between Jeannie and Saira.

'There's no need for the gun. Why don't we go into the bar for a chat? There's so much for us to catch up on.' A few tears trickle down Jeannie's face. 'I'm so happy you're here, I really am. You're alive. Nothing else matters.'

I start to lower my arm. I don't want to hurt Jeannie. A tumour of loneliness and bitterness inside of me threatens to burst open at the kind words from my first friend.

'What about Saira?' I ask.

'We can lock her in my office. I've got the key.'

I'm about to put my gun on the floor when Saira warns, 'No, Jeannie, don't trust her, she killed Adam!'

I swivel round in Saira's direction and step towards her, intending to push her to the office and lock her in. When I'm barely a couple of steps away she pulls a serrated knife out of her bag and stretches her arm out, holding her weapon inches from my face. On instinct, I pull my spray can out of my open shoulder bag, more illegal stuff from the internet, this time pepper spray, and press firmly on the button to release its contents. She screams and falls to the floor. My body trembles as I stand over her. I hadn't planned on harming her. If only she hadn't pulled out that knife . . .

I'm about to bend down to help Saira up to a chair when a massive blow hits the back of my head, knocking me sideways. Time slows down, I reel from the shock and start to fall, desperately trying to get my balance but failing and I crumple onto the floor. There's a loud crack as the side of my skull hits the wooden parquet.

My hands scrabble around in confusion. I've dropped the gun and spray. An excruciating pain blares in my head. I look around, not knowing what has happened. Saira's near me, crying and rubbing her eyes, blinking ten to the dozen. Standing over me is Jeannie, going in and out of focus.

She's holding a rolling pin.

The end is red with my blood.

Chapter 24

Jeannie

'I'm sorry, I'm really sorry but I couldn't let you kill Saira too. The knife, you know I don't like knives.' My words tumble out along with my tears.

On the floor in front of me is a slightly overweight middle-aged woman with brown hair streaked with grey cut in a chin-length bob. She's wearing black trousers and a matching T-shirt. The contrast to the image of her in the cardboard cut-out is remarkable. Her face is makeup free, lined around the eyes and below is a soft double chin. It's her eyes that told me it was Tania. Blue, striking, defiant.

'Jeannie, help me!' Saira begs. I take my eyes off Tania, making sure I've kicked the gun and spray out of her reach. Quickly, I go to Saira, pass her her walking stick and help her up, guiding her to a comfy chair where I pass her the glass of water she filled earlier. 'Bathe your eyes with it. It'll help,' I tell her. 'So it was you who took the knife.'

'Good job I did,' Saira sobs, her eyes streaming. 'I took it last night before I went to bed. I didn't feel safe going upstairs on my own, the whole night had creeped me out.'

Tania lets out a quiet moan and I go back to her and sit down on the floor next to her, not sure of what to do. Blood is seeping out of her head wound, fanning out across the carpet. Her stricken eyes try to focus on my face. Whatever she's done I wish to God it hadn't come to this. I'm not a killer.

'Why did you do it, Tania?' I ask softly, taking her hand. Despite her age I can still see remnants of my young best friend from all those years ago.

'Someone betrayed me. I needed to know who it was and when I discovered you'd organised this weekend I wanted to find out the truth. It was Adam. He was the reason I had to fake my death or I would have gone to prison. He as good as killed me.'

She's not making sense. The Adam I knew wouldn't hurt a fly.

'Prison? What did you do?'

'I went to the pub because there was a message on the fridge to meet me there. He called the police with an anonymous tip-off. When the police did a drugs raid I panicked, ran away and hit a policeman with my car.'

The blood flow from her head wound is getting heavier. I daren't move her in case I make it worse.

A moan escapes from her lips, which are now turning white. The blood has drained from her face. I fear her life is slipping away.

'What did the message say?' I ask.

'To meet at The Dark Horse pub,' she replies in a low voice.

'I saw that message on the fridge that day, when I came back home for lunch,' says Saira, still sniffling.

The Dark Horse pub. Adam mentioned it last night. So Tania was involved in what went on there.

'It wasn't Adam who left that message, Tania.'

Tania coughs and draws a creaking breath. 'How do you know?

I take a deep breath.

'Because it was me.'

Chapter 25

Saira

Jeannie bends further down so her lips are near Tania's ear. My stomach churns at the sight of the blood staining the floor. I've seen lots of fake deaths on TV but nothing could prepare me for the horror of seeing this in real life.

Jeannie speaks soothingly. 'I left that message on the fridge asking you to meet me, but it wasn't a set-up. None of us tipped off the police, we all loved you. That pub was dodgy, the police knew drugs were often sold there. I wanted it to be just the two of us again. I should have asked to meet you somewhere else but I knew The Dark Horse was a place where your other friends wouldn't be.'

Tania's mouth moves. 'You?' she whispers.

Jeannie nods. 'I'm sorry. I missed the bus from campus and the next one was full. I thought you'd just gone home. When you didn't come back to our house I was frantic. You might have irritated all of us a little sometimes but didn't we do the same to you? Honestly, we all adored you. I've never had a best friend since.'

Tania sighs and the exhale of breath seems to render her a little smaller. It's hard to make out what she's saying. I strain to hear what she says next.

'I'm so sorry. Oh my God, I killed Adam. I've been wrong all along? You know, you were the one person I didn't really suspect. I never thought you'd betray me. You really were my best friend.'

The blood on the carpet is starting to clot, darkening to a ruby red.

'Did you use all the insulin?' Jeannie asks. Tania weakly tries to shake her head.

'You can make it right, you can still save Johnny. Tell me where the insulin is and I'll take it to him.'

'My bag,' she whispers and slowly moves her left-hand forefinger to point at her shoulder bag, still wrapped round her beside her body. Jeannie carefully zips it open and tips some of the contents out. What I assume is an insulin pen appears.

'Take this to Johnny, quickly,' Jeannie says to me.

'I can't see very well, my eyes hurt,' I groan.

'Just do it, go up in the lift. Hurry.'

I stand up hesitantly then hobble towards Jeannie, leaning heavily on my stick, and she passes me the pen with outstretched hands, deliberately not looking in the direction of the serrated knife I let go of when I collapsed to the floor. Slowly but surely, I make my way towards the lift and I wait until I hear its doors close to breathe a sigh of relief.

When the doors open again, I rush to Johnny's room, shouting outside the door that it's me and I've got insulin.

The chef unlocks the door and lets me in, his face lined with worry. 'Where's Keren?' I ask.

'Back with her husband,' he replies shakily.

'I've got the insulin pen, there's some left in it.'

My hand trembles as I walk towards Johnny. When I lean over him his eyes flip open.

'Tania, is that you?' he says, his eyes struggling to focus.

'It's Saira. I've got insulin,' I tell him. The room feels unbearably hot. I fold back the duvet covering Johnny's torso and panic.

'What do I do?' I ask the chef.

He shrugs his shoulders. 'Put the needle in his arm, I guess. Quickly. Will you stay with him please? I need to see if I can help downstairs.'

I take a deep breath then jab the pen into Johnny's arm and press down firmly until I think it's empty. Johnny's eyes close. I pull the pen out and drop it on the floor with a thud.

Eerik leaves the room and I sit on the side of the bed holding Johnny's hand, willing Jeannie to find a way to call for an ambulance.

Johnny does not look well.

I don't want to be the one he dies on.

Chapter 26

Jeannie

Tania's fingers have little strength in them as I hold her hand, willing her to stay with me.

'I'm sorry,' she gasps. 'You're the only one who liked me for who I really was, before I changed my hair and wanted the others to like me. I should have left things as they were in that first term at St Mark's, just the two of us. I can see now that I took you for granted. You're the only best friend I've ever really had.'

'It's all in the past,' I tell her kindly, tensing as I see her eyelids flicker and she struggles to take a breath.

'I was so wrong to kill Adam. Consumed by revenge. I'm so sorry. I've got everything wrong. Please forgive me,' Tania implores.

I squeeze her fingers again, not able to say I do.

'You can try and make things right, Tania. The router, where is it? I need to call an ambulance for Johnny and you,' I beg. 'You can still save him.'

Her voice is weaker. It takes a few attempts for her to reply.

'I did love Johnny, truly I did. The router is in the far room on the top floor. I've been hiding there.'

'Thank you, for telling me,' I say.

'I don't blame you for hitting me. You stopped me from hurting Saira. You've done me a favour really. I'm dying. I'm terminally ill – the doctors can't do anything more for me. I had to put my mind at rest, to know who set me up before I go. That's why I risked coming over to England on a fake passport. At least now I don't have to sit and wonder how long I've got left.'

'Don't say that. I'll call an ambulance,' I tell her, but in my heart I know it's true. She seems to be getting weaker and blood is still seeping from her head wound. I wince as I spot a red rivulet slithering stealthily out of her ear. Willing to transfer some of my strength to her so she can survive until an ambulance and the police arrive, I squeeze her hand even harder. However heinous her crime, her death won't bring Adam back. Two wrongs don't make a right.

'Thank you for being kind to me,' Tania whispers faintly. Her eyelids flutter then close.

'Hold on, Tania, hold on. Talk to me. Stay awake.'

'Tell . . . that I love him.' I strain to hear but can't make out the missing word.

'Who? Tania, tell me who,' I say forcefully but she doesn't reply. Her chest isn't moving. She's taken her last breath.

I clasp my hand to my mouth to stifle a sob. I killed her. I shuffle backwards and sit motionless for a minute, watching Tania in case I'm mistaken and she gasps for breath.

She doesn't.

Frozen in position, I let out a silent sob. My brain can barely take in all that's happened in the last few hours. Tania remains still. Was it Johnny she wanted me to tell that she loves him? A brief pang of jealousy and guilt envelops me. For a minute I sit paralysed, my body unable to function. Then I remember the router. I have to find it and call an ambulance for Johnny.

I take the stairs two at a time as I rush up to the top floor. It's rare that I come up here because it's not a guest space, more of a storage area for spare furniture and cleaning equipment. I pop my head around a few doors until in the small room with pale green striped wallpaper that avoided the hotel's renovation I see a sleeping bag on top of a mattress. Beside it lie a few black items of clothing and a small backpack. I hurriedly try to unzip it but the fabric gets caught in the zipper. 'Come on!' I shout impatiently as I try to yank it free. The zip opens at my third attempt and I tip the contents out onto the mattress. There's not much in there, a few toiletries, a novel, and, hallelujah, the router, but it's the final thing my eyes are drawn to.

In a small, white plastic frame is a photograph of a woman and what looks like a teenage boy. Both are smiling at the camera. The woman is undeniably Tania. The boy? His hair is longer and face more youthful but I recognise him straightaway. I drop the frame in shock.

There's a squeak as the door opens and a man walks in.

'Jeannie . . .' He stops as he sees the photo on the floor, lying face side up.

My whole body tenses up with trepidation.

'Eerik, why is there a photograph of you and Tania together?' I ask him in amazement.

Chapter 27

Eerik

I'm dumbstruck. Jeannie has found out. I came up here to gather together Mum's things, so she can steal away before any more damage is done. Before she appeared in the hall I hadn't seen her since last night. Things were never supposed to go this far and Mum promised me she'd keep me out of it. I love this job. I just love Mum more.

'Is Tania your mother?' Jeannie asks me incredulously. I take a step towards her and she curls up backwards like a cornered cat.

With horror I realise she thinks I'm a threat.

I step backwards raising my palms. 'I'm not going to hurt you. Yes, Tania is my mother. I'm sorry, Jeannie. I didn't lie to you, I just didn't tell the whole truth.'

'That's just as bad,' she replies, picking up the router. With shame, I see a mixture of hurt and fear in her eyes. 'I'm going to take this downstairs and plug it in so I can call an ambulance and the police. Why are you here?'

The police? Mum needs to get away first. Hopefully she has done so already. I look at the detritus of her small bag of things. She'll have the hire car keys on her. She can manage without the backpack. Mum was supposed to stay hidden, just watch, only that.

'I came to get Mum's bag for her so she can leave. Look, I know she took some of Johnny's insulin but it wasn't her who injected Adam with it. She wouldn't do that.'

Jeannie looks at me in confusion, then walks towards me and places a hand on my shoulder. 'Eerik, Tania did kill Adam, she admitted it to me. And she can't leave. She's dead.'

I stagger back in shock. 'What? No? She can't be. She's in the hall downstairs after letting you two go.'

Jeannie shakes her head sadly. 'She didn't let us go. She tried to attack Saira. I had to stop her. I'm sorry, Eerik. I had no choice.'

I desperately want my boss to be lying. I won't believe it until I've seen it. I run downstairs followed by Jeannie and retch when I see Mum's body on the hall floor. She's not breathing and the carpet is stained with her thick, warm blood. 'No, no, Mum, Mum,' I cry, willing her to wake up. This can't be happening.

Mum has a gaping head wound. I remember the first aid training I went on. What was it, the nose first, yes that's right. I roll Mum slightly to the side so she's on her back, pinch her nose and breathe into her mouth, despair rising in me.

'She's gone, Eerik, it's no use,' Jeannie says. I desperately try a few more times but nothing happens. Mum doesn't breathe on her own. I sit back on my heels in shock, my hands dashed with Mum's blood.

I turn towards her. 'You killed her?'

Jeannie bends down on the floor next to me and takes my hands, as if talking to a young child. There's blood on her hands too.

'She hurt Saira and she murdered Adam. Johnny's very ill because she took his insulin. I'm so sorry, but I had to stop her. I wish to God I didn't have to but I was frightened, I didn't know what she'd do next.'

'There must be some mistake. No, no, my mum wouldn't kill anyone. She just wanted to see you all again, that's all, that's why I let her in. She would never have murdered Adam.'

Jeannie's pupils narrow into a tiny black ball. 'She confessed, Eerik. You concocted this plan together, did you? Did you know what she was going to do?'

Shaking my head, I wipe my eyes and runny nose with the bottom of my shirt. I've never lied to Jeannie – she just never asked the right sort of questions. Jeannie's a good boss, a kind woman.

'I let her in through the back door and told her where she could sleep. When she found out about the reunion, she really wanted to see you all again. All she could talk about, after I got the job and she looked on the website and saw you worked here, was the old days and her friends. She told me she only wanted to see you all again, to watch from the sidelines.' I think back to when I snuck her in the hotel, how happy she seemed to be here with the prospect of being near her old friends again.

'Look at me, look at me, Eerik.' I turn to Jeannie.

'How long have you worked here? How long have you known me? Do you trust me?'

I do. My eyes feel red and raw. Mum is lying lifeless next to me. Words don't come. All I can do is nod.

'She admitted to me she killed Adam. Do you believe me?'

I don't want to but deep in my heart I know Jeannie would not lie. She's not that kind of woman.

I never thought I'd become that kind of man.

'Did you help her, Eerik? Did you know she was going to harm Adam and Johnny?' I shake my head violently. Mum can't have been thinking straight.

'Did you tell her about the insulin?' Jeannie asks.

How I wish I hadn't. 'Yes. I was in the kitchen when Johnny put it in the fridge. I wasn't going to say anything but after he was rude to you at dinner I mentioned to Mum that a little time without it might teach him a lesson. I never imagined she'd actually take it or use it on Adam. I thought it must have been someone else.'

Jeannie sighs. 'When Johnny and Adam became ill, didn't you suspect it was because of Tania? Did you know where she was?'

I'm torn between loyalty to my mum and my boss, but looking at Mum's body I realise with a gasp that I can't protect her any more. Finally, I open my mouth. 'I looked for her in the attic room this morning, but she wasn't there. Her handbag was gone. I thought maybe she'd left, was frightened by what had happened. I was worried about her, not thinking that she was involved. I heard your friends arguing last night. I thought it must have been one of them who harmed Adam.'

'How could they have done, when it was Tania who had Johnny's insulin?' Jeannie says quietly. 'When you came with your torch to help last night when the lights went out, was that on purpose?'

I nod. 'I thought Mum might be frightened, what with her not knowing the hotel layout, so I came to look for her when I found she wasn't in the upstairs room. Instead, I found you and Grant trying to sort out the electrics.'

I've been so blind. Switching off the lights must have been another part of Mum's plan that she hadn't told me. I look at Mum, the only parent I've ever known, and still can't really believe she could have killed someone. She looks so small, so defenceless. The metal tang of her blood reaches my nostrils and I gag, snorting back grief.

'I've been so foolish. I'm so sorry. I should have realised, should have stopped her.'

'I believe you,' Jeannie says compassionately. 'I'm going to plug in the router now and call the emergency services. I pray it's not too late for Johnny. How could you look after him when you knew it was your fault?'

'Like I said, I told Mum about the insulin but didn't think she'd taken it.'

'Tania was holding a gun, Eerik, didn't that shock you?'

'It was just for show. She had it in Estonia. It's fake, she bought it to scare off intruders after we were burgled once. Yes, I did start to worry she was going too far, but then I couldn't do anything more when I had to take Johnny upstairs. I assumed she was going to speak to you and Saira before getting out of the hotel. The fake gun was just to protect herself.'

'How was she going to leave when the doors were padlocked? Oh, but it was her who did that, wasn't it? She had the keys,' says Jeannie.

I think back to the backpack Mum brought with her. Could they have been in there? When I saw the doors were locked I thought it must have been one of the others, until a nagging doubt set in. We'd all been together in Adam's room. How could one of them have disappeared to padlock the doors? I let out an anguished wail as I realise I've been so stupid.

Jeannie says to me in her soft voice, 'I'm sorry to say, Eerik, that your mother used you just like it appears she did everyone else.'

Did she? I don't want to believe it. She loved me.

I sit vacantly beside Mum's body while I hear Jeannie calling 999 and asking them to send the police and an ambulance.

In a daze, I walk to the breakfast room and pick up a clean tablecloth from the ironed stack in the corner. Carefully, I unfold it and lay it over Mum's still body. The cloth turns red where it touches her blood. I think back to how excited she'd been for me when I told her I'd got an interview here. This position, head chef, was a step up for me. When I got the job and moved a fortnight later she called me and told me that the manager was an old friend of hers, but that I mustn't say anything in case it helped the police track her down.

Since I'd reached adolescence, I'd suspected that Mum was hiding something. She was open that she and my dad split before I was born, although I don't know who he was, and that it was just the two of us against the world. My childhood in Estonia involved us moving every year or so from town to town or village, never staying long enough to put down roots or for me to make good friends.

'It's because of work,' she told me. 'We need money to eat and we go where the jobs are.' Mum taught English to adults. None of her students ever came to our house. She'd hire a room or a church hall for her lessons. I grew tired of always changing school and never settling but Mum would tickle me out of my bad mood and tell me that she had my best interests at heart. We'd watch TV together, eat home-cooked food and everything would be OK again.

We never travelled out of Estonia. In my teens I wanted to but Mum said I was too young and anyway, I didn't have a passport. At school, my grades were low, not surprising since I'd moved so many times. At sixteen, I left to go to catering college. For a few years I'd already been head cook at home, trying out different recipes in books I borrowed from the library. Other boys read dirty magazines or horror stories. I read cookbooks. Just before I turned eighteen I received my diploma. I was top of the class. All I wanted to do was to go to England, where some of the best restaurants in the world are, to find a job. Thanks to Mum my English was nearly fluent. I begged her to give me the documents I needed to apply for a passport.

On the day I became an adult, Mum made me a rhubarb cake,

my favourite, to celebrate. When I think back I can still taste the exquisite tart and sweet combination. She handed me an envelope wrapped with a blue ribbon. I undid the bow and opened the envelope excitedly. It was what I wanted, my birth certificate, proof of address and the passport application form. With it was a pile of banknotes.

'I know you want to go to England. You have my blessing, my wonderful son,' she told me. 'But there's something you need to know first.'

I listened as she explained that she ran years ago from the British police because of a misunderstanding and no one must know who she really was or where she lived. She told me my grandfather was still alive and lived in Devon and apologised that she'd previously said he'd died in the car crash with her mother. She hadn't wanted to lie to me but had to wait until I was old enough to keep it a secret. All the little, strange things I'd noticed over the years made sense to me then and I vowed I'd always keep her safe.

Outside, it's still daylight. I hear the call of a bird, I swear they sound different here than at home. How can life carry on seemingly as normal when Mum is dead?

Ten minutes must have passed when I hear Jeannie's footsteps coming towards me.

'I've checked on Johnny, he's sleeping and there's a bit more colour in his cheeks. The ambulance is on its way,' she says.

I'm filled with remorse at my petty action telling Mum about the insulin because he'd insulted the food. Thank goodness he's still alive.

'Eerik, we'd better wait by the front door for the police. I don't think Saira, Keren and Johnny will want to be in the same room as you. Best stay with me.'

We both walk over to the upholstered bench nearest the door and sit down. My stomach rumbles; it's a long time since we last ate. In the kitchen the food I prepared for lunch and started for dinner is untouched.

Jeannie's eyebrows rise as she has a thought. 'I remember now, it was you wasn't it, who mentioned having a gathering of my old friends when I told you about Tania? We were having a drink in the kitchen after a busy night. You asked me about friends from uni and I told you about Tania. You wondered if I'd thought about meeting up with the old St Mark's gang.'

I nod. 'Yes. Mum wanted to see you all again. It would make her happy. I put the idea in your head, but it was you who chose to do it.'

'I do believe you that you didn't know what Tania had planned. I don't understand though why you didn't tell me earlier that she was here.'

That's a simple question to answer. 'Because Mum swore me to secrecy. If the police knew she was in the country they'd have taken her away. She was supposed to have died years ago. Mum was always looking over her shoulder in case someone found her out. I thought she'd left this morning,' I tell her.

'If you don't mind me asking, how did she manage to fake her death? There was a cremation and a gravestone. If it wasn't her in there, then who was it?'

Talking about it to someone else makes me realise the extent of the lies Grandfather told.

'I didn't know until I turned eighteen. Grandfather told the world she disappeared when she went swimming. Mum confessed to me that a couple of months later a badly decayed body of a young woman washed up on a beach nearby. The police called Grandfather. Mum's name was top of the missing persons' list. They can't have done DNA tests then. Nobody else came forward, so Grandfather said the body was Mum and had her cremated. He was respected in the community. No one doubted him. Mum told me she sometimes wondered sadly who the woman really was, perhaps someone without a family or friends, but at least she got a decent funeral.'

We sit in silence for a few minutes.

'I am sorry for your loss, I really am,' Jeannie says. 'It must have been hard for her being terminally ill.'

'What?' I exclaim.

Jeannie looks startled. 'She told me she was dying and that's why she was so keen to see her old friends again. She thought one of us set her up the night of the pub raid.'

'No, you've got it wrong. She was healthy, she never told me she was ill.'

Jeannie's cheeks turn pink like a blushing rose. 'She probably didn't want you to worry. She honestly did tell me that she was dying. I'm sorry I mentioned it.'

So many things I thought I knew about my mum have been proven wrong today. How can I work out what is true and what isn't? I long to be able to ask Mum myself. I let out a moan then clench my lips to keep the rest inside.

Jeannie puts her hand on my arm. 'The last thing Tania said was to tell someone she loved them. She spoke so quietly I couldn't make out the name. I think she meant you, Eerik. She wanted me to tell you she loved you.'

I rub my eyes with the back of my hand, thankful to have that piece of information to hold onto. A minute later I speak out loud what comes into my mind.

'Will I lose my job?' I ask my boss.

She sighs ruefully. 'I think we both will. The police will want to question you as to what you knew. As you let an uninvited guest stay in the hotel, I'm pretty sure it breaches your contract. The police may charge you too for abetting a murderer. And I'm the manager of a place where two people were killed, one by me, even if it was in defence of someone else. I doubt I'll get a job in hotel management again,' she says ruefully.

'Maybe I'll go to York to see if I can get a job near Ian,' I reply, trying to find some hope, desperately avoiding the thought that I could go to prison.

I need to bury Mum. Grandfather died last year, perhaps Mum can rest with him. I went to his funeral and stood at the back, missing the gathering afterwards to avoid being asked who I was and how I knew the deceased. Mum was very upset but she couldn't risk going. Someone, perhaps one of her father's old friends, might have recognised her.

'What will you do?' I ask Jeannie, remorseful that my actions may have cost her her job.

She shrugs her shoulders. 'I have no idea. I've saved up quite a bit of money because I haven't had to pay rent living here or in the previous hotel I managed. I've enough to think about buying a house, a bed and breakfast maybe or a tea shop. Somewhere by the sea would be nice. Maybe on the Yorkshire coast. I've grown to like it here. I don't have anywhere else to go. I haven't got any friends.'

'Yes you have,' I tell her. 'I'm your friend.'

'I'm your boss,' she replies straightaway.

'Yes, and my friend. What about the times we've watched films together on our time off, or had a drink at the bar when all the guests had gone to bed? You've always been kind to me.'

She smiles sadly. 'Thanks, Eerik, I appreciate that.'

The ring of the doorbell startles both of us.

'Police!' shouts a voice outside.

Jeanie jumps to her feet and shouts, 'The door is padlocked inside, we can't open it. I told the 999 operator. Please be quick.'

'Stand back, madam. Make sure everyone is well away from the door.'

'We are,' she shouts back.

For a few nervous seconds there's silence until a loud ram batters the doors. Once, twice, three times I count until the hinges on the right-hand side break from the wall and it opens from the wrong side.

A paramedic in a jumpsuit runs in carrying a small bag with a cross on the side. 'Where's the patient?'

'Room seven, second floor,' Jeannie tells her breathlessly. Two police officers appear followed by a male paramedic who points at Mum's body under the tablecloth.

'This the perpetrator you reported?' he asks.

'Yes. Her name is Tania Armstrong-Jones. We all thought she died twenty-five years ago.'

The officers put on gloves and look round. 'I'll secure the firearm, you bag the can, knife and the rolling pin,' one says to the other and bends down to pick up the gun. He turns it over in his hand, aims it at the wall away from us and pulls the trigger. I wince with fear. There's a loud bang but no bullet.

'A toy. A realistic-looking cap gun. If you didn't know anything about firearms you'd be easily fooled.'

I exhale with relief that at least I was right about the gun. Mum never intended to shoot anybody.

'Where's the other body?' the paramedic asks Jeannie.

'First floor. Room four. His wife is very distressed. Please take care of her.'

'Will do.' With that he heads up the stairs carrying a medical bag.

The officer who bagged up the rolling pin and spray can starts taking photos and talks on his radio. With a loud crackle in the background I can't follow what he's saying.

The other turns to Jeannie and me.

'Do either of you need a medical check?'

We both say no.

He pulls out his notebook. 'Right then. Some more officers are on their way to secure the scene. Stay right here and tell me what's happened.'

I think it's going to be a long night.

Chapter 28

Keren

The family liaison officer brings me a mug of hot, sweet tea. She's been with me at my home in London for two days now. I wrap my fingers around it, grasping on to the pottery as if for dear life. For a few minutes I know what to do. Drink the tea – that's all my shut-down brain can manage. After that is no man's land. I have no idea how to carry on this evening, tomorrow, or the next month without Adam.

'I've had news from the hospital. Johnny's up and walking round the ward. The doctors think he will make a full recovery,' the officer tells me in her Geordie accent that's laced with sweet sympathy. It can't be empathy because she's single, there's no wedding ring on her finger. Her husband hasn't been murdered. Scarlett she's called, here to support me when I told the kids that their dad would never be coming home. She's sticking around now they're out with Mum and Dad for a couple of hours. I don't know where they've gone. Scarlett said the police needed some time to talk with me about things that aren't appropriate to say in front of the children, even though I gave a statement at the hotel. The new officer Scarlett mentioned hasn't arrived yet.

Tania killed my husband. There's nothing more to say other than I wish she'd really drowned in the first place.

I sip the hot tea. It burns the roof of my mouth but I don't care, it's nice to actually feel something.

'Jeannie's stayed with him the whole time in hospital apparently.

It's good that he's had an old friend with him,' she continues, as if she expects me to reply saying how lovely that is.

I carry on drinking my tea, each mouthful a jolt to my system.

I don't tell Scarlett that Johnny and Jeannie (sounds like an American sitcom or a sixties pop duet, doesn't it?) were never really friends, that they only hung around in the same group two and a half decades ago, and that the most time they'd ever spent together alone was a drunken one-night stand on Friday night. Or maybe it won't turn out to be a one-night stand. If Jeannie's been holding a vigil at Johnny's bedside then perhaps she thinks there could be more to it.

One couple ends and another begins. No, I can't go there.

Ow! I take a large gulp of my drink to drown my thoughts and this time it scalds.

'You OK? Too hot?' Scarlett asks. I nod and she scuttles off to bring me a glass of water, which I drink quickly to soothe my throat.

She sits down next to me on the sofa, right where Adam usually does. Even though I plump the cushions up every week there's still an indentation where he should be. I manage to stop myself from telling her to move to another chair.

Adam's mum is too distraught to visit. His brother Bobby is looking after her.

The police arrested Eerik, who apparently confessed that he'd let Tania into the hotel and hidden her, though he says he didn't know what her real plan was. He thought she only wanted to observe her friends. He's probably lying but I can't help feeling sorry for him losing the life lottery and having her as his mum. I know how good she was at charming people and manipulating them into doing what she wanted. But still, he let her in the hotel and if she hadn't been there, she wouldn't have killed Adam. I'll never forgive him for that.

The police are still deciding whether Jeannie acted in defence of Saira. Scarlett says it's unlikely she'll be charged with anything, what with the evidence from Saira that Tania attacked her first.

Saira's phoned a couple of times. Everything I know about what happened after we went to the hospital is from her. Scarlett took the calls, I'm not ready to speak to her yet. An ambulance took Saira and me to hospital to be checked over. Jeannie went in another with

Johnny. Once we were in A & E we were separated into different cubicles. The hospital called Hannah, who was still down as Saira's next of kin. Saira's now staying at her old house with Hannah and Emily to recuperate, Scarlett says. Sounds like Saira's near-death experience has persuaded Hannah to forgive her.

I know how she feels. I'd forgive Adam anything if it would bring him back, not that there was anything to forgive, of course. He didn't set Tania up, she was obsessed with her own importance, wanting everyone to be in awe of her.

'I'm sorry the DS is taking so long,' Scarlett says to me. I shrug my shoulders in reply. She pats my hand and I jerk my arm away. I don't deserve compassion.

This is all my fault.

When Jeannie explained to us all about the message that Tania had found on the fridge her eyes briefly flicked to meet mine. Typical Jeannie. She lied to spare Tania's feelings, trying to find some good in her even after everything she'd done. When the ambulance person checked me over while two others took away Adam's body, Jeannie turned to me and opened her mouth to say something but then closed it with a knowing look, as if she'd guessed my secret but had decided to keep it because revealing it would serve no useful purpose.

It was me who put the message on the fridge. I was angry that the hallowed invitation to stay with Tania for a week in Devon was really an expectation that I'd teach her everything she hadn't bothered to learn on our course. It didn't take long to dawn on me that what she wanted wasn't company but a free tutor. When we got back to our student house, I went alone to the library to revise, before she got up, to avoid wasting hours explaining yet another historical era to her. You didn't say no to Tania. Then of course she took my pills. How could she be so self-righteous about drugs when she smoked dope, had all the time in the world to revise and daddy would pay for another course if she failed? I'd already had a low mark on my assessment. I needed to do well in my exams, as otherwise I wouldn't be able to get in to my PGCE course. I didn't have the luxury of a millionaire dad. I *needed* to make sure I'd do well and those pills helped me concentrate and gave me energy to stay up longer into the night after my bar job to revise.

My anonymous call to the police was only supposed to shake her out of her privileged ivory tower for half an hour. A drugs raid seemed fitting payback. How dare she call me a druggy when she often smoked joints in her room? I didn't know she'd be so stupid to smoke them in The Dark Horse though, or that she'd run away when the police arrived and knock over a police officer. I didn't even know at the time that had happened.

I do now.

The ripples of what I did all those years ago led to her killing my husband.

My children are fatherless because of me and I don't know how I'm going to live with it.

The doorbell rings. Scarlett jumps up to open it. 'That'll be the DS.'

I raise my mug to my lips. It's empty.

Acknowledgements

First of all, thank you to you for reading this book. Authors write to have their stories told, and for that we need readers. Thank you too to all the booksellers and librarians who have supported me, particularly at Kenilworth Books and Warwickshire Libraries.

After I began writing this book, my dad was diagnosed with a terminal illness. Thank you to all the hospice at home nurses who supported him, and us, in his final days. I promised Dad I'd dedicate this book to him and it's a promise I'm proud to have kept.

It takes a team to create a book and I have one of the best at Embla. My thanks go to all of them, particularly my commissioning editor Melanie Hayes, managing editors Anna Perkins and Emma Wilson, marketing manager Katie Williams, copyeditor Sandra Ferguson and cover designer James Macey. My author friends, including the d20s (a group of us whose debut books came out in 2020) and Emma Scullion, have been brilliant in supporting me during the writing process. Mark Bailey was kind enough to share with me details about living with diabetes and its care and management.

As ever my love goes to my family and my husband Chris who always champions and encourages me in my writing career.

If you'd like to subscribe to my author newsletter to find out about what I'm writing next then I'd love to have you. Please sign up at www.pennybatchelor.co.uk.

Read on for an exclusive extract from *My Perfect Sister...*

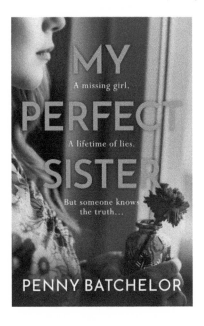

Thursday 4th May 1989. 4.15 p.m.

Out in the garden Annie enjoyed the feel of the sun on her skin in the dappled afternoon sunlight, relishing casting off her red gingham dress and lying down on the grass in the back garden playing horizontal starfish. The grass tickled her as she moved her legs and arms sideways in tandem, pretending she was floating in the sea; a feared creature of the big, wide ocean. Free to float away to a desert island.

The school day was over. Above her head a cabbage white butterfly flapped its wings, teasing her by flying back and forth almost rhythmically towards her nose but never quite trusting to land. Annie giggled with delight and opened her mouth, pretending to swallow the butterfly in one. It flew away towards the fence separating their garden from next door and disappeared into the pink blossom on a tree.

Annie bathed in the warmth of the sun against her skin and started to doze, dreaming about chocolate ice cream. Perhaps her mummy would take her to the corner shop to buy one when she got out of bed. All would be well with the world.

Suddenly a shadow covered the sun, cooling her face, causing her to wake up and sit bolt upright.

'Oh!' she said, startled. 'It's you.'

~ 1 ~

2014

I stand in my childhood bedroom, though little remains of what it used to be. On the walls where in my teenage years I had Blu-Tacked Nirvana and Oasis posters there's now pale blue wallpaper with a small, white, peony pattern. The old cider-stained taupe carpet has gone, replaced by a dark blue plush version. Instead of my vanity table placed against the side wall there's a modern sewing machine on a stand, surrounded by neat, stacked plastic boxes containing threads and fabric. Lots of flowers and pink. Everything has a place and is rigidly in it.

The pencil marks on the door frame recording my height over the years have been emulsioned over. A white flat-pack wardrobe stands where my old wooden one used to be. Inside are empty hangers, the kind bought in a multipack, not plastic ones taken from high street shops on a Saturday afternoon shopping trip. No cast-off underwear destined for the laundry lounges on the floor. The childhood books I left behind are long gone, as is the small bookcase. Only the single bed remains as a remnant from what the room once was to testify that I slept here. Even that, pushed up against the back wall instead of jutting out into the room, is covered in a patchwork quilt no doubt sewn by my mother to show her crafting skills off to guests.

If she ever has any.

This is not my room anymore; it's the spare bedroom. In fact, it's as if I never was here, as if I didn't exist.

On the contrary, it is Gemma who probably doesn't exist, but you wouldn't know it by looking in 'her' room. I shut the spare room door behind me and push open the brown door with a pottery multi-coloured 'Gemma' sign still stuck on it. Behind that door is a lost world, a museum piece from a distant decade that should be covered Miss Haversham-style in dust and cobwebs but is as spick and span as if it were cleaned yesterday.

No doubt it was.

Presents lie on the floor next to the bed where her shoe collection used to be – one for each birthday and Christmas she has been gone. For goodness' sake. Does Mother think Gemma is going to come back from the dead and open them?

Her pop posters still line the walls, her lipsticks, mascara and eyeliner neatly sit on the dressing table below its mirror (I hate to think of the bacteria on them), and from the back of her dressing table chair hangs her mini-rucksack, the black one she took out with her when meeting her friends. Scruffy, the mangy fluffy dog Mother said Gemma was given as a baby, guards her pillow. It's the same bed linen, purple with white swirls that she once slept in, but freshly washed and ironed. This is a sanitised teenage girl's bedroom, without the smell of perfume, freshly washed hair, sweaty cast-off clothes or a cup of once warm coffee. Without breath. Without life.

I look at the pinboard resting on top of the desk. There are photos pinned there, photos I haven't seen for all those years I've been away. Photos from a real camera, the kind where you point, shoot and don't know what the picture will turn out like until it comes back from the developer's. In the middle of one faded rectangle Gemma smiles at the camera, her dark brown hair pulled back in a ponytail, her eyes laughing at something the photographer must have said. She is in the park, I think. The evening light dances on her cheekbones, striped pink in that eighties fashion; her cut-off T-shirt shows off a tanned midriff above a pair of pale blue ripped jeans; she's raising her arms in the air as if to say this is mine. This is all mine.

The other photos show a mixture of permed girls and mulleted boys in a variety of fading situations: someone's house, the park again, and one where they wear white school shirts with fat, short ties. She smiles out from the pictures, frozen at sixteen.

As I turn to leave I notice another picture at the bottom left-hand corner, one of my parents looking much younger, sitting on the step outside the front of this house. Mother is curled up on Father's knee and they are smiling for the camera, their happy faces belying what I can remember from my childhood. I peer closer inquisitively then remove the pin and pull the photo away from the board. The corner of another photo had covered part of the image. I take a sharp breath when I see which part hasn't been viewed by the world for twenty-four years. Here the colours are bright and stand out next to their muted neighbours.

To the right of Father, a real-life gap of about twenty centimetres away, there's a little girl with a ginger ponytail and a brown pinafore dress looking the other way, not part of this cosy family scene. Me.

Gemma must have taken it.

I hear the front door close softly.

Occasionally I think that if she weren't already dead I'd want to kill Gemma myself.

~2~

I close the bedroom door quietly and walk to the stairs. The old swirly red and green stair carpet has gone, replaced by a dark beige industrial one, the practical kind that won't show up the dirt. I remember as a young girl sitting on the stair third from top, rubbing my face against the carpet, half-closing my eyes and watching the red and green dance together millimetres from my eyelashes whilst a policewoman spoke to my parents in voices muted by the closed kitchen door. Every ten seconds or so loud sobs punctuated the mumbling. 'Stay upstairs until I say so,' my father had said, ushering me into my bedroom. Time passed, was it minutes or hours? A minute can feel like millennia to a young child.

I'd ventured as far as the stairs but no further, as if there was an invisible barrier holding me back, fixing my eyes on the carpet pattern. There I'd stayed until Father came to get me and told me I had to have an early night. You see, that's what I remember from my childhood, not picnics, birthday parties or trips to the park but the police coming round when my sister didn't return home and the pervading shadow it cast everywhere. Except that shadow, that gloom, that tiptoeing around death never left. I did instead.

When I walked out of the red front door for the last time I may have lived on this planet for a month longer than Gemma ever did. I left at soon as the bell had rung on my final day at school and didn't come back, ever, to this house.

7

I returned from Leeds over a decade later to see my father in hospital after his stroke, and although she had left the message on my mobile to let me know which hospital he was in I hovered in the darkest recess of the corridor until my mother had left. A dying man's bedside isn't the place for a row, or more likely the silent treatment. My mother is more passive-aggressive than the dramatic argumentative type.

The smell of the disinfectant stuck with me, pinning itself to my recollection of the day. Whenever there's that scent in the air I think of my decaying father. He couldn't talk well but squeezed my hand and a tear ran down his cheek; he then pulled on my arm, gesturing that he wanted to tell me something. I bent down to his level, so close that I could feel his shallow breaths on my ear.

'Forgive your mum,' he said. Thirty seconds passed whilst he drew upon some more energy to speak his final words to me. 'She loves you, she just couldn't show it. Look after her when I'm gone. Please.'

I smiled at him, a wide smile that didn't stretch to my eyes, and nodded – a panacea for the dying. Like hell I'd keep my fake promise. His last words to me were about her, not some words of love and wisdom for me. He'd been the buffer between me and her, but even on his deathbed he took her side. What about me, I wanted to scream. What about me?

Nine days later I went to the church funeral but skipped the pub buffet and reminiscences about what a decent bloke he was by old colleagues, neighbours and those who wanted a free lunch. Instead I went home, got drunk and remembered Father in my own way as the quiet, smallish man who tried, but never quite hard enough. Did I love him? I think so. But I can't say that his passing made much of a difference to my life, it now being so far removed from the bad old days.

And yet, despite all my remonstrances, here I am at 22 Greville Road, the place I'd swore I'd never return to.

With great sadness and faint hope I pat my back jeans pocket where my mobile is. It hasn't vibrated and there's still no text or voice message from Shaun begging me to come home. Or rather back to his home – the one he asked me to leave in no uncertain terms after what I did, the situation he couldn't understand and I won't bring myself to think about.

Greville Road is now the only semblance of a home I have left. That's how low I've sunk.

I walk down the stairs, steadying myself for the inevitable moment when I'll come face to face with my mother for the first time in, how long? I've lost count. In fact, I never bothered to start counting: far away from here, living a different life, I didn't have to think about facing up to what I'd spent so long running away from, being the left over one, the daughter who was still around, a stark reminder to them that their wonderful, beautiful, preferred Gemma was not. How could I possibly ever live up to the memory of a dead saint?

My childhood key, the bronze one with the stripy plastic cover at the top 'to show you this is the key to home,' Father had said, still worked and when I arrived she was out. So they hadn't changed the locks, but then that was probably nothing to do with me. Mother will have kept the locks the same just in case Gemma turns up with her key, a bunch of flowers, a husband, family and a dashing tale to tell about what she's been up to since that summer day when she never came home.

Downstairs now, I walk into the kitchen, which is still the

same and looking none the better for it. Mother is standing at the sink with her back to me making a cup of tea. The noise of the kettle may have covered my footsteps.

'Hi,' I say a bit louder than necessary, steeling myself. Why am I nervous? Should I have agreed to come here at all?

She turns around, balancing a tea bag on the end of a teaspoon. If this had been another situation it would have almost been comic.

'Oh Annie . . .' she says, her words tailoring off to a soft silence. The first thing I notice is that her knitted cardigan is hanging off her once plump frame in swathes. She looks like a child dressing up in adults' clothes. She is pulling the edges of her right sleeve with her left hand: fidgeting, twisting, rubbing. Her eyes, surrounded by a panda bear's black rings, seem to have sunk into her skull, whilst her crumpled skin is stark white, almost translucent, criss-crossed by red, angry veins in a spider's web fashion. Her once golden-brown hair is now grey and cropped shortly to her head. She is gaunt, haggard and shrivelled.

I gasp in shock, and then cough to try to cover up my initial bad-mannered reaction. I hadn't expected it to be true, I'd assumed that her wheedling pleas were just a manipulative pretence to guilt trip me into returning and the reason I could give for heeding them.

Mother really did have cancer. Or rather cancer had eaten her up and was preparing to spit her out, used and desiccated, into the grave.

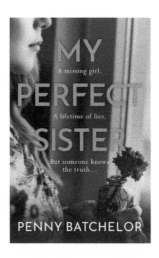

Annie is five when her beloved big sister, Gemma, leaves for school and is never seen again.

The police search for weeks and Annie never gives up hope that Gemma will one day come home to her.

Now, twenty years after her sister mysteriously vanished, Annie returns to her childhood home to care for her ill mother.

Opening the door to Gemma's room, Annie finds it untouched from the day her sister disappeared, with her makeup still on the dresser and her books open on her bed.

Annie is certain that the answers to what happened to Gemma are here in her old room.

But in the search to finally find Gemma, will Annie discover her perfect sister is not who she thought she was? And will her quest for answers put her in deadly danger?

Someone knows the truth. And they will do anything to stop Annie from finding it . . .

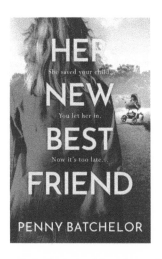

She saved your child...

You let her in.

Now it's too late...

HER NEW BEST FRIEND

PENNY BATCHELOR

Mum-of-two Audrey only looks away from the stroller for a moment, as her daughter runs off across the park. But the next thing she knows, her baby son is rolling towards the lake.

When Claire steps in to prevent disaster, Audrey is beyond grateful. She can't imagine what would have happened if Claire hadn't been there that day.

As Claire and Audrey grow closer, Audrey couldn't ask for more from her new best friend.

But when tragedy strikes for a second time, Audrey discovers that Claire wasn't who she thought she was . . . **and now it's far too late . . .**

About the Author

Penny is the Amazon bestselling author of psychological thrillers *My Perfect Sister* and *Her New Best Friend*. She is currently writing her fourth. Her short story, 'The Dilemma,' appears in *UnLocked*, an anthology to raise money for The Trussell Trust. Penny is a co-founder and judge of the ADCI Literary Prize for adult fiction by a disabled/chronically ill novelist.

She lives in Warwickshire with her husband.

Web: www.pennybatchelor.co.uk
Facebook: @pennyauthor
X: @penny_author
Instagram: @pennybatchelorauthor

About Embla Books

Embla Books is a digital-first publisher of standout commercial adult fiction. Passionate about storytelling, the team at Embla publish books that will make you 'laugh, love, look over your shoulder and lose sleep'. Launched by Bonnier Books UK in 2021, the imprint is named after the first woman from the creation myth in Norse mythology, who was carved by the gods from a tree trunk found on the seashore – an image of the kind of creative work and crafting that writers do, and a symbol of how stories shape our lives.

Find out about some of our other books and stay in touch:

X, Facebook, Instagram: @emblabooks
Newsletter: https://bit.ly/emblanewsletter

.

Milton Keynes UK
Ingram Content Group UK Ltd.
UKHW050638220624
444517UK00001B/3

9 781471 416354